**Oh, Baby!**

Maggie wanted her new neighbors to accept her as
an everyday person who led a quiet, everyday
life. Standing in the midst of a gaping,
questioning crowd, in a sexy negligee with a
screaming baby at her feet, repeating, "I just
found it on my doorstep," Maggie knew her wish
had a snowball's chance in hell of coming true.

"Pick her up."

Maggie's head turned to the right, then up. Way up.
It was the guy she'd noticed on the elevator. Maggie
was again struck by his good looks—and his
intimidating frown.

"What?"

"Pick her up. She needs to be held and comforted.
Or she needs a bottle and a diaper change. Don't
you know anything about babies?"

Maggie wanted to retort that she knew plenty, but
decided to demonstrate. She picked up the baby and
smiled down at her. Maggie expected an immediate
response. She'd always been good with kids.

And the baby responded. After a brief silence, the
baby blinked, took a deep breath and let out an
earsplitting scream.

## ABOUT THE AUTHOR

Emily Dalton lives in the beautiful foothills of
Bountiful, Utah, with her husband of twenty-one
years, two teenage sons and a very spoiled American
Eskimo dog named Juno. She has written several
Regency and historical novels, and now thoroughly
enjoys writing contemporary romances. She loves
old movies, Jane Austen and traveling by train. Her
biggest weaknesses are chocolate truffles and crafts
boutiques.

**Books by Emily Dalton**

**HARLEQUIN AMERICAN ROMANCE**
586—MAKE ROOM FOR DADDY
650—HEAVEN CAN WAIT
666—ELISE & THE HOTSHOT LAWYER
685—WAKE ME WITH A KISS
706—MARLEY AND HER SCROOGE

Don't miss any of our special offers. Write to us at the
following address for information on our newest releases.

Harlequin Reader Service
U.S.: 3010 Walden Ave., P.O. Box 1325, Buffalo, NY 14269
Canadian: P.O. Box 609, Fort Erie, Ont. L2A 5X3

# Dream Baby

## EMILY DALTON

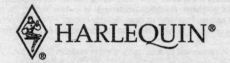

# HARLEQUIN®

TORONTO • NEW YORK • LONDON
AMSTERDAM • PARIS • SYDNEY • HAMBURG
STOCKHOLM • ATHENS • TOKYO • MILAN • MADRID
PRAGUE • WARSAW • BUDAPEST • AUCKLAND

If you purchased this book without a cover you should be aware
that this book is stolen property. It was reported as "unsold and
destroyed" to the publisher, and neither the author nor the
publisher has received any payment for this "stripped book."

To the good-looking Ford boys—
Dana Jerry, Douglas James, Darrell Jon and Duane Jay
From the one thing you still have in common.
Me. Your good-looking sister.

ISBN 0-373-16738-5

DREAM BABY

Copyright © 1998 by Danice Jo Allen.

All rights reserved. Except for use in any review, the reproduction or
utilization of this work in whole or in part in any form by any electronic,
mechanical or other means, now known or hereafter invented, including
xerography, photocopying and recording, or in any information storage
or retrieval system, is forbidden without the written permission of the
publisher, Harlequin Enterprises Limited, 225 Duncan Mill Road,
Don Mills, Ontario, Canada M3B 3K9.

All characters in this book have no existence outside the imagination of
the author and have no relation whatsoever to anyone bearing the same
name or names. They are not even distantly inspired by any individual
known or unknown to the author, and all incidents are pure invention.

This edition published by arrangement with Harlequin Books S.A.

® and TM are trademarks of the publisher. Trademarks indicated with
® are registered in the United States Patent and Trademark Office, the
Canadian Trade Marks Office and in other countries.

Printed in U.S.A.

# Chapter One

"Was that the doctor on the phone, my darling? What did he say? Was it good news?"

Count Alexander Tolstoy, played by *Soap Beat* magazine's September choice for "Hot Hunk of the Month," actor Greg Moran, was regally decked out in a black silk robe, his thick, dark hair slicked back from his noble brow. Obviously restraining his eagerness, he gently clasped Maggie's shoulders and turned her to face him.

As the camera zoomed in to catch her reaction, Maggie ignored an almost irresistible urge to scratch her nose, then assumed Monica Blake's customary stricken expression. She was an old pro at this—her eyes readily welled with tears and her bottom lip quivered. Dressed in a lacy, pale-pink peignoir, and fully made-up despite the fact that she'd barely risen from bed, she was a vision of elegant tragedy.

"Do you have to ask, Alexander?" Maggie whispered brokenly. "The in vitro didn't work! *Nothing* works! I'll never get pregnant! I'll never be able to give you the son you want so desperately! I don't know how you can still love me. I'm only *half* a woman!"

Maggie gave a weak show of trying to wrench herself from the Count's grasp. Suddenly his face was a mere inch from hers and she was blasted with the strong scent of breath spray as he hissed, in an accent that sounded something like a mixture of Hungarian and an east Texas drawl, "Don't ever say that again, Monica! God knows you're more woman than any woman I've ever loved. More woman than any woman that's ever walked the earth. More woman than—"

Maggie held her anguished look with difficulty as the Count broke eye contact and shifted his gaze to the TelePrompTer behind her. Although they'd gone over this scene twice in rehearsal, she couldn't blame him for forgetting his next line. The point had been made, for pity's sake! And in Maggie's opinion, Monica Blake was more woman than any woman in her right mind would ever *want* to be!

There had been too many diamonds and designer duds, too many lovers, and too many husbands over too few years. Not to mention the comas, paralysis from the waist down, blindness, murder trials, drug addiction, amnesia, and multiple personalities....

As Greg struggled to find his next line, Maggie saved the scene by clamping his face between her hands and firmly "coaxing" him to look at her instead of the TelePrompTer. "You're too generous, Alexander," she said. "But I know how important it is to you to pass on your noble title to a son. After all, without a male heir, who will inherit the castle in Carsovia?"

Maggie wondered for the umpteenth time where the writers had come up with the name of the Count's own personal principality. "Carsovia" always sounded to her like a suspicious mole you had your doctor remove.

Grateful for the save, the Count assumed *his* usual stricken expression...minor variations of which Greg Moran had used for everything from stepping in horse manure in his lavish stables to learning of the death by decapitation of his evil twin brother, Voris. Then he released her and walked away to stand morosely in a window embrasure, his head hung in mute resignation.

The camera panned back to Maggie. It was the end of the scene and she knew the camera would stay on her for several interminable seconds as they faded to a commercial. Now her nose *really* itched....

During the entire twelve years she'd worked on the highly rated "The Rich and the Reckless," the most difficult acting Maggie had ever done was to hold her expression for those few seconds before commercial. She had learned to use the time productively...mentally listing and evaluating all the bad dates she'd been on, for example, or fantasizing about sweet and creative ways to break her perpetual diet. But in real life she knew that no one stood, speechless and unblinking, in one spot for so long. But soap operas were not real life...thank God.

"Okay, that's a wrap. You looked great, Maggie," the director, Allen Bannock, told her, pinching her cheek affectionately as she passed him, headed for the dressing room.

"Thanks, Allen," Maggie called over her shoulder as she rubbed her itchy nose. "How long have I got till we tape again?"

Allen looked at his watch. "The next scene is a killer, and you'd have to change into an evening gown, so let's call it quits early today. I know you want to get out of here at a decent hour so you can get settled in your new apartment.''

"Thanks, Allen," Maggie said, turning to throw him a kiss. "I owe you one."

"Need some help unpacking?" Greg asked her, dabbing away the sweat on his forehead from the heat of the overhead lights, as he hurried to catch up.

Greg was a notorious womanizer and, besides, Maggie made it a rule never to date soap opera studs...especially while they enjoyed their month-long reign of glory as "Hot Hunk." She'd been politely fending off Greg's advances for the past two years as they'd shared interwoven story lines, but lately he'd been more persistent.

Maggie suspected Greg's intensified interest had more to do with wanting to capitalize on the popularity of their "couple" image on the screen for publicity purposes than a real attraction on his part. Either way, *she* wasn't interested. Throwing him a careless smile, she said, "Thanks, Greg, but there isn't much to unpack. I'll manage."

Greg tried again. "We could practice our love scenes," he suggested teasingly. "Making babies takes *lots* of romantic love scenes, Maggie."

"Not the way *we've* been attempting to make babies," Maggie retorted, still going full speed ahead down the hall. "There's nothing romantic about test tubes and petri dishes."

Greg gave up and, with a disgruntled wave of his hand, turned back. She heard him asking Allen, "How did my pores look in that last close-up?" and, "Do you think I need a clay mask?"

"We've got the viewers in the palms of our hands,"

said Morty Shuback, the show's executive producer, matching his stride to hers as he joined Maggie from an office door midway down the hall. Maggie decided that he could walk pretty darn fast for a middle-aged guy with a paunch, but he talked even faster. "They're still loving this infertility story line! Have you seen the ratings from last week, Maggie?"

"If they're good, I'm glad," Maggie answered. "I just hope we're giving this subject the serious consideration it deserves. There are a lot of people out there who can't have babies who really want them."

But, thank goodness, she wasn't one of them, she added to herself. Too bad the more avid fans of the show continued to confuse her character with her real self. Last week some woman had sent, by Quickie Express, a jam jar of her husband's sperm packed in ice. The woman's accompanying note explained that, as a mother of five, she knew "Joey's stuff" was the most potent around, and, as long as he didn't supply needy women with sperm the "traditional" way, she didn't mind sharing it!

Then there were all the letters from fans advising her on sexual positions and other methods for getting pregnant, as well as women who wanted to be surrogate mothers for Monica and the Count. Maggie frequently found herself shaking her head over these letters, amazed by how wrapped up some people got in the life of fictional soap characters.

"Well, we've certainly explored the infertility issue from every angle," Morty said, sounding a bit dejected.

Maggie slid him an amused look. "What's the matter, Morty? The writers running out of material? Worried about how we're going to keep such a popular story line going? Why not go on to something else…like a vampire loose in the soap city of Pleasant View?''

"We don't *do* gothic," Morty said in a beleaguered tone. "We do realism and issues on 'The Rich and the Reckless.'"

"Relatively speaking," Maggie murmured. She turned at the door of her dressing room and gave Morty a kiss on the cheek. "Gotta go, Morty. It's Friday and I've got a whole weekend ahead of me to live my *real* life."

Morty looked at her worriedly. "You sound a little jaded, Maggie. Need a vacation? Please don't tell me you're ready for prime time. The show wouldn't be the same without its biggest star."

"Don't worry," Maggie assured him, smoothing the lapel of his gaudy checked jacket. Her lips curved up in a teasing smile. "New jacket?" Morty was a flashy dresser—to put it kindly—and he wore white shoes year-round.

"Yeah, it is. Like it?" But Morty was distracted for only a minute, then he was back to business. He crossed his arms over his chest—till he realized he might be putting a crease in his yellow polka-dot tie—and said firmly, "Never mind the threads, Maggie. Tell me why I shouldn't be worried."

"The show's been good to me, Morty. I'm not the least bit tempted to move from New York to L.A. to pursue a prime-time show or a movie career. Someone has to be Monica Blake, and it might as well be me." She laughed. "The truth is, I love playing Monica. She makes my boring life away from the show such a treat to go home to."

"How *is* your real life?" Morty asked her, still

looking concerned. "Is it as boring as you make it out to be?"

Maggie shrugged. "Actually, right now my life's a little more exciting than usual."

Morty's sparse gray brows lifted. "You got a new man, sweetheart?"

Maggie wrinkled her nose. "No. It's *much* better than that. I've got a new apartment."

"You mean you're finally moving out of that tiny hole you've euphemistically referred to as an apartment all these years? It's about time. I don't pay you peanuts, you know. You could have afforded something better much sooner than this."

Maggie just smiled and said nothing. Morty didn't know it, but her more than adequate salary had always had plenty of places to go besides her personal bank account. But now that three of her four sisters were out of school and holding down jobs of their own, there would be less of a drain on her income.

"Bye, Morty," Maggie said in a friendly but firm tone. "I've *really* got to go."

Morty turned away with a weary smile, lifting both palms skyward. "So go, already."

Maggie had her heavy makeup off and her sweats on in no time at all. She eased her tired feet into a pair of Reeboks. Without the obligatory high heels Monica always sported, Maggie was definitely on the petite side...but she didn't mind. Her mere five-foot-two-inch height sometimes helped hide her from the fans. Television made you look "bigger than life" in many ways.

She put on her sunglasses and shoved her long brown hair into a Mets baseball cap. Waving to other cast members on her way, she hurried out the back entrance of the studio and stepped inside the waiting limousine.

"*Home*, Jeeves," she said, affecting a majestic tone, then smiled teasingly at the driver's reflection in the rearview mirror.

The driver, whose real name was Chuck, smiled back. "That'll be the new address, right, Ms. Stern?"

"Right," Maggie said emphatically. "I've got scads of room in my new place, Chuck, and I can't wait to start arranging my stuff."

"Pretty roomy, huh? Two bedrooms?"

"Yes...*and* a study."

Chuck grinned again, his straight white teeth gleaming in the mirror. If the kid weren't all of nineteen years old, Maggie would definitely have a crush. Tall, blond and good natured, Chuck was to die for.

"I'm happy for you, Ms. Stern. You're a nice lady. You deserve the best."

"Thanks, Chuck."

"Now, sit back and relax. With this Friday afternoon traffic, it'll be a few minutes before I can get you home to that new palace of yours."

Maggie took Chuck's advice. She leaned back in the soft leather seats of the limousine and gazed out the window at building fronts and throngs of people. Where the studio was located in downtown Manhattan, it was hard to tell it was autumn because there just weren't many trees around. But soon they were traveling the perimeter of Central Park and the golds and reds of the leaves inside the park were breathtaking.

During this pleasurable interval of quiet, Maggie was glad she'd given in to Morty's insistence that she use the limo to get back and forth from work. Even dressed down in sweats and a baseball cap, she couldn't take the subway without being recognized by fans, which was sometimes a pleasant experience of signing autographs and accepting accolades and sometimes not—depending on her current story line.

For example, when Monica was having an affair with her best friend's husband, several elderly women on the subway had cornered Maggie and lectured her on the wickedness of her ways. One of the ladies wept openly and another, angrier one kept punctuating her points by jabbing Maggie in the ribs with her umbrella.

As for cabs, even soap stars had trouble flagging them down during rush hour. But still Maggie had resisted the limousine till just over a year ago. She knew other actors on the soap used a limo, but she had tried hard not to take her star status too seriously, getting caught up in the glamorous traps and ego trips that had ruined the lives of lots of other actors she knew.

In her humble opinion, she was just a stagestruck girl from Long Island who'd been lucky enough to win the role of the ingenue, Monica Blake, straight out of acting school. She'd stuck with the role through every personal disaster a soap character could endure, and been rewarded for it with two Emmys.

Maggie was proud of those Emmys. She'd put her whole heart and soul into her acting, especially those first few years. But lately she wondered if she wasn't just sleepwalking through some of her scenes.... Despite her love for the over-the-top role of Monica Blake, recently Maggie had felt a vague dissatisfaction with life in general. And she didn't know if the dissatisfaction had to do with her professional life or her personal life.

Maggie chuckled to herself. *Personal life? What personal life?*

As the limo pulled up in front of Maggie's new building, she stared up at the high-rise and felt excitement flood through her. This new apartment was a real treat, and the first major indulgence she'd allowed herself since moving to New York. She couldn't wait to get inside.

She couldn't wait for Chuck to open the door, either, so she stepped out and threw him a breezy wave before hurrying toward the door of the building. Recognizing the newest tenant, Dennis, the doorman, bowed and wished "Ms. Blake" a good day as he opened the door for her. Maggie inwardly sighed at being called by her character's name instead of her own, but it happened so often she was forced to be forgiving about it. She smiled and, taking off her sunglasses, headed for the elevator.

She shared the elevator for the first few floors with a woman who stared at her during the entire ride. And when the door opened for the woman's floor, she didn't move.

"Is this your floor?" Maggie asked politely.

"Oh! Yes. Yes, it is," the woman admitted, flustered.

Hoping to put the woman at her ease, Maggie extended her hand and smiled. "Since we're going to be neighbors and riding the elevator together now and then, perhaps we should introduce ourselves. I'm—"

"Yes, I know who *you* are," the woman interrupted. "You're Monica Blake."

"Actually, I'm Maggie Stern," Maggie gently corrected. "And you are?"

"Nice to meet you, Ms. Blake. Hope you like it

here," the woman stuttered, completely forgetting to introduce herself and not even seeming to notice Maggie's extended hand. Then she stumbled backward out of the elevator, still looking dazed.

Maggie sighed and let her hand fall to her side. Sometimes she thought she preferred it when people politely ignored her. She definitely didn't feel that meeting *her* ought to make anyone nervous and flustered. After all, she wasn't really the ultrachic Monica Blake. The sweat suit she was wearing ought to be proof enough of that!

The elevator finally stopped at the twenty-first floor at the top of the building. Maggie eagerly stepped out, immediately colliding with a tall man who was so busy reading something, he wasn't looking where he was going. Their collision caused him to drop a whole slew of papers. They scattered, half of them in the lobby, half of them on the elevator floor. A few papers even caught in the closing doors, bending and tearing as the elevator whisked down the shaft to another floor.

"Oh, dear," Maggie exclaimed, stooping to pick up papers. "I'm so sorry. Were these papers important?"

"I'm the one who should apologize," the man insisted, setting down his briefcase and also stooping to retrieve papers. "I wasn't paying attention." He chuckled self-derisively. "Most of the tenants know how distracted I can be and keep a sharp eye out."

"Well, I'm new here," Maggie admitted as they both straightened up. She held the papers out to him and smiled. "But now that I've been warned, I'll keep a sharp eye out for you, too."

The man took the papers hesitantly. Suddenly he was staring at her as if he'd just seen a ghost...or something worse. Perhaps he recognized her, but didn't know from where and was dredging his memory for a name. Maggie was about to introduce herself, put him out of his misery by giving a name to her face, but she was feeling a little bemused herself....

His eyes were a nice blue, Maggie decided. *Very* nice. And they were made all the more striking by the wire-rimmed glasses he wore. His hair was blond, longish and wavy, and he was wearing an oxford-cloth shirt, a wool tie, and a nubby tweed jacket. His trousers were double pleated in the front, and he wore suede Hush Puppies. The overall effect was very Ivy League. Very professorial.

But Maggie had always pictured professors as balding and myopic with narrow shoulders and a "chalky" pallor. If she'd thought they were as square-jawed, tanned and handsome as this guy, she'd have skipped acting school and gone to college! Was it too late to register for a few classes?

"You're the new tenant?" he said, still looking stunned and...yes, there was no denying it...disapproving.

"Er...yes," Maggie answered uncertainly.

"On this floor?"

"Yes. Apartment 2101. I do have the right floor, don't I?"

He ignored her question, his eyes flitting over her petite figure swathed in jade-green sweats. "*You're* Monica Blake?"

"No, I'm *not* Monica Blake," Maggie succinctly replied. "I'm Maggie Stern...the *actor*. I only play Monica Blake on a soap opera."

"I never watch soap operas," the man quickly and emphatically informed her.

Maggie's chin lifted. "Oh? Then how did you know who I was?" She saw a muscle tick in his jaw.

"I was told you were coming," he answered morosely, sounding a lot like Winnie the Pooh's dour friend, Eeyore. Then he just stood there with that grim look on his face, silently observing her.

"I suppose Mrs. Fernwalter, the building supervisor, told you about me," Maggie suggested, still trying to be pleasant despite the fact that the handsome stranger wasn't returning the favor. He hadn't even told her his name. "I knew it would get around sooner or later, but I was hoping for later. Sometimes being even a little bit 'famous' can be inconvenient."

"But I imagine being a little bit famous can also come in pretty handy now and then."

Maggie couldn't miss the sarcastic edge to his voice. "I'm not sure what you're getting at, but...are you angry with me about something?"

The man picked up his briefcase and jabbed the elevator button. "You'll like your apartment, Ms. Stern. It's got the best rooms in the building and the best views of Central Park. There's even a study off the living room that will come in very handy when you're memorizing your scripts. *I* had planned to use it as a home office. God knows I need one."

The elevator door opened and the man stepped on. He turned to face her, his expression deadpan. The doors began to close, but Maggie propped her foot against one side to hold them open. The door bounced off her Reebok and "pinged" insistently while she stared back at him.

"Are you trying to tell me that *you* wanted my apartment?" she demanded to know.

The man released an irritated huff. "It was prom-

ised to me by Mrs. Fernwalter four years ago. I signed
a lease on my present apartment with the handshake
agreement that she'd give me 2101 as soon as it was
vacant. Obviously Mrs. Fernwalter's promises don't
hold up very well against the pressure of pleasing a
soap diva who thinks her star status entitles her to
anything she wants, regardless of prior claims.''

"But I—"

In her confusion and distress, Maggie unconsciously
removed her foot from holding the elevator open, and
the doors closed. Before she had a chance to explain,
the man was gone. But, on reflection, what explanation
could she give? Mrs. Fernwalter had said nothing
about a prior claim to the apartment. She'd been more
than eager to sign Maggie up for a five-year lease.

But as Maggie walked down the hall, she remembered thinking at the time of that telephone conversation that it was amazing that the popular building
had a vacancy just when she needed one. Long waiting
lists for premium apartments were the norm in New
York. But she'd been so excited to hear that Mrs.
Fernwalter had just what she wanted, she hadn't given
a thought to a prior claim. Besides, wasn't it Mrs.
Fernwalter's job to keep track of that? Why would she
conveniently forget she'd agreed to give the apartment
to someone else?

But Maggie knew why. Mrs. Fernwalter was a fan.
She couldn't have made that any clearer to Maggie
over the phone. And, later, when Maggie had come to
the building to look at the apartment and sign the
lease, Mrs. Fernwalter had gushed and babbled and
stared till Maggie was embarrassed and uncomfortable. Mrs. Fernwalter had been watching "The Rich
and the Reckless" since its inception twenty-five years

ago. She knew the show's history better than Maggie did. And Monica Blake was her favorite character.

There it was…apartment 2101. Maggie fitted her key in the lock, trying to ignore the damper her run-in with the man had put on her excitement about moving into her new apartment. She couldn't help what Mrs. Fernwalter had done, and there was nothing she could do about it anyway, now that she'd signed the lease. Obviously the man thought she'd exerted her influence to cheat him out of his prior claim. Hopefully she'd eventually be able to explain the situation to him…if he ever gave her the chance. Or maybe, since it was a big building, she'd be lucky enough never to "run into" him again.

JARED AUSTIN WAS still picking up papers off the elevator floor when the doors opened at the main lobby. As luck would have it, Billie McKenzie stepped on just as he was rising to his full height, treating him to a close-up, traveling view of her curvaceous figure.

"Hi, Doctor J," she cooed, tossing back the long blond bangs of her short shag cut and smiling demurely. Her luxuriously-lashed blue eyes batted the usual come-hither signals, and he could have sworn he saw her roll her shoulder just like a femme fatale from an old-time movie. She was wearing her customary tight-fitting sweater and leggings.

"Just back from rehearsal, Billie?" Jared asked politely. Billie was cute as hell, but she was a dancer in the Broadway hit, *Beauty and the Beast,* and that qualified her as "show-business" people. Show-business people like Monica Blake…or Maggie Stern or whoever she was. Or like Claire and her gaggle of weird friends.

"Yep," she answered perkily. "But I'm not too tired to check out that new espresso bar down the street. You game?"

"Not today, Billie," he replied with a weary smile. "I have a meeting. Maybe some other time."

Billie gave him a wry look and shook her head. "But don't hold my breath, right?" Then a sly gleam came into her eyes. "Although if I fainted, you'd have to *resuscitate* me, wouldn't you? You doctors have an oath to uphold."

"I can always spot a faker," he warned her. "You'd feel pretty foolish if I walked away from your prostrate body and left you alone on the elevator."

"Foolish *and* disappointed," she admitted. She kept the elevator open with one hand and added with a sigh, "But if you really could just walk away from my prostrate body, it must be true what they say about you."

Jared raised his brows, edging around her to exit the elevator, his chest barely missing skimming her breasts. "What do they say? And who's 'they'?"

"People say you don't date anyone in show business. They say actors and dancers to you are taboo." She cocked her head to the side. "Hey, that rhymed, didn't it? Anyway, they say you won't even give the time of day to the mime on the corner. Is that true?" When he hesitated, she urged him, "You might as well tell me, Doc. It would save us both a lot of time if you just came clean with me."

"They" were absolutely right. When he'd moved back to New York after attending medical school in Boston and completing his internship and residency there, Jared had made a firm promise to himself never to get romantically involved with any woman even remotely connected to show business. He'd kept his promise...with the exception of those two dates he'd been coaxed into and would just as soon forget.

His ban included any woman who had to be in front of a camera or required an audience to make a living. But he hated to publicly admit such a prejudice because, as a pediatrician in Manhattan, he took care of the children of lots of show-business people. And, being the highly sensitive folk they were, that "star" portion of his clientele might take umbrage at his little rule against dating among their glamorous ranks.

But Jared had had enough exposure to show business to know that he didn't want it to be any more a part of his life than it already was. Big egos and general eccentricities went along with all that glamour, and he already had enough of that baloney to deal with because of his renewed relationship with Claire.

And Ms. Stern's piracy of his apartment just reinforced his general opinion of the "beautiful people." That sweat suit and baseball cap she'd been wearing was just a disguise to get her in the building without being mobbed by fans. He easily recognized the striking woman beneath that humble outer façade, and he would bet a year's salary that along with the gorgeous face and figure came an ego the size of Yankee Stadium.

"Well, Doc?" Billie prompted him, her lips curving in a coy smile. "Is it true?"

"Billie, I don't date much of anyone these days," he hedged. "I'm far too busy. See you later."

Then he quickly turned and walked away. He wasn't lying. He dated infrequently, and it really was largely because of his busy practice. But he'd certainly make time for a nice girl with the everyday values he'd learned growing up in a blue-collar home on Long Island, just he and his dad. Trouble was, where in Manhattan was he going to find such a woman?

## Chapter Two

By eleven o'clock that night, Maggie had managed to get at least the kitchen and living room in order and stood back to survey her work with satisfaction. The minute she'd entered her apartment that afternoon, she'd taken off her Mets cap, pulled her hair into a ponytail, rolled up her sleeves, donned rubber gloves to protect her manicure, and gone to work with a vengeance. Now she used her dusting cloth to wipe the sheen of sweat off her forehead, then propped her fists on her hips.

"Not bad, Margaret Morgenstern. Not bad at all," she murmured to herself. "If you ever have to give up acting, you could move furniture and clean houses for a living."

She'd had all her furniture sent over earlier that day while she'd been at the studio, but the movers hadn't shown much taste in arranging it. She'd pushed around the couch, chairs and antique tables several times before finding just the cozy look she wanted. She ended up creating a sort of conversation-friendly grouping around the fireplace.

The Victorian prints and pillows she preferred suited the airy room perfectly. There was even a place for her dining-room set at the far end of the living room near the windows that overlooked Central Park. The lacy swags she'd hung there would let in plenty of sunshine. Tomorrow she would tackle her bedroom and the study.

Thinking of the study reminded Maggie of the man she'd run into in the lobby. Picturing his handsome, frowning face always took the edge off her happiness. Even though she wasn't responsible for what had happened with the apartment, she still managed to feel guilty about it.

But she hated the idea of the man feeling disappointed and cheated and…worst of all…blaming *her* for the whole thing! She had a feeling she would have enjoyed being friends with him. Until he'd found out who she was, he'd actually been quite pleasant.

Maggie jumped when the doorbell rang. She'd never heard it before and the melodic chime took her by surprise. The doorbell in her old apartment sounded something like a scratchy wheeze. But who would be visiting her at eleven o'clock at night?

She moved cautiously to the door and peered through the peephole. A woman with short blond hair, chewing energetically on a wad of gum and holding a plate of some sort of food, stood waiting. It was no one Maggie recognized. But since the apartment complex was secured and all outside guests were announced via intercom, she figured the woman was one of the other tenants and probably just there to welcome her to the building. Despite the late hour, Maggie was eager to see a friendly smile on the face of one of her neighbors, and she opened the door.

"Hi, I'm Billie," the woman announced, breezing past Maggie into the apartment. While Maggie was still holding the door, Billie continued on into the kitchen and set her plate of goodies on the counter. "I'm your next-door neighbor in apartment 2100. I hope you like marshmallow treats. I love 'em myself." She took out her gum, stuck it to the counter top, then picked up a sticky marshmallow square and took a bite. "Got any diet coke?"

Amused by the way Billie had immediately made herself at home, Maggie closed the door and joined her at the counter. "No. I haven't had time to go shopping yet. I just moved in today. All I've got is bottled water."

"That'll do," Billie said with a shrug. "These things are great, but you gotta have something to wash 'em down or they stick in your throat like a hair ball. My dog, Brenda, choked on one once and we had to do the Heimlich. It was hard, too, 'cause she was so fat we couldn't find the right spot to press."

Maggie laughed and got a bottle of water out of the fridge and handed it to Billie. "It was kind of you to go to all the trouble of making marshmallow treats. I love them, too. I used to make these all the time when I was growing up."

"Don't get too choked up about it...no pun intended," Billie advised her with a crooked grin. "I didn't actually buy the cereal, melt the marshmallows and stir the mess up. They sell these yummy goodies in individually wrapped squares now. I just bought a box and unwrapped them all, then put them on this plate. Makes it more personal that way, don't you think?"

"Absolutely. And they're all the same size, too," Maggie pointed out, trying to keep a serious face.

"Fancy me living right next door to the actor who

gets to live vicariously through a character like Monica Blake," Billie went on, giving Maggie a thorough once-over as she took a swig of water. "I see you around town now and then, and sometimes I catch the show, but—" She interrupted herself and rolled her eyes. "Man, that Count Tolstoy is some hunk. Is he a good kisser?"

"Greg Moran? Yes, actually he is," Maggie admitted with a judicious nod. *But not good enough to tempt me to get involved with such a conceited and self-serving man,* Maggie added to herself.

Billie nodded back, looking wistful and distracted for a moment, then continued. "I'd have that guy's baby *any* day. Well, anyway—as I was saying before I interrupted myself—this is the first time I've seen you up close. You've got good skin...which is pretty surprising considering how many years you've had to pack on all that makeup. Some TV stars look like hell without their paint. Know what I mean?"

"Sounds like you've had a little experience with stage makeup yourself," Maggie observed, picking up a marshmallow square, taking a bite, then sliding onto a stool. She just realized that she hadn't eaten since her salad at lunch, and she had a real weakness for anything sweet. "Are you an actor, too?"

"Nope. A dancer. Seen *Beauty and the Beast?*"

"I have. I love it, but then I've always been a sucker for fairy tales."

"Well, I'm one of the spoons in the big dinner extravaganza scene. You know, when Lumiere sings 'Be My Guest' and all the dishes and silverware start dancing and singing?"

"I love that scene! Wasn't there a show tonight?"

"Yeah, but it's not my night, so instead I went

shopping. I ran into some friends, had dinner, then rushed home, unwrapped my marshmallow treats, and hurried over here to do the neighbor thing.''

"Well, sit down and let's get acquainted," Maggie suggested, gesturing toward the stool opposite her.

"Can't," Billie said, whisking her hands together and popping her gum back into her mouth. "I've got a date and I still need to shower and put on my face."

"At this hour?"

"He's a waiter-slash-actor and doesn't get off till midnight," Billie explained, then smiled coyly. "Makes for a late night, but he's worth it."

"I see," Maggie murmured with a responding smile.

"But I ought to be up and around by one or two tomorrow. You'll need a break by then from all this hard labor. Maybe we could do lunch?" She reached inside the back pocket of her tight jeans and pulled out a business card. "Here's my phone number. It's private, so guard it with your life! But you know all about fan harassment, don't you?" She handed Maggie the card and headed toward the door. "Call me."

"Okay, I will. I wish you could stay longer…but thanks for the treats," Maggie said, a bit dazed by the whirlwind visit.

"No biggy," Billie waved airily. "See you tomorrow, Maggie."

"Yes, see you tomorrow," Maggie answered. "And thanks again."

"For the marshmallow treats?" Billie waved a scornful hand.

"No, not for the marshmallow treats," Maggie clarified. "Although they *are* delicious. Thank you for calling me Maggie instead of Monica. So many people don't seem to get the difference.''

Billie smiled and nodded her head understandingly. ''People can be a little strange about that, can't they? Don't worry, Maggie. *I* get the difference. See ya around.'' And with a last cheerful wave, Billie was gone.

Maggie smiled as she closed and locked the door behind her, grateful that at least one of her neighbors was friendly and wasn't mixing her up with her soap character.

Six marshmallow treats and a hot shower later, Maggie couldn't wait to crawl into bed. She was definitely a flannel fan when the temperatures started dipping, but she hadn't organized her bedroom yet and couldn't remember in which box she'd packed her pajamas. With a tired sigh, her gaze strayed to the open closet and fell on the long white nightgown and matching robe Morty had given her last Christmas.

The low bodice of the nightgown was hand-beaded, with a few sequins thrown in for glamour, and the raglan sleeves of the robe were trimmed with real ermine. It was definitely not your everyday night wear, and if it had come from any other middle-aged man than Morty, Maggie would have thought the gift inappropriate and refused it. But the costly and elegant peignoir set was one Monica had worn twice on the show and, therefore, couldn't wear again, and Morty thought Maggie might enjoy owning it. He'd said it made her look like a sexy angel. Maggie thought the metaphor a little blasphemous, but took the gift with a grateful smile, never expecting to wear the thing. After all, why dress up for bed when there was no one to impress?

Maggie moved to the closet and ran her hands over the soft satin fabric of the nightgown. It was definitely something Monica Blake, *not* Margaret Morgenstern, would wear to bed, Maggie thought with a wry smile. But never having slept in such a getup, Maggie got the sudden urge to find out how it felt. It would be a way of christening her new apartment, she decided. Besides, she was way too tired to look for her pajamas.

Minutes later Maggie went to bed in a much improved state of mind than earlier that evening. She wasn't sure if her contentedness had more to do with the sugar buzz she was enjoying, the decadence of sleeping in a satin nightgown, or Billie's visit, but she was actually able to close her eyes without seeing the upsetting image of the handsome stranger and his angry frown. Well...*almost.*

MAGGIE SLEPT like a rock and didn't wake up till nearly nine. Pulling the filmy matching robe over her shoulders to ward off the chill of the apartment till the furnace kicked in, Maggie stumbled to the bathroom mirror, ran a comb through her hair, brushed her teeth, then stumbled into the kitchen. She was never one to be perky in the morning.

There was no coffee to help wake her up, either, so she grabbed another marshmallow square and another bottle of water from the fridge. She was definitely going to have to get to the store that morning and buy some decent food. To keep herself in Monica's size two wardrobe, Maggie had to constantly watch her diet and exercise regularly.

After eating six marshmallow treats last night—not to mention the three she'd just devoured for breakfast—Maggie knew she shouldn't miss her morning jog. But on her way to the bedroom to change into another pair of sweats, she remembered that she'd arranged to have the *New York Times* delivered to her new address and she backtracked to the living room.

Covering a yawn with her hand, she opened the door. There on her doorstep was the rolled-up morning paper, and beside it was...a baby carrier. She immediately recognized the scoop-shaped device; her two married sisters used baby carriers...to carry their *babies*.

Maggie bent down and blinked at the carrier. All she could make out at first were a bundle of multicolored blankets dotted with teddy bears, ducks and balloons. Then, horrified, she detected the tip of a tiny pink nose and a set of pale, feathery eyelashes above the hem of a folded blanket. The rest of the sleeping baby's face and its hair—if it had any—were covered up. It looked so peaceful, so angelic, so—

"What's going on here?" Maggie rasped out. Such things didn't happen in real life, she reminded herself, trying to calm her quickly escalating state of panic. Only on a soap did people leave babies on your doorstep! But Maggie couldn't help but glance down at her sexy, elegant white nightgown and wonder if by wearing Monica's clothes to bed she'd somehow crossed over to another dimension...the Soap dimension. She couldn't think of a more terrifying episode of "The Twilight Zone" than to find herself actually living Monica Blake's soap-opera life!

"Don't be ridiculous, Maggie," Maggie continued to talk to herself in a hoarse whisper. "This isn't real or a "Twilight Zone" episode. You're just dreaming. That's it. All the sugar from those marshmallow treats sent your adrenaline into overdrive and you—"

But in the midst of Maggie's feverish explanation to herself, suddenly the baby stirred. She watched, fascinated and fearful, as a little mouth and two small fists cleared the top of the blanket. As the baby yawned, it stretched its arms and pushed its chest out like a strutting pigeon in Central Park.

Then those feather-lashed eyes blinked open and stared at Maggie.

Maggie stared back. As the eldest of five children, she'd had plenty of experience with babies. It was the main reason she didn't want any rug rats of her own…at least not yet. They were darling, but oh-so-demanding, and she didn't think she could combine motherhood with a career and be successful at both. Not that she'd even thought that much about it!

Maggie's gaze shifted quickly up and down the empty hallway. Dream or not, she had to get this baby into her apartment and out of sight before someone called the *National Intruder* and she and the kid and her sexy white nightgown were splashed all over the front of every tabloid in the country.

"Okay, dream baby, you can come in," Maggie said, reaching to lift up the carrier by its handle. "But not to stay. Ever ride in a patrol car? I'm calling the cops. Surely this is just somebody's bad idea of a joke," she grumbled.

Apparently the baby didn't like Maggie's tone of voice, or he or she didn't like the idea of fraternizing with the fuzz, because suddenly it let out a shriek that could literally wake the dead. And since most of the tenants on Maggie's floor probably weren't dead, or even asleep at that hour, doors opened and heads began to poke out into the hall.

Maggie supposed she could have, at this embarrassing point, scrambled into the apartment with the baby, furtively dragging the accompanying diaper bag along behind her, but she knew Mrs. Fernwalter would soon be knocking on her door anyway and demanding an explanation. After all, this was a no-children-or-pets-allowed building. Leaving the baby on the doorstep where she'd found it while she made an explanation would hopefully support her story and make her sound more believable.

Maggie continued to stand as motionless as if she were fading to commercial and watched helplessly as people began to leave their apartments and approach. Soon she was standing in the middle of a babbling, excited crowd. If they didn't know before that Maggie Stern, a.k.a. Monica Blake, was moving into their apartment building, they knew now…and what an introduction!

Maggie's dearest wish had been to be accepted by her new neighbors as an everyday person who, away from her job, led a quiet, everyday life. Standing in the midst of the gaping crowd, draped in a sexy negligee with a screaming baby at her feet, and fielding numerous questions with a blank stare and the repeated phrase, "I just found it on my doorstep," Maggie knew that her wish had a snowball's chance in you-know-where of coming true now.

"Pick her up."

Maggie's head swiveled to the right, then up. Way up. About six feet, three inches up. It was the man from the elevator. He'd changed clothes and was wearing a cream-colored sweater and tan Dockers…but he was still frowning.

"What?"

"Pick her up. She needs to be held and comforted.

Or she needs a bottle and a change of diaper. Or maybe all four. Don't you know anything about babies?''

Finally nudged out of her stupor, Maggie wanted to retort that she knew plenty about babies, but she decided she'd rather demonstrate her ability. She bent to pick up the baby, then cradled it in her arms. Pulling the blanket back from the crown of the baby's head, she exposed a halo of fine blond curls. Smiling down at the infant, Maggie expected an immediate response. After all, she'd always been good with children.

Well, the baby responded, all right. After a brief hiccuping silence, it blinked through its tears, took one look at Maggie, then cried even harder.

A sudden flash made Maggie flinch. As she searched the crowd for a camera so she could ask the amateur shutterbug to please refrain, the baby's cries rose to an ear-shattering crescendo.

"Great," the man drawled. "Looks like you've got just about enough maternal instinct to fill a thimble. Hoping for a photo opportunity, are we? Give her to me."

"Look, Mr.—whoever you are," Maggie said irritably, "why should I give the baby to you? You don't look where you're going, and you drop papers all over the floor. Why should I trust you to hold something far more fragile?"

"Trust me," he said above the din of the screaming child. "I'll do a much better job than you're doing."

And with that, he slipped his hands under the baby's head and bottom, removed her from Maggie's embrace, and tucked her snugly against his chest. The baby immediately stopped crying. Maggie stared at the baby's face, then up at the man. There seemed to be an instant chemistry going on. He smiled and the baby smiled back, her tear-dampened cheeks rounding like a couple of small, shiny apples.

"Why haven't you taken her inside?" the man said with a brief, disapproving glance at Maggie, then turned back to the baby again. "All this confusion and noise can be very upsetting to an infant."

"I was waiting for Mrs. Fernwalter," Maggie defended herself. "And what makes you think this kid is a 'she?' She's not wearing pink."

"Call it a hunch," said the man. "I'm usually right."

Maggie lifted her eyebrows. "You go around guessing babies' sexes? Sounds odd to me."

"Could we please just go inside?" the man hissed. "Or are you waiting for the real paparazzi to show up?"

She couldn't imagine why the man thought she wanted her picture taken, but his question had awakened Maggie to the actual threat of news exposure that she definitely didn't want. It was a secured building, but reporters and photographers always seemed to find a way to get where they wanted to go, and to get pictures of whatever chump happened to be a hot property at the moment.

"All right. Come in," Maggie said, picking up the diaper bag and baby carrier and leading the way. The man followed her inside her apartment and closed the door with his foot. The immediate dulling of the jabbering crowd outside calmed Maggie's nerves somewhat. She wasn't sure why she hadn't come in sooner. She supposed she'd just been in a state of shock and couldn't function very well. That, and the lack of real food for nearly twenty-four hours, could make a person a little fuddled.

Without further invitation, the man carried the baby into the living room and laid her on the sofa. Maggie set the carrier down and followed with the diaper bag. She watched as the man unwrapped the blankets around the baby and began to unsnap her yellow sleeper. The baby's eyes were still fixed adoringly on the man and she wasn't making a single peep. If she'd been a cat, she'd have been purring.

"Give me a diaper," the man ordered, without looking away from his task.

Maggie obeyed.

"Are there wipes in there, too?" he inquired brusquely.

Maggie found some wipes and handed one to the man. "Well?" she said. "*Is* it a girl?"

The man efficiently and quickly changed the baby, resnapped her sleeper, then lifted her against his shoulder and stood up. With one large hand splayed securely over the baby's back and the other cupping her head, he turned and looked frowningly at Maggie. Despite his frown, Maggie couldn't help but admire his deftness at holding a baby. Greg Moran—an ex-football jock, no less—couldn't even hold a prop doll without fumbling it.

"Yes, it's a girl. Did she come with a note?"

Maggie shook her head. "I...I didn't see one. But maybe there's one in the bag." She sat down on the sofa and began to go through the bag's contents. As she searched through bottles, binkies and bibs, she felt the man's gaze boring into her. She didn't know if he was just watching her search...or if he'd noticed how low her neckline was. Trying not to appear obvious about it, with one hand she tugged her robe together in the front.

"I can't find a note," she said finally, surprised to realize how reluctant she was to meet the man's gaze again. His obvious dislike of her was disconcerting, especially since she felt no urge to dislike *him*. He was so good with the baby, so gentle, so capable.

"Why would someone leave a baby with you?"

Maggie's head reared up. "Why *not* leave a baby with me?"

He sighed. "I'm sorry if I sounded rude, but I frankly don't understand what's going on."

Maggie stood up and spread her hands. "That makes two of us." But then a terrible thought occurred to her. "Unless...."

"Unless what?"

Maggie glanced at the man's expectant face, then at the baby. Looking utterly content, she'd laid her head on the man's shoulder and seemed ready to doze off again.

Gulping hard, Maggie wondered if she dared tell him what she was thinking. She could hardly take it in herself.

"Well?" he prompted impatiently.

"It's possible...just *possible*, mind you...that whoever left this baby at my doorstep did it because—" Again she found it difficult to go on.

"Because?" he repeated irritably.

"Because they got me mixed up with the character I play on 'The Rich and the Reckless'...Monica Blake," she blurted out. "And it's so stupid, too, because I'm *nothing* like Monica Blake!"

*Sure you're not,* Jared thought sarcastically, eyeing her nightgown. He supposed she thought *everyone*

wore a getup like that to bed every night. Only if
"everyone" meant Ivana Trump, Princess Stephanie,
and RuPaul. But he had to admit she looked damned
good in it. Her long, loose hair, fresh-scrubbed skin
and large, dark, unmade-up eyes were perfectly com-
plemented by the white satin and lacy silk. But it was
hardly an outfit for baby-tending. A little spit-up on
those ermine cuffs would probably produce a star-
caliber fit of hysterics in Ms. Stern.

"So why would someone leave a baby with Monica
Blake?" he finally asked her. "Don't tell me she runs
a foundling home?"

"Well, she did once," Maggie Stern mumbled as
she fidgeted with the front of her robe. He wished
she'd stop doing that. It was damned distracting. "But
that was right after her recovery from drug addiction
and she was really into community service. Of course,
she always *did* have an interest in abandoned children
since she, herself, was abandoned as a child and later
adopted. Of course, she didn't know she was adopted
until she nearly married her own brother—"

"Could you get to the point?" Jared interrupted.

Ms. Stern bit her lip and hesitated before finally
saying, "You're right. I should get to the point. Monica's story line for the past several months has been
about…infertility. Someone may have left this baby at
my doorstep because they wanted Monica to…
er…raise it as her own."

"That's crazy," Jared said. "What kind of person
thinks a soap character is real?"

"Most soap fans are just normal people who like
good melodrama," Ms. Stern explained. "But occasionally someone will get too wrapped up in the story
and forget it's just entertainment they're watching.

Suddenly they see the soap characters as real people with real problems."

"You have to call the police," Jared stated grimly.

"Yes, that's what I'd planned," Ms. Stern replied. "But I was waiting for Mrs. Fernwalter."

"What for? This baby needs to be placed in a foster home where she can be given proper, experienced care as soon as possible. If her mother's nuts enough to give her away—" He'd almost said, *to someone like you,* but stopped himself just in time. However, it looked as if she had read his thoughts, or guessed them.

"You act like I'm the witch from Hansel and Gretel or something," she accused. "I don't plan to shove the poor little thing in an oven and eat her. I can take care of a baby perfectly well. In fact—"

"Just call the police, Ms. Stern, then we can argue about your baby-tending skills. Maybe while we wait for the cops to show up, you can prove yourself by giving her a bottle. She's trying to suck on my ear...which indicates to me she's hungry."

Ms. Stern got a militant gleam in her eye. "Okay," she said, heading toward the phone on the kitchen wall. "I'll call the police, then I'll feed her. You'll see. She and I, we'll do fine together."

She made the call, then returned to the living room and pulled a bottle of premixed formula out of the bag.

"Heat it till it's just warm, not hot," Jared instructed her.

She raised a brow. "Do I look like an idiot?"

After warming the bottle under the tap, she tested it by shaking a few drops on her wrist. "Just right," she said. "Now give me the baby."

A little mollified by her proficiency in preparing the

bottle, Jared gave her the baby. Since he was quite sure the child would be whisked away as soon as the police showed up, he wasn't too worried about a single feeding at the hands of Monica Blake...*that is,* Ms. Maggie Stern.

Besides, he was there to rescue the poor little thing if Ms. Stern screwed up.

But Ms. Stern didn't get a chance to screw up. As soon as he handed her the baby, the baby started screaming at the top of her lungs again.

"Are you supporting her correctly?" Jared asked.

"Of course I am! I know how to hold a baby."

"Well, I'm not so sure—"

The doorbell rang and Jared took the opportunity to snatch the baby back. She stopped crying right away.

Glaring at him, Ms. Stern went to the door and peered through the security peephole. "How'd they get here so fast? It's the police," she revealed. But when she opened the door, not only did two of New York's finest enter the room, but so did Mrs. Fernwalter and a middle-aged man in a loud coral-colored jacket, white pants and white patent leather shoes.

Jared recognized the type. "Oh, God," he moaned under his breath. "Show business people."

# Chapter Three

Jared watched as the policemen, Mrs. Fernwalter and "Mr. Showbiz" entered the apartment and immediately made Maggie Stern the center of their attention. Everyone spoke at once and no one seemed to even notice him...or the baby.

"Figures," Jared grumbled, moving away from the noise and confusion to sit down in a chair by the sunny window where he angled the baby for feeding purposes and offered her the bottle. "You need to eat anyway, don't you?"

As soon as the rubber nipple touched her lips, the baby began to suck greedily, her big blue eyes staring up at him as she made short work of her breakfast.

"Guess even an abandoned child has to take the back seat when there's a 'star' in the room, eh, squirt?" he crooned to the baby. "Even a bright beam of sunshine like you."

The baby reached up and caught hold of his thumb where he was holding the bottle, but she didn't stop sucking for even a second. Jared smiled at the baby, then looked across the room at the others and noticed that Ms. Stern seemed to have taken control of the conversation. He shook his head. "Look at the way those cops are drooling," he whispered in the baby's ear. "And they haven't got your excuse, Sunshine. They cut *their* teeth years ago."

But Jared knew the policemen had their own, very grown-up, reasons for drooling. They seemed mesmerized by the sight of Ms. Stern in her negligee...especially the younger cop with a neck the size of an Easter ham. He might be big and burly, but Ms. Stern's luminous presence had turned him into what amounted to a hungry-eyed pup looking at a juicy bone. And the other, older cop wasn't behaving much better. He was holding a notepad and pencil, but, though Ms. Stern was obviously telling her tale, he wasn't writing down a single word. He seemed, in a word, starstruck.

Then there was Mrs. Fernwalter...who must have been taken by surprise that morning because she wasn't exactly dressed for company. With her hair in sponge rollers, wearing an old sweater over a simple housedress, she was gazing at Ms. Stern as if she were a heavenly messenger, or something equally divine. And considering Mrs. Fernwalter's account of her initial encounter with Ms. Stern, which had shed a very unflattering light on the soap star, this surprised Jared.

The landlady had reported that even when she'd tried to explain that apartment 2101 was already promised to someone else, Ms. Stern had been adamant and downright nasty in demanding that it be given to her. And, although Jared still blamed Mrs. Fernwalter for giving in to pressure from the soap star, he could imagine how intimidated she'd felt in the face of such selfish high-handedness. Yet now she appeared to have forgiven Ms. Stern everything and even seemed in awe of the woman!

As for Mr. Showbiz in the neon jacket, he was avidly listening to everything being said…and pulling a big fat cigar out of his pocket. For Jared, that was his cue for finally getting noticed.

"Don't light that in here," he commanded, standing up as he spoke and still holding the bottle for the baby's feeding. "Secondhand smoke isn't good for an infant."

Everyone turned and stared. Mrs. Fernwalter started when she saw Jared—a guilty reaction, he supposed—but the others simply seemed surprised to discover someone else in the room.

"This is the child that was left on your doorstep?" the young cop asked Ms. Stern.

*What amazing powers of deduction,* Jared thought dryly.

"Yes," said Ms. Stern. "And this man is one of the other tenants in the building. I don't know his name—"

Jared opened his mouth to reveal who he was, but the cops didn't seem interested. "Ms. Stern," the older officer said, turning his back on Jared, "did you find a note anywhere?"

"No, but—come to think of it—I didn't look in the baby carrier, just the diaper bag." As she spoke, she moved across the room toward the baby carrier, her nightgown and diaphanous robe flowing around her like mist and clinging oh-so-subtly to her curves. When he was finally able to wrench his own gaze away from those shapely, satin-sheathed hips of hers, Jared noticed that both cops had goofy looks on their faces.

"Maybe under the pad—" She got down on her knees and slipped her hand under the pad, doing what the cops should have been doing if only they'd been thinking with their brains instead of their...er... libidos. "Yes! There *is* something!"

Ms. Stern stood up, triumphantly waving an envelope.

"Well, read it out loud!" Mrs. Fernwalter exclaimed, pressing her fists together under her chin in a fever of excitement. "Oh, this is just like an episode of 'The Rich and the Reckless'!"

"It's definitely giving *me* ideas, lady," Mr. Showbiz admitted with a speculative glint in his eyes.

"Yes, read it, Ms. Stern," the young officer beseeched her, seeming more than eager to listen to every syllable that dropped out of her mouth.

Ms. Stern nodded, quickly opened the envelope, and pulled out a single sheet of hot-pink paper. She held it in front of her and began, "'Dear Monica....'" At this point, Ms. Stern paused and flitted an embarrassed glance toward Jared. Jared gave her a disapproving look in reply, which, surprisingly, made her blush as deeply as the sheet of stationery paper she was holding.

"Go on," Mrs. Fernwalter urged her. "Please go on!"

"Yeah, this is getting interesting," Mr. Showbiz murmured, rolling his cigar between his fingers.

Ms. Stern threw Jared a defensive look, lifted her chin and continued. "It reads, 'Dear Monica. Over the past few months I've watched, my heart breaking, as you and the Count have suffered through the trials of infertility. No two people deserve a child more than you do. Your love has risen above every test of endurance. I was especially touched when the Count nursed you through that bout of malaria and the resulting amnesia that caused you to take on the identity of an exotic dancer.'"

"Yes, I *loved* the way he dragged you off the stage at the Hoochie Koochie Bar and carried you home in that dreadful thunderstorm," Mrs. Fernwalter enthused, her hands now clasped at her ample bosom, her eyes taking on a dreamy look. "And how lucky for you that that bolt of lightning stunned your brain and brought back your memory!"

"...er, yes," Ms. Stern mumbled, dashing another embarrassed glance Jared's way.

"Finish the letter, Ms. Stern," Jared prompted impatiently. By now his armful of sunshine had finished her bottle and he gently placed her over his shoulder and patted her back.

"Yes, please continue reading, Ms. Stern," the older officer seconded, belatedly seeming to remember that he was supposed to be in charge.

Maggie nodded. "The letter goes on to say, 'Because a child would make your lives together complete, and because the Count needs an heir for Carsovia—'"

"Oh, but the heir has to be male!" Mrs. Fernwalter interrupted agitatedly. "Is the child a boy?"

"There's no such place as Carsovia, Mrs. Fernwalter," Ms. Stern reminded her, "so I don't think it much matters." Then she continued reading. "'—I'm leaving my niece, Sarah Jessica, with you. Her mother...my sister...died five months ago when Sarah was born.'"

Ms. Stern looked up again, but this time at the baby. By the pitying, distressed expression in her eyes, Jared could almost believe she had a heart. But how could he be sure? After all, she was an actor and she was playing to a captive audience at the moment.

"'No one knows who her father is,'" she presently continued. "'I'm single and have a full-time job and can't give Sarah the kind of life she deserves. I want her to grow up like a princess with you, Monica, and with the Count. I'm Sarah's legal guardian and I have every right to give her away to whomever I choose. I choose you, Monica Blake. I know you'll love her and take good care of her always. Devotedly, C.'"

"C?" Jared repeated.

Ms. Stern's eyes remained on the paper. "That's all it says. Doesn't give us much of a clue as to the note writer's identity, does it?"

"We have ways of finding things out," the young cop bragged, moving forward with a bit of a swagger and taking the note from Ms. Stern. "We'll start our investigation by talking to the doormen who worked last night and early this morning. And, with our computer systems, we have access to information on babies born all over the country. We'll start by looking up births in local hospitals approximately five months ago. We'll be able to track down Sarah's aunt sooner or later."

"If that's who the woman really is," Jared put in. "Maybe she's actually Sarah's mother. Or Sarah might even have been kidnapped."

"That's true," the older cop agreed, tapping his blank notepad with the pencil. "Every possibility will have to be checked out. In the meantime—"

"Sarah will go to a state-appointed foster home...right?" Jared said. "Then hopefully she'll be adopted by a loving couple with a firm handle on reality."

"But aren't *you* going to keep her?" Mrs. Fern-walter exclaimed, looking horrified at Ms. Stern. "I know she's not the son Alexander has always wanted, but—"

Ms. Stern opened her mouth to say something, but Mr. Showbiz spoke first. "Of course she's going to keep her."

"What?" Ms. Stern said.

"*What?*" Jared echoed.

"You don't want this little angel going into a strange foster home, do you, Maggie?" Mr. Showbiz asked her, gesturing toward the now sleeping baby and making a sad face.

"Well, I—"

"After all, her aunt wanted you to have her. If she finds out you *dumped* her in a foster home, she might get mad and snatch the kid away again, no matter where the authorities tried to hide her. If she could find out where *you* lived, Maggie, and got inside a secured building like this one, she's a smart one." He tapped his forehead with his finger. "Smart, but with a screw loose…if you get my drift." He turned to the cops. "You know the type, I'm sure."

Then, before the officers could reply, Mr. Showbiz continued. "Besides, as producer of a daytime drama that deals with these sorts of family issues, I've researched the foster care angle and I know how scarce good homes are. Sometimes, to take up the slack or because it's the best alternative for the kid, relatives or family friends of a homeless child are made temporary foster parents. Couldn't Ms. Stern be made a temporary foster parent…just until the kid's aunt is found or the courts decide what to do? It seems to me that it would be the best thing for the child, don't you agree, officers?''

''Or don't you mean the best thing for the show?'' Jared suggested grimly. Now that he knew that Mr. Showbiz was the producer of ''The Rich and the Reckless,'' he had no trouble understanding the man's motives. Ms. Stern taking in an abandoned child—particularly in conjunction with her infertility story line on the show—would be a publicity tour de force.

''I would never use this child's predicament for publicity purposes,'' Ms. Stern heatedly informed him.

''No, sweetheart, you'd be taking her in because you care what happens to her,'' Mr. Showbiz assured her soothingly. ''Everyone knows how much you love kids.''

''It's obvious on the show that you'd make a super mom,'' Mrs. Fernwalter gushed. ''Your motherly instinct stands out like a beacon!''

''A beacon or a pecan?'' Jared mumbled, getting a dark look from Ms. Stern in response.

''Besides,'' Mr. Showbiz continued, ''you feel personally responsible for this little angel's predicament, don't you, Maggie, m'girl? Becoming her foster mother till the authorities find her a permanent home is the *least* you can do…right?'' He hunched up his shoulders and held both hands out as if he were testing for rain. ''I'll give you all the time off you need.''

''It could be arranged, Ms. Stern,'' the older officer told her. ''If you really do want to be this child's temporary foster parent, a couple of quick phone calls and a follow-up visit from a social worker Monday morning could cinch it. Shall I make the calls?''

Jared was dumbfounded. He couldn't believe what was happening! Mr. Showbiz had worked them all like lumps of play dough, molding the situation to his greedy purposes with the finesse of a snake oil salesman. Both police officers and Mrs. Fernwalter were gazing adoringly at Ms. Stern, waiting for her answer and fully expecting her to agree to the foster parent idea.

Jared stared at her, too, his lowered brows and sternly held mouth communicating his opinion of such a harebrained idea. He could only pray that she'd do the right thing...give the baby to people qualified to take care of her. Surely she would realize that she was the last person on earth who should be taking on the responsibility of a—

"I'll do it," Ms. Stern said, returning Jared's astonished expression with a defiant glare. "I'll take care of Sarah till a permanent home is found for her. Morty is right. I *love* children."

"But this is a no-children-or-pets-allowed building," Jared blurted, desperate. "It's against the rules to keep an infant in your apartment!"

"Exceptions can be made to all rules," Mrs. Fernwalter sniffed, giving Jared a repressive look. "Besides, I'm the one who interprets the rules around here and I say it's okay. After all, this is just a temporary situation."

Stunned and disgusted, Jared handed the sleeping baby to Ms. Stern and headed for the door without saying another word. With the police and the building manager on the soap star's side, there was nothing he could do to reverse the decision. He would just have to trust in the probability of Ms. Stern calling the police tomorrow, or even later today, when she realized that the demands of taking care of a baby seriously interfered with her glamorous life-style.

A HALF HOUR LATER, Maggie sat on the couch with a sleeping Sarah in her lap and a sinking sensation in her stomach. Morty sat across from her in a chair, inspecting his cigar.

"What have I done?" Maggie whispered. "What have you tricked me into doing, Morty?"

"I don't know what you're talking about, sweetheart," Morty calmly replied. He took a long whiff of his cigar. "You sure I can't smoke this thing in here? The kid's asleep."

"But she's still breathing," Maggie retorted. "I absolutely forbid you to light that cigar. That man, that *irritating* man...whoever he is...was right about secondhand smoke being unhealthy for the baby. You'll have to wait till you're outside."

"Well, I was about to leave anyway," he announced as he stood up.

"Sure, just take off...now that you've saddled me with this baby!"

"Maggie, keep your voice down, sweetheart. You'll wake her up," Morty said reasonably. "Besides it was your decision to take care of her."

"After you made me feel guilty about the idea of *dumping* her in a foster home," Maggie pointed out. "You only wanted me to become Sarah's foster mother so you could use it as publicity for the show."

Morty shrugged and had the grace to look a little sheepish. "It won't hurt the show, that's true. But I meant everything I said about the kid being better off with you."

"Not everyone thinks so," Maggie said sulkily, remembering the horrified look on *that man's* face when the older officer said it could be arranged if she wanted to be Sarah's foster mother.

If Maggie was totally honest with herself, she'd have to admit, too, that part of the reason she agreed to take Sarah was to defy *him* and to prove that she was perfectly capable of taking care of a baby…despite appearances to the contrary. She and Sarah had just got off to a bad start, that's all. Now that things were more calm, she was sure Sarah wouldn't cry the minute she woke up and looked at her.

"Who was that guy, anyway?" Morty asked.

"I still don't know," Maggie said with a frown. "I should have asked Mrs. Fernwalter, but she ran off to find me a crib for Sarah before the thought even crossed my mind. All I know is that he resents me because he wanted this apartment and didn't get it." She pursed her lips, thinking hard. "But there's more to it than that. Even if the apartment issue didn't exist, I still don't think he'd like me."

"Then he's one strange and unique individual," was Morty's opinion.

"So says you and the president of my fan club," Maggie grumbled with a smile. But she had to admit, it felt good to be reassured that not everyone shared the man's poor opinion of her.

"You're not worried about taking care of her, are you?" Morty asked. "You were just complaining yesterday about your life being boring—"

"Believe me, it wasn't a complaint," Maggie clarified.

"—but if she's too much for you, Maggie, just give the authorities a call and they'll find her another place to crash till the poor kid's life somehow gets straightened out. Obviously no one's going to think her aunt's a suitable guardian after pulling a trick like this, and with no mom...."

Maggie looked down at Sarah's angelic little face. The baby was so sweet and innocent and helpless. She truly did want to help the child, and not just because she felt guilty about the aunt's delusions about her actually being Monica Blake. Just holding her in her arms made Maggie feel protective toward her...kind of like the "motherly instinct" the man accused her of having only a minuscule amount of. Well, evidently he was wrong.

"I grew up with four younger sisters," Maggie finally said. "I know more about kids than I'll ever need to know. I'm sure I can handle taking care of one little baby girl for a few days."

"Good," Morty said, tucking away his cigar and smiling down at Maggie.

A little worried about Morty's satisfied look, however, Maggie added, "But I won't do interviews and I won't have pictures taken. I don't want to exploit this child for ratings. Understand, Morty?"

"Sure, sweetheart," Morty agreed, but then added, "only this is something you won't be able to keep under wraps. The press already knows. How do you think I found out about it so fast this morning? You think I'm psychic or something? George Spader from the *Planet* called me. One of your neighbors probably scooped the story for a little cash."

Remembering the flash of a camera as she stood in her doorway holding Sarah that morning, Maggie nodded back. "Yeah, I'm sure you're right. But I won't initiate or encourage publicity."

*I won't do anything to support that horrid man's negative views of me,* she added to herself.

"Well, I gotta go, sweetheart," Morty announced. "I can't wait any longer to smoke this cigar."

With Sarah still sleeping in her arms, Maggie stood up and walked Morty to the door. "You were serious about the time off, then?" she asked him.

"Sure," he replied, sticking his cigar in his mouth and reaching for his lighter. "The writers will just have to beef up the other story lines for a few days. Take care, sweetheart, and call me and Marge if you need anything…anything at all." Then he gave her a peck on the cheek and was gone.

Maggie shut the door and looked down at Sarah. Her warm little body felt so good in her arms. She smiled. Maybe this was just the diversion she needed in her life. She'd been coerced into this little baby-sitting gig, but, upon consideration, maybe it was just the respite she needed from her hectic schedule.

All she'd been doing for the past twelve years was work, work, work. Now she could spend several lovely days rocking this sweet baby, playing with her, giving her baths, combing her silky hair. There would be no conflict with work at the studio, so it would all be as easy as pie.

Maggie walked to the couch and sat down. She gazed at Sarah till suddenly those feathery lashes of hers blinked open. Maggie smiled and said, "Hi, sleepyhead. Ready for some lunch?"

Sarah blinked a few more times, her blue-as-the-sky eyes fixed on Maggie. Suddenly her face crumpled like a wadded piece of newspaper and she let loose with a gut-busting yell that made Maggie's ears ring.

THREE HOURS LATER, Sarah was still crying and Maggie was exhausted and desperate. Bouncing Sarah up and down and holding the phone receiver between her chin and shoulder, she punched in Morty's number one more time. As it had every other time she'd called his number that afternoon, the phone just rang and rang.

"Sure, Morty," Maggie grumbled. " 'Just give you a call if I need anything.' You don't tell someone that and then leave town!"

Maggie hung up the phone with a bang, shifted Sarah onto her shoulder, and began to walk the floor from one end of the room to the other. She figured she'd wear a hole in the carpet by day's end if this kept up. But she'd tried everything to make Sarah stop crying and nothing worked. The child didn't want a bottle, her diaper was dry, and she seemed to have absolutely no interest in the rattle and the little ring of plastic keys Maggie had found in the diaper bag.

She was beginning to worry that Sarah might be sick, but with no thermometer in the house there was no reliable way for Maggie to check her temperature. Along with diapers and formula, she should probably buy a thermometer, too…but how? She hadn't thought to ask Morty to pick up some things at the grocery store while he was here, and now he couldn't be reached.

She'd also tried to reach a couple of friends, but with no luck. Since it was such a gorgeous fall weekend, everybody was probably out enjoying it. As for her sisters, the married ones lived in Connecticut, and she didn't want to involve her youngest sister—who was shy—in anything that might end up on the front page of a tabloid. Mrs. Fernwalter was gone, too, no doubt finding the perfect crib for her celebrity tenant's unexpected guest.

Maggie didn't dare attempt to go to the store herself, since with a screaming baby in tow she couldn't exactly shop incognito. Worse than a tabloid picture of herself in a sexy negligee with a baby in her arms would be a tabloid picture of her in sweats and a ballcap with a *screaming* baby in her arms. While she hadn't gotten into this with ratings in mind, she knew that such negative publicity would not be good for the show and she definitely wanted to avoid it.

She supposed she would have to have the groceries delivered, but with Sarah crying non-stop it was difficult to look up the number of a delivering grocer nearby, much less try to talk to him over the phone. And she hadn't even changed out of her negligee!

In addition to baby essentials, Maggie thought it would be nice to have some food in the house, too. It was now more than twenty-four hours since she'd had a meal. Marshmallow treats just didn't help much when your body was craving real nourishment. She supposed she could call out for Chinese or something, but how could she eat with Sarah carrying on so? What she really needed was to find out what was bothering this baby and go from there. Colic, maybe? But should she call her own doctor, or try to find a pediatrician that took new patients on a Saturday afternoon?

"Fat chance, Maggie," Maggie grumbled to herself. "You might as well face it. You're in a corner. You've got to call your mom."

Calling Lorena Morgenstern was definitely a last resort for Maggie. She loved her mother dearly, but the woman was a busybody with a capital "B." Ever since her husband died ten years ago of a heart attack, she had devoted herself completely to her five daughters...and that meant having an opinion about everything from their choice of eye shadow to their sex lives. Once she found out about the unexpected little bundle that had showed up on Maggie's doorstep, she'd probably set up camp in her eldest daughter's living room indefinitely. But it was a risk Maggie had to take.

However, as she punched in the familiar number, the doorbell rang. "Saved by the bell," she muttered, trudging tiredly to the door. Peering through the peephole she saw Billie standing there. Now, why hadn't she thought to call Billie? Maggie heaved a sigh of relief and opened the door.

"Why didn't you call me? I thought we were going to lunch? You're not even dressed yet," Billie observed as she breezed through. "Nice nightgown, though. You always sleep in satin? Hey, who's the kid?"

Maggie felt a hysterical urge to laugh, but that would take energy she didn't have. It was pretty comical the way Billie had noticed the nightgown first and the screaming baby second.

"Her name is Sarah," Maggie said, "and she's been crying for three straight hours."

"No kidding?" Billie replied casually as she eased down into a chair in the living room.

"You mean you live next door and you haven't heard this child screaming at the tops of her lungs? The walls can't be that thick."

"I thought I heard a cat," Billie said with a shrug.

"No such luck," Maggie groaned. "A cat would be much easier to take care of."

"Then why didn't you get a cat?" Billie inquired ingenuously.

"I didn't even 'get' this baby, Billie," Maggie blurted, exasperated. "She was left on my doorstep this morning. Didn't you hear the ruckus in the hallway this morning?"

"I sleep like the dead," Billie admitted, then pulled her feet up under her and leaned forward with an eager smile. "But this sounds like a great story. Tell me all about it, Maggie."

As she continued to walk Sarah up and down the room...to no avail...Maggie told Billie about her day, finishing with her concern that Sarah might be sick.

"She needs to be looked at by a doctor. Do you think you could help me get her to the emergency clinic at St. John's Children's Hospital? You could hold her while I change clothes."

Maggie attempted to hand over the baby to Billie, but Billie pressed back in the chair and firmly shook her head. "Nope. No way, Maggie. I don't have a clue how to hold babies...especially when they're crying. I'll do anything for you but *that*."

"I'm desperate, Billie," Maggie admitted, on the verge of tears herself. "So desperate I was even ready to call my mom. What am I going to do?"

"If your mom's anything like my mom, you *are* desperate," Billie said, her forehead furrowing. "Too bad doctors don't make house calls anymore...." Suddenly Billie's eyebrows lifted and her lips curved in a wide smile. "Why didn't I think of this sooner? I know *exactly* what to do. There's a doctor...a pediatrician, no less...that lives right here in the building. In fact, he's your neighbor on the other side—number 2102. If he's home, I'm sure he'll come over and look at the baby."

Maggie's eyes drifted shut on a relieved sigh. "Oh,

thank you, Billie. That would be perfect. Let's just hope he's home."

"I'll go right now and find out," Billie announced, jumping to her feet. "Boy, this is great! I've been wishing for a long time to have a good reason to knock on that guy's door. You can only deliver so many plates of marshmallow treats before a man begins to question your motives."

"What *are* your motives?" Maggie asked, watching suspiciously as Billie stopped at the mirror by the door to fuss with her hair. "Have you got the hots for this guy?"

Billie turned and smiled, her eyes sparkling with excitement. "Of course I do. And, once you see him, you'll understand perfectly." Then she was gone.

Three minutes later there was a brief knock on the door and Maggie hurried to open it. As usual Billie waltzed right in, but the tall man she'd brought with her remained outside. Maggie just stared at him, unable to believe her rotten luck.

It was the man from the elevator! The one who had wanted her apartment! The man who thought she didn't have enough motherly instinct to fill a thimble!

"What are ya waiting for, Doctor J?" Billie asked him. "Come on in and meet my friend, Maggie Stern. Maggie, this is your next-door-neighbor, Jared Austin...the baby doctor."

Dr. Austin's mouth curved up in an ironic smile. "Nice to meet you, Ms. Stern. I understand you might be needing my assistance?"

# Chapter Four

Jared waited while Ms. Maggie Stern absorbed the shock of finding *him* at her door. He tried to appear as nonchalant as he sounded, but he was itching to snatch that baby out of her arms. It had been very difficult listening to the child's cries through the thin walls that separated his apartment from hers. He had been on the verge of coming over, or even calling the police and telling them what a mistake they'd made by leaving a defenseless baby with a soap opera star, when Billie showed up at his door.

"I was hoping I was wrong about your lack of skill at baby tending," Jared couldn't resist saying. "But I guess I wasn't."

"That's not fair," Ms. Stern shot back, tossing a lock of dark hair out of her eyes. "I'm no expert...like *you* are, apparently...but I think Sarah may be sick."

Jared frowned and came into the apartment, shutting the door behind him. "So Billie tells me. But why do you say that?"

"Isn't it obvious?" Ms. Stern snapped. "She's screaming at the top of her lungs."

Jared narrowed his eyes. "She looked the picture of health this morning. Are you sure she isn't wet? Hungry? Feeling neglected?'' While in his apartment, listening to Sarah cry, he'd pictured her being left on the sofa while her glamorous guardian took a bubble bath.

Ms. Stern's eyes flashed angrily. ''I've checked her several times and changed her twice. She's dry. She might be hungry, but she won't take a bottle. And as for being neglected, she hasn't been out of my arms since you left this morning. I've walked her, rocked her, talked to her, and sung to her. I've done everything but stand on my head, but she just won't stop crying.''

Jared was forced to abandon the mental picture he'd had of Ms. Stern relaxing in a tub while Sarah cried for attention. She might appear as alluring as ever, but she didn't look like she'd just stepped out of a bubble bath. In fact, she looked a little frazzled, and she still hadn't changed out of her negligee.

But then maybe she routinely wore such get-ups around the house all day long on the weekends? Frequently when he'd stop by Claire's on a weekend, she'd be floating around in a silk caftan or some other flamboyant loungewear or sleepwear, complete with chunky diamonds as accessories. Claire took her celebrity status very seriously, even when she was vegging out at home.

''I know you're the last person on earth who would be eager to grant me a favor…*Dr.* Austin,'' Ms. Stern said, ''but for Sarah's sake, could you…?''

''Give Sarah to me,'' Jared said briskly. ''I'll check her out, but don't consider it a favor to you, Ms. Stern. You're right. I'm doing this for Sarah's sake.''

''Say, you two know each other,'' Billie declared

belatedly, staring with surprise from one tense face to the other.

"Barely," Maggie muttered.

"Not even that," Jared added.

Billie's eyebrows lifted. "But you've been quarrelling since I brought Doctor J over here. Geez, if I didn't know better, I'd think you two were married or something."

"That's a good one," Jared snorted, ignoring Ms. Stern's piqued look as he handed his bag of instruments to Billie, then held out his arms for Sarah. Although she seemed relieved to relinquish the wailing bundle to him, Ms. Stern did follow closely behind as he carried Sarah to the sofa. Jared was speculating about colic versus an ear infection, but by the time he'd sat down, Sarah had stopped crying.

"Hey, that's some trick, Doctor J," Billie observed as she stood over them. "How'd you do it?"

Holding her with one hand supporting her neck and head, and the other cupping her small bottom, Jared peered into Sarah's tear-streaked face. "I don't have a clue," he admitted. "But, lo and behold, the child seems about to crack a smile."

"You've got to be kidding," Ms. Stern murmured as she and Billie bent near to look at Sarah, too.

"I knew I didn't nickname you Sunshine for nothing," Jared said to the baby as she did, indeed, break out in a huge smile. "Sarah Sunshine is a perfect moniker for someone with such a sunny disposition."

"My experience with her certainly doesn't bring such a nickname to mind. 'Stormy Sarah' is more like it," Ms. Stern grumbled. "There must be some reason why she's been crying all this time. I still think you should check her out…er…*Doctor*."

"I intend to," Jared informed her. "Billie, my bag, please. And you, Ms. Stern, could you prepare another bottle for Sarah? If she hasn't eaten since the formula I gave her this morning, she's probably ravenous."

"I tried to get her to eat, but she wouldn't swallow a drop," Ms. Stern said plaintively.

Jared gave her a beleaguered look over his shoulder. "Just fix it, all right? Maybe Sarah will take the bottle from me."

Ms. Stern turned away and went to do as she'd been asked, but Jared could hear her muttering under her breath. While she was gone, he unsnapped Sarah's sleeper and checked her diaper for dampness. Just as Ms. Stern had claimed, the baby's bottom was perfectly dry. And, at the moment, even her eyes were perfectly dry. Sarah was smiling at Jared and happily flailing her arms in the air.

"I knew you had a certain charm, Doctor J," Billie said wonderingly. "But I didn't know it extended to females of such a young age."

"I'm a pediatrician, Billie," Jared said modestly, smiling back at Sarah and catching hold of one of her tiny fists to kiss it. "Babies are my business." But Jared had to admit, he was as surprised and flattered by Sarah's instant liking for him as Billie was. He'd had his fair share of screamers in the office who wanted absolutely nothing to do with him. But, thank goodness, such cases were definitely in the minority. Sarah, though...she was something special.

"Here's the bottle," said Ms. Stern, handing it to Jared. "I've checked it. The temperature is just right."

Jared said, "Thanks," then rechecked before giving it to Sarah.

"I told you I'd checked it," Ms. Stern objected.

Jared didn't reply. He just watched as Sarah gulped down the formula as though she hadn't eaten in a week.

"This baby was starving," he said, throwing Ms. Stern an accusing look.

"I tried to feed her," Ms. Stern insisted. "I told you, she just wouldn't take the bottle. Have you checked her ears?"

"If her ears were infected, she wouldn't be chugging this stuff down so fast. The suction makes infected ears hurt like the devil. But I *will* check them...as soon as she's done eating."

Jared settled back in the sofa cushions and watched Sarah emptying the bottle in record time. "Slow down, Sunshine," he advised her soothingly. Halfway through the bottle, he gently plucked the rubber nipple from her mouth and placed her over his shoulder. After a few pats on the back she let loose with a burp loud enough to be heard above the strains of a marching band.

"Way to go, Sarah!" Billie cheered, laughing at the baby. But when Jared looked at Ms. Stern, there was no trace of humor on her face. She looked tired and confused and...hurt? Jared quickly scuttled that idea out of his brain. If anything about Ms. Stern was hurt, it was only her pride. She was offended because Sarah obviously liked him better than her. Didn't "stars" always want to be the center of attention?

"Now, Billie, why don't you hold her and give her the rest of the bottle while I check her out?" Jared suggested.

Jared was surprised when Billie immediately backed away. "No, not me. I'm no good with babies. Have Maggie hold her."

As if *she's* good with babies? Jared wanted to ask, but he refrained. "You want to give it another try, Ms. Stern?" he felt beholden to say, not expecting her to jump at the chance.

"I guess so," she said, looking doubtfully at Sarah. "She seems to be doing much better now."

Jared handed Sarah to her and he could have sworn the soap star had a profound look of relief and pleasure on her face when Sarah did not scream bloody murder.

"So far, so good," he muttered. "Now just keep her happy while I check her out...if you think you can handle it."

Ms. Stern scowled at Jared, but he ignored her and put on his stethoscope. Well, maybe ignored was too strong a word. Ignoring a beautiful woman like Maggie Stern was probably impossible, especially when he was standing so close to her and could smell the scent in her hair. Lilacs? And from his vantage point, he could actually see down the front of her gown. That is, if he cared to look...which, of course, he didn't. Well, maybe he *did* want to look, but he wouldn't.

He listened to Sarah's heart and lungs and found everything normal. Once she was finished with her bottle, he took out his otoscope and examined her ears. Everything checked out normally there, too. There had been no signs of abuse on her arms and legs, and her stomach was flat and pliable...which seemed to indicate she wasn't troubled with colic. He peered down her throat, too, and it was as normal as they come. Lastly, he took her temperature. It was a perfect 98.6. There appeared to be no medical explanation for Sarah's crying.

"She's as fit as a fiddle," Jared pronounced as he stuffed his instruments back inside his small black bag.

"My recommendation is for mom—the *temporary* foster mom in this case—to take two aspirin and *don't* call me in the morning."

"But I don't understand," Ms. Stern said, her eyebrows knitting together. "Why was she crying?"

"My guess would be that she was unhappy, Ms. Stern," Jared said.

"About what?"

"Being separated from her aunt, perhaps?"

"She seems perfectly happy now...but I wonder for how long?"

"Till the doc leaves is my guess," Billie suggested with an arch look at Jared. "I know *I'll* be heartbroken."

Jared smiled back at Billie, but he did not reply to her flirtatious comment. "I've got paperwork to do, ladies." He bent down and gently pinched Sarah's fat cheek. "You be good, Sarah Sunshine." Then he turned and had only taken two steps away when Sarah's smile crumpled and she began to cry.

"She really doesn't want you to go, Doc!" Billie exclaimed.

His brows knitting, Jared turned back and approached the baby again. Sure enough, Sarah stopped crying as soon as he drew near.

"Hey, the kid sure knows how to get her own way, doesn't she?" Billie observed, obviously impressed. "Maybe I should try crying sometime when a date wants to leave too early!"

"Maybe it's not me she objects to so much," Ms. Stern suggested with a troubled look at Jared. "Maybe it's just that she wants *you* around all the time."

"She barely knows me," Jared objected, gently stroking Sarah's downy curls.

"That's probably in your favor," Ms. Stern murmured. When Jared scowled, she hurriedly added, "Seriously, though, you were the one who comforted her right after she was dropped off at my door. You must have bonded with her, or something. Maybe you ought to be the foster parent."

Jared let go of Sarah's fist and stepped back, firmly shaking his head. "Hey, unlike some people, I know my limitations. I get emergencies at the hospital that sometimes take hours to resolve. Who would take care of Sarah then? Besides, you volunteered, not me. Why don't you just call the police and tell them you can't do the job?"

"If Sarah cries whenever you're not around, why would another foster parent be better than me?" Ms. Stern retorted, her chin set at a stubborn angle. "She just needs to get used to me, that's all. Just like she'd have to get used to anyone else."

"Suit yourself, Ms. Stern," Jared said stiffly, turning to go.

"Wait...please."

Jared reluctantly turned back and stared down into large brown eyes full of supplication. He could almost imagine he saw the sheen of tears collecting. Damn, she was good. "What, Ms. Stern?"

"Can't you stay till she goes to sleep again? I desperately need a shower and to order some groceries. There's no food in the house, and I'll need my strength to care for Sarah, you know. And she'll be out of diapers and formula soon."

Jared sighed. "Can't Billie—?"

"I've got rehearsal," Billie quickly said, moving toward the door. "I don't know the story behind you two, but you'd better sign a temporary truce for

Sarah's sake. Looks like she needs you both.'' She threw Maggie an apologetic look. ''Much as I'd like to help, I'm no good with kids, anyway. Besides...you know...I've got rehearsal.'' Then she quickly exited, closing the door firmly behind her.

''She's got rehearsal all right...in about three hours,'' Jared grumbled.

''She really is afraid to hold Sarah for some reason,'' Maggie told him, ''so she wouldn't be much help.''

''Which she freely admits,'' Jared said dryly. ''Like me, Billie knows her limitations.''

''Can't you at least quit taking potshots at me long enough to see that this child needs your help?'' Ms. Stern admonished, her brown eyes now sparking with anger. ''I know you don't want to help *me,* but by helping me you'll be helping Sarah. Would it kill you to stick around till she goes to sleep? In the meantime I could order groceries and take a shower. You could leave the minute she nods off. Is that too much to ask?''

Jared wanted to be difficult, but he couldn't because he cared too much about Sarah's well-being. ''Fine,'' he said with an exaggerated sigh. ''But make it snappy, will you?'' He set down his bag and held out his arms.

While he was trying hard to appear as put-upon as possible, Jared could tell Ms. Stern was trying just as hard not to look happy and relieved by his capitulation. The truth was, he didn't mind baby-sitting Sarah. He only wished it wasn't necessary, and that the poor kid was in a proper home where she felt secure and loved.

''I'll call the grocer's first,'' Ms. Stern said as she

handed Sarah over to him. "Do you know one around here that delivers?"

Jared sat down in a chair, fitting Sarah into the crook of his arm. "Angelo's delivers," he offered grudgingly. "But make sure you know what brand of diapers and formula Sarah uses before you call. There's all kinds of both, you know."

Ms. Stern gave him another look that seemed to say, "I'm not a complete idiot," then got out the Manhattan telephone directory, sat down across from him, opened the huge book on her lap, and began to look for Angelo's number.

While rocking Sarah in his arms, Jared couldn't help but observe Ms. Stern as she pored over the phone book. With her head bent, her long dark hair fell forward onto her shoulders, the ends curling toward her pale cleavage. The flowing skirt of her negligee swirled at her feet, and her bare toes peeked out at the lacy hem, one foot overlapping the other. It was a demure pose and Jared couldn't help the cynical suspicion that it was practiced. But there was no denying that she presented quite a fetching picture. He was surprised and aggrieved to feel his groin tighten with desire.

Then, as she found the number and began to punch the buttons on her phone, he quickly looked away. As he gazed around the apartment, he fueled his dislike of her by taking in the superior attributes of her apartment over his. Although he was just next door, strategic placement of trees and balconies made her view much better. And her apartment was just bigger and airier, the floor plan more open. And then there was the study.... To think that for four years he'd planned on this great apartment being his. *Four years!*

"I've placed the order. They'll be here in half an hour."

Lost in his thoughts, Jared was taken by surprise when Ms. Stern spoke. He looked up, his brow still furrowed in a frown from contemplating his ill-usage at the hands of this soap diva and his landlady.

Seeming to feel the rebuke in his expression, Ms. Stern's gaze wavered and fell away. "And since Sarah's asleep, you can go now. Thank you for staying with her while I called Angelo's."

"I thought you wanted to shower?" he said gruffly.

"I do, but—"

"Go ahead. She's only been out for a minute, so I'll make sure she's really asleep before I lay her down, then I'll let myself out."

"Mrs. Fernwalter hasn't brought the crib yet. The carpet is soft. Better lay her down there or in the baby carrier rather than on the sofa where she might fall off."

"I'd thought of that already," he assured her dryly. "Just take your shower, okay?"

"Okay…and thanks again," she muttered, turning to go. Then she disappeared down the hall that led to what Jared knew was a large bedroom with huge closets and a deep, whirlpool tub.

"Damn," he muttered under his breath. "How'd I get suckered into this?" He gazed down at Sarah, who was peacefully sleeping. "Normally I'm a pretty nice guy," he whispered to her, skimming his thumb along the edge of her small, shell-shaped ear. "But this whole situation just makes a guy grouchy…you know?"

Sarah responded with a soft sigh, and snuggled closer. Jared contemplated laying her down on the carpet, but he didn't have the heart. Not yet, anyway. She just seemed so darn comfortable. And he frankly didn't like leaving her unattended for any amount of time, even though she was asleep. At her age, she couldn't crawl off or anything, but still....

No, he'd better stick around till Maggie Stern finished her shower. But it was aggravating being in the apartment that should have been his, helping a woman he didn't even like to accomplish something he heartily disapproved of. He just hoped everyone involved would eventually come to their senses and Sarah would end up where she really belonged.

But where was that? he wondered, gazing down at her. Judging by the blissful expression on her tiny face, she appeared to think she belonged with *him*.

Maggie would have loved to stand under the stream of hot water for a couple of hours, but knowing Sarah was alone in the living room, she hurried through her shower and quickly wrapped herself in a large pink towel. She hadn't been able to find her shower cap in the as yet unorganized bathroom, so she'd pinned her hair into a haphazard knot on her head. Now wet strands had loosened, falling into her eyes and onto her shoulders.

"Sarah won't care how you look, Margaret," she lectured her reflection, just before she padded down the hall toward the living room. She just wanted to check on Sarah, but she was not about to venture out if Dr. Jared Austin was still on the premises, so she stopped and listened first, then peeked around the corner.

By now it was late afternoon and the light in the living room was dim, but she could plainly see Sarah's little form on the carpet in the middle of the room, well away from any tables or chairs. She lay perfectly still on her back on top of a blanket with another blanket covering her, her little fists in the air and her head turned to the side.

It appeared that the irascible "Doctor J" had settled her safely before he'd abandoned ship, but Maggie just wanted to snatch a reassuring look at her before she went back to her bedroom and searched through boxes and suitcases for something to wear.

She looked around the room once more, and when she saw no tall, angry pediatrician lurking in the shadows, she tiptoed into the living room toward Sarah. Standing over her at last, she peered down at the baby's sleeping face and smiled.

Despite what the child had put her through that afternoon, Maggie couldn't help but think she looked like an angel. If only she'd behave like one when she was awake and Maggie was the only person around to care for her! But Maggie told herself that Sarah would get used to her...in time. She just hoped, for both their sakes, it was sooner than later.

"Do you always dress so casually when you have guests?"

Maggie clapped her hand over her mouth and whirled around, nearly losing her towel in the process. Standing at the door of the kitchen, with a marshmallow treat in his hand, was the good doctor.

"*You!*" she croaked. "I thought you were gone!"

"I didn't want to leave Sarah alone," he explained. She felt herself blushing as his gaze slid slowly down her barely covered body. He raised a brow. "First a negligee, now a towel. What next, Ms. Stern? But possibly there's an explanation.... Are you hosting a pool party this afternoon?'' He raised both brows. "No? Then perhaps an orgy?''

Clutching her towel to the front of her, Maggie decided to play the scene like Monica would. Standing tall, she affected a tone of haughty disdain. "I suppose you think you're being quite amusing. Forgive me if I fail to see the humor. As you can obviously see, I've finished my shower and, since Sarah is sleeping, you can go now.''

He'd been dismissed, but Jared Austin made no move toward the door. He just stood there and looked at her, his blue eyes keen and unwavering, his expression unreadable. Maggie felt herself blushing deeper than ever, her body warming from the roots of her hair to the tips of her damp toes, and her heart ticktocked like an out-of-control metronome. Outwardly she pretended to be unembarrassed, but inwardly she was dying.

Despite the fact that on "The Rich and the Reckless" she'd done endless love scenes and had cavorted in towels and in tubs and on the tops of tables with her fictional lovers, she never became confused about the difference between fantasy and reality. The trouble with most of her dates was that they frequently *did* become confused, and expected Maggie to act just like Monica did on television.

But Maggie was no Monica. And Jared Austin's continued scrutiny was getting to her in a big way. She felt like a deer caught in headlights, frightened but mesmerized...and he seemed just as stalled, just as reluctantly transfixed. Despite her outward bravado, Maggie wished the floor would just open up and swallow her.

However, since a complete collapse of the build-

ing's concrete structure seemed unlikely, Maggie sent
a prayer winging heavenward that something...
*anything*...would break the strange spell she and Jared
Austin were caught up in.

Suddenly the intercom buzzed and Jared flinched,
then shifted his gaze away from Maggie. Finally she
could move. Heck, finally she could breathe.... Her
prayer had been answered. Twelve years of attending
Sunday school had finally paid off.

"Maybe that's Morty," Maggie murmured hopefully, clutching her towel and moving with as much
dignity as she could muster to the intercom on the wall
by the door. Trouble was, she had to walk past Jared
to get there...and he was watching her again. She
avoided eye contact and managed to take the necessary
steps without tripping or otherwise mortifying herself.

She pressed the intercom button. "Yes?"

"Hey, Maggie, it's me! Can I come up?"

Maggie could not mistake the voice of her on-screen
love interest. But why was Greg suddenly showing up
at her building? She'd certainly made it clear that the
passion between them was strictly dictated by the soap
script and limited to the studio.

"Greg, I'm not dressed...." she began, flustered.

"Perfect," he drawled into the intercom.

Maggie snatched a nervous glance at Jared, who had
folded his arms and was listening with obvious interest, those brows of his again lowered disapprovingly.
"Hey, if you need privacy," he offered with a shrug,
"I was just leaving anyway." He moved toward the
door.

"No, you don't understand," Maggie said agitatedly. "I wasn't expecting company." *Least of all*

*Greg Moran!* "Sarah might wake up before I'm finished—"

Jared glanced toward Sarah as if suddenly remembering her and said, "Before you're finished *what?*"

Maggie heaved an exasperated sigh. "Before I'm finished dressing, of course."

"Don't go to all that trouble for me, doll," came Greg's voice over the intercom.

"Oh, be quiet, Greg!" Maggie implored him, at the end of her rope. "Is Dennis there?"

"The doorman? Sure."

"Put him on, please."

"Yes, Ms. Blake?" came the doorman's voice. "You want I should send Count Tolstoy up?"

"Count Tolstoy?" Jared repeated, rolling his eyes. "The guy from your soap?"

Ignoring Jared, Maggie ordered, "Send him up in ten minutes, Dennis, but not before."

"You shouldn't keep *Soap Beat* magazine's Hot Hunk of the Month waiting, Maggie," Greg said teasingly. "After all—"

But Maggie impatiently clicked off the intercom before he got his sentence out and rounded on Jared.

"Will you stay, Dr. Austin, just till I get dressed?" she asked him, brisk and businesslike. "Ten more minutes is all I'm asking for."

Jared stared at Maggie Stern's cool-as-a-cucumber expression. Apparently it didn't bother her nearly as much as it bothered him that she was standing in front of him in nothing more than a towel. And what if this Count Tolstoy jerk with the Texas accent came up before she was finished dressing? They cavorted on television in front of millions, so who knew what they did together in private? For Sarah's sake…yes, for

*Sarah's* sake...he'd better stick around and make sure that absolutely *nothing* happened.

"All right, Ms. Stern," Jared said, moving to a chair in the living room and sitting down. "I'll give you ten minutes."

"You're all heart," she said with sweet sarcasm, then marched sedately out of the room. But despite her upright stance and proudly jutting chin, her cute, round rear still had an enticingly feminine wiggle to it beneath the pink towel. His thoughts couldn't help but wander....

Jared impatiently jerked his gaze away and his thoughts back in line, then crossed his arms and trained his narrowed eyes on the front door. He couldn't wait to get a look at this so-called "Hot Hunk."

## Chapter Five

Jared had expected to be kept waiting in the living room trying to make small talk with the Hot Hunk while Ms. Maggie Stern, soap star extraordinaire, took her time applying makeup and picking out a suitable outfit with matching jewels. So it was quite a surprise when, a mere nine minutes later, she walked briskly into the room, pushing up the sleeves of a pale lavender sweater.

She wore matching pants and black flats and had combed her hair into a loose pageboy that rested on her shoulders in shiny waves. She had on lipstick, but he couldn't tell if she'd put on eye makeup and all that other stuff or not. She appeared to be a woman who could look good with or without the "other stuff." The only jewelry she wore was a pair of delicate, old-fashioned gold earrings and a watch.

Jared had to reluctantly concede that Ms. Stern apparently was not the stereotypical "star" when it came to being obsessed with her appearance...yet she still managed to look like a million bucks.

"That was fast," he said.

"I told you I only needed ten minutes. Thank you

for staying. You're free to go," she replied with cool politeness.

Jared stood up, but he didn't move toward the door. He had expected to at least get a look at the Hot Hunk before leaving. In fact, he'd expected to have to stay longer than he wanted to, so Ms. Stern's quick-change routine was a bit...well...*unexpected*. And disappointing.

As he hesitated, Ms. Stern gave him a questioning look and he was forced to speak. "I thought you'd want me to stay till the groceries are delivered." He gestured toward Sarah. "She might wake up before you have a chance to put everything away."

Ms. Stern raised a brow. "I thought you had paperwork to do?"

"I do, but I suppose I can wait a few more minutes till the groceries arrive." *Besides,* he added to himself, *I'm not sure I like the idea of leaving Sarah here with you and the Hot Hunk.*

Ms. Stern's eyes narrowed suspiciously. "I know what you're thinking."

Jared endeavored to look as innocent as possible. "What do you mean?"

Resting her hands on her hips, her cheeks flaming, her eyes flashing, Ms. Stern said, "You think...you arrogantly *assume*...that Greg and I—"

But before she could finish her sentence, the doorbell rang, followed by insistent knocking. "Hey, doll, it's me," came a muffled, masculine voice from the other side of the door.

Ms. Stern looked annoyed and headed quickly for the door, mumbling a sentence or two that contained the words "men" and "morons" in unflattering juxtaposition. She opened the door and a tall, dark-haired man stepped purposefully into the apartment and, without saying a word, yanked Ms. Stern into his arms and kissed her like a sailor who'd just been granted shore leave after months at sea.

No, make that *years* at sea, Jared amended as the kiss went on and on. True, Ms. Stern seemed more stunned than an active participant in the kissing marathon, but she wasn't pushing the Hot Hunk away. Jared was thinking it was a darn good thing he'd stuck around to make sure Sarah wasn't forgotten while her guardian cavorted with her costar, but he was also beginning to feel like a voyeur.

And then there were all those other surprising and uncomfortable feelings.... Suddenly his heart was beating out of control, there was a knot in his stomach the size of a casaba melon, and most of his blood supply seemed to have pooled behind his eyes. He was either having a heart attack or Ms. Stern and the Hot Hunk's passionate display was making him madder than he had any right to be.

But since his hands had balled into sweaty fists and he was gritting his teeth till his jaw ached, he was forced to admit his symptoms had more to do with anger than with a coronary occlusion. Hell, if he didn't know better...if it wasn't the most ridiculous idea in the world...he'd think he was jealous.

Then Jared saw the flash. And another. Then another. In just a few quick steps, he was at the open door, staring into the lens of a camera.

"What the hell—?"

"Hey, get out of my way, mister," the photographer complained, waving Jared aside. "I'm missing some great shots."

Maggie didn't know what to do. She'd finally managed to squirm out of Greg's strong embrace and firm lip-lock, but instead of demanding an explanation and giving him the indignant lecture he deserved, she had to make "nice" for the camera. A picture of her and Greg screaming at each other was the kind of publicity that might harm the show. And, after twelve years, she did feel a certain loyalty to Morty and the entire cast and crew of "The Rich and the Reckless."

Maggie smiled and forced herself to look relaxed while the photographer clicked away, but inside she was seething. How dare Greg invite this man up to her apartment without her permission? How dare he kiss her and wrap his arm around her shoulder so possessively? And why did all this have to happen when Jared Austin was there to see it?

He looked as angry as she felt, but didn't dare show. No doubt she was just reinforcing his bad opinion of her, but she figured she was only making the best of a bad situation. If she looked like she was enjoying herself, well, that was just because she was a good actor. He, on the other hand, couldn't seem to keep his true feelings from showing on his face. If she didn't know better, she'd say he was not only angry, but jealous, too. But that, of course, was a ridiculous idea.

"So, where's the abandoned baby?" the photographer inquired, craning his neck to look past them into the apartment.

"Yeah, doll, let's get a few shots with the three of us...you, me and the kid," Greg said enthusiastically. "Just one big happy family."

Instantly feeling a fierce protectiveness, Maggie began, "Greg, *absolutely* n—"

"That won't be possible," Jared said, interrupting

Maggie before she could finish her firm refusal. He stepped in front of the photographer and stared down at him from his impressive height, his arms folded over his broad chest.

"Who are you?" the photographer inquired belligerently.

"I'm the child's personal physician and I'm ordering you to leave the premises immediately."

"But this is *your* apartment, Maggie," Greg objected, eyeing Jared with suspicion and dislike.

"Ms. Stern, please, just let me get one shot of the kid and I'll leave happily," the photographer begged with a beseeching smile.

Maggie had never had any intention of allowing the photographer to take pictures of Sarah, but Jared was giving her a warning glance as if he thought her intentions were quite the contrary. She frowned at him, then turned back to the photographer with a smile. Unlike Dr. Austin, she believed in using tact whenever possible. "I'm sorry, Frank, but photographing the baby is out of the question. The police haven't even determined yet who her legal guardians are. So until I hear from them, for her protection—"

"Oh, come on, Maggie," Greg cajoled, snaking his arm around her shoulders again. "All babies look alike. One little picture won't make any—"

"Are you guys deaf or something? You heard Ms. Stern. There will be no pictures taken of the baby," Jared said in a tone that brooked no opposition. He glared at the photographer. "And if you value that camera you're holding, you'll take it somewhere else...*now*."

*So much for tact*, Maggie thought. But she couldn't help but admire Jared for taking a firm stand, and at least Greg and the photographer had finally backed down.

"These pictures will be in the Monday edition of the *Weekly Spectator,* Ms. Stern," the photographer said, quite unnecessarily reassuring Maggie when she'd much rather his entire roll of film accidentally fell down a sewer hole. "Thanks for your cooperation."

She smiled and waved him away, then eagerly moved to close the door behind him.

"Wait," Jared said, sliding between Maggie and the door. It startled her to suddenly find her nose practically pressed against Jared's chest. She could feel his warmth, smell his nice scent. A quiver went through her and she backed away in a panic, looking up into his blue eyes with startled awareness. Oh, if only he'd smile! She'd love for him...*just once*...to look at her with a less hostile expression in his eyes!

"I have to get back to my place," he said tersely.

Now Maggie was panicking for other reasons. Vivid memories of Sarah's incessant crying rushed into her consciousness. "But you said you'd wait till the groceries came."

Jared flitted a disparaging glance toward Greg. "I'm sure your friend the Count, here, will help out."

"But it's not him, it's you she—"

"Remember, though," Jared interrupted, as he turned to go, "the groceries will be delivered *any minute.* I wouldn't get too *wrapped up* in anything, because you're bound to get interrupted."

Maggie could not mistake Jared's implication. She felt her face flood with warmth. *How dare he...?*

"Good luck, Ms. Stern," he finished, closing the door behind him. Seconds later, Maggie heard his own apartment door open and shut...perhaps with just a little too much force.

"The kid's doctor lives next door?" Greg inquired.

"It's a long story," Maggie said with a sigh as she walked into the living room.

"What a killjoy," Greg muttered, following her.

Maggie stood looking down at Sarah. "He was just watching out for Sarah."

Greg stood close to Maggie and stared down at Sarah, too. "So this is the little rug rat, eh?"

"Keep your voice down," she admonished in a whisper.

"I still think they all look alike, but I guess this one's kinda cute," he offered. Then, as if the "warm-fuzzy" moment had inspired him, he slipped his arm around her shoulder again.

Maggie firmly removed his arm and gave him a scathing look. Now that the photographer was gone, she could give her presumptuous costar the lecture he deserved. "I resent you using this circumstance to make passes, Greg. And I resent you using it for pub-licity, too, particularly since you didn't ask my per-mission to bring that photographer to my apartment! Furthermore—"

"Maggie, don't be mad. I couldn't resist," Greg pleaded. "I'm hot right now and 'more is better' when it comes to publicity. And don't raise your voice, you'll wake up the baby."

But it was too late. Sarah was already awake and peering bleary-eyed about the room. Almost as if she were looking for someone....

"Quick, Greg, pick her up," Maggie suggested. She was hoping that maybe it wasn't Jared in particular Sarah wanted. Maybe she was just a pint-sized Mae

West and liked all men better than women. Better than her, anyway.

"Me?" Greg said, balking.

"Don't worry about dropping her. I'll spot you," Maggie reassured him.

"Well, okay," Greg finally agreed. "But I don't know why you couldn't have made this suggestion while the photographer was still here." He stooped to pick up Sarah, managing with Maggie's directions to hold her correctly.

Maggie hovered near, her hands stretched beneath Greg's just in case he was as clumsy with a real baby as he was with the prop doll at the studio. But he was doing fine, and Sarah seemed to be doing fine, too. She wasn't smiling as she stared earnestly into Greg's face, but she wasn't frowning or crying, either, and that was more than Maggie had hoped for.

"Hey, I think she likes me," Greg announced triumphantly, lifting his head and smiling at Maggie.

Maggie smiled back...tentatively. Then, sure enough, when she looked at Sarah again, her smile vanished. All the warning signs were there; the wrinkled forehead, the downturned mouth, the quivering lip. The storm was gathering. Sarah was getting ready to cry.

"Oh, jeez! Take her," Greg exclaimed, staring horrified into Sarah's red face as she screamed at the top of her lungs. *"Quick!"*

JARED TRIED not to listen, but it was impossible. Sarah had been crying for over an hour...almost from the minute he'd left Ms. Stern's apartment. He sat in the living room with his papers strewn on the coffee table, trying to work, but he finally threw down his pen and paced the floor.

What the hell was that woman doing to make Sarah so unhappy? He had half a mind to call the police and complain. He certainly hoped Ms. Stern wasn't so foolish or irresponsible as to be...well...*entertaining* the Hot Hunk while Sarah cried for attention. The very idea made him furious.

But Jared had to admit he'd find it hard to believe that Maggie would do such a thing. *Maggie*. When had he begun to think of that impossible woman...Ms. Stern, the glamorous soap diva...as simply Maggie? He grimaced. But if Mrs. Fernwalter hadn't told him how overbearing Maggie had been about the apartment, just from his experiences with her so far, he'd have never guessed she was the prima donna his landlady made her out to be. Stubborn, yes. But not a prima donna who stomped over everyone else's feelings and rights.

*However,* he reminded himself, *she sure ate up that photo opportunity with the Hot Hunk....*

Jared was relieved when the phone rang and he could quit thinking about Maggie Stern...sort of. Sarah's continued crying made it impossible to put either of them out of his mind.

"Hello?"

"Jared? Is that you, dahling?"

"Yes, Claire, it's me," Jared answered warily. "I usually answer my own phone." He settled in his favorite easy chair for what he was sure would be a long conversation.

"Oh, dahling, you're so droll. Just like your father."

Jared made a face. "I'm not sure how to take that."

"It was meant as a compliment, of course. I never belittle people I love. Not in this life, nor in any other of my previous lives, was I ever cruel to the people I love."

"Spit it out, Claire," Jared advised her wryly. "You're buttering me up for some reason. You want something, don't you?"

"Have I told you lately that I think you're much handsomer than that other pediatrician, the heartthrob on that terribly popular TV show? And I should know, we had drinks the other day—"

"Claire...."

"Just having you back in my life has meant everything to me, dahling. You know that. But I want to see you happy. I want you to find a lovely girl and have a meaningful relationship with her. You'll have other lives, it's true, but there's no point in wasting this one, is there?"

"I won't let you set me up again, Claire. The two dates you conned me into last spring were total disasters. No offense, but you don't seem to understand what I'm looking for in a woman."

"No offense taken, dahling. But I beg to differ. This time, I have the perfect girl for you. Even my psychic agrees."

"Well, then," Jared said with a chuckle, "that settles it."

"Oh, dahling, does that mean you'll go?"

"No, that means I won't go."

"But she's nothing like the others—"

"You mean she won't be a hopeful starlet, so deeply immersed in her current role she takes on the character's personality...like Rhonda did?"

"Dahling, how could I know Rhonda would take

off all her clothes when you walked through Times Square? She takes all her parts very seriously and she absolutely adored playing a stripper in that off-Broadway play.''

"Obviously," he murmured dryly. "The bump and grind she did for the police was Oscar-caliber."

"Kimberly was...er...*better,* wasn't she?"

"Well, she didn't take off her clothes in public, if that's what you mean. I took her to dinner, as you may recall. She ordered lobster and ate only three bites. Then she spent fifteen minutes out of every hour in the bathroom redoing her hair and makeup. She even changed her dress midway through the evening. Hell, she acted like the host of an awards show, making wardrobe changes during commercials. And, just like an awards show, the night seemed to go on forever. All she could talk about was getting her 'big break.'''

"Did I ever tell you, dahling, that I found out later that Kimberly is actually...a man?"

Jared dragged his hand down his face. "No, Claire, you never mentioned that. Maybe that's why she kept having to reapply her makeup...to hide her five-o'clock shadow! Thank God I never kissed her...I mean, him."

"Oh, dahling, I've utterly failed you, haven't I? First your dreadful, lonely childhood, now this!"

"Don't get dramatic, Claire. As you know, I had a great childhood, even though you weren't there. And you don't have to try to make anything up to me, if that's what you're worried about."

"But I've already arranged for this girl...this *lovely* girl...to meet you at André's."

"Claire—!"

"She's not in show business, Jared," Claire rushed

on. "Candace is my accountant's niece. She works at his firm as a receptionist. She's very quiet and reserved and traditional. Very boring. Just your type, dahling!"

"How flattering," Jared drawled. "But I won't—"

"But you must, dahling. It's already arranged. She's probably already on her way to the restaurant. You mustn't disappoint her…or *me,* for that matter. And I guarantee that this one is really a woman. Just this once, dahling. I promise you you won't be sorry. Please, dahling."

Jared sighed deeply. Once again Claire DeSpain, the great stage actress, would get her way. "All right… since it's already arranged. But never again. Do you understand, Claire?"

"Yes, Jared. I understand. Now hurry along, you haven't got much time to get ready. You have to be there at seven. And please don't wear something dowdy. I love you, dahling."

"I love you, too, Mother," Jared replied resignedly.

"I adore it when you call me that," Claire cooed. "It makes me feel so…maternal. Ta-ta, dahling."

Jared put down the receiver and smiled with wry affection. But soon the smile fell away. For a couple of minutes he'd managed to block out Sarah's crying. Now he was hearing it loud and clear again. It really troubled him, but he wasn't sure what to do. He figured she was bound to stop crying eventually, even if she simply fell asleep from exhaustion. Then tomorrow maybe he could talk Maggie into giving her to the police to be put in a proper foster home.

Jared headed for the shower, glad at least that this blind date afforded him the opportunity of getting away from the apartment for a few hours. However, that was the only thing he was looking forward to about the date. He couldn't trust Claire's judgment when it came to setting him up with women. Even the term "setting him up" made him nervous. With the other two dates, that's exactly how he'd felt…"set up."

But he knew that Claire had just been trying to fulfill her ideas of what a mother should do. He was just grateful that this time the woman his mother had chosen for him wasn't in show business.

As Jared went into the bedroom to undress, he ruminated about his reunion with Claire four years ago. Shortly after Jared's return to New York to set up his practice in the city he loved, his father had died of cancer. But before he died, he encouraged Jared to get in touch with his mother.

Claire DeSpain—whose name was Irene Jensen Austin before she had it legally changed—and Victor Austin had divorced when Jared was only a year old. Claire gave Victor full custody of their son, admitting to herself and Victor and the judge that she was too driven to pursue a career on the stage to be a proper mother to him.

Victor never remarried and did a marvelous job of raising Jared on his own. He never mentioned Claire, and, over time, Jared pretty much forgot he'd ever had a mother. Then, when he was old enough to realize that Claire DeSpain, the famous stage actress, was his mother, he considered the information interesting but unimportant.

Jared respected his father's dying wish and got in touch with Claire. He didn't expect to like a woman who had deserted him and his father thirty years before, but she eventually won him over. He realized that the situation was more complicated than a simple matter of abandonment, and was sorry that his parents had had to find out the hard way that they were two very different people who should never have married.

Jared suspected that, despite their differences, his father never quit loving Claire and had lived a lonely life because of it. He was determined never to make the same mistake.

Despite this tragic history and his mother's eccentricities and weird friends, Jared grew to love Claire. Sometimes he even called her "Mother."

In his bedroom—a much smaller bedroom than the one in 2101, with no whirlpool tub in the adjoining bathroom and only enough space in the closets to hang half his clothes—he quickly kicked off his loafers, stripped off his sweater and undershirt, and was taking off his belt when the doorbell rang.

Since no one had buzzed from the lobby, he assumed whoever was at the door was another tenant. "I hope it's not Billie," he muttered as he padded across the living room carpet in his stocking feet. But as he approached the door, he noticed that the sound of Sarah's crying seemed to get louder and louder.

Sure enough, when he opened the door without bothering to look through the security peephole, there stood Maggie holding Sarah. She looked desperate.

"Look, Sarah," said Maggie, lifting the baby to face Jared. "It's your friend, Doctor J. Look at him, honey, and *please stop crying!*"

Instinctively, Jared took the baby out of Maggie's arms. After a minute Sarah realized what was going on, and when she finally opened her swollen eyes far enough to see who was holding her, she stopped crying.

The transformation from Stormy Sarah to Sarah Sunshine was fast and dramatic. There was no longer a shred of doubt in Jared's mind that for some inexplicable reason Sarah had decided that he was essential to her happiness. Flattered but frustrated he looked at Maggie, who was sagging against the doorjamb.

"What are we going to do, Dr. Austin?" she asked him, her eyes reflecting how exhausted and discouraged she was. Even though she'd got herself into this fix in the first place, Jared couldn't help but feel sympathy for her. Damn it.

"Hell, I don't know," he grumbled, frowning into Sarah's face and getting a radiant smile in return.

"She wants to be with you. She's *determined* to be with you."

"So it seems."

"Maybe if you gave her a bedtime bottle and held her till she dozed off, she'd sleep through the night," Maggie suggested hopefully.

"I can't," Jared replied. "I've got a date."

Maggie pushed away from the doorjamb and stood before him, wringing her hands. "You do?" she said worriedly. "Well, what if Sarah and I just hung around till you left, then? She doesn't seem to mind if I hold her as long as you're within sight. What do you say, Dr. Austin? I'm *desperate!* And I just *hate* hearing her cry."

"So do I," Jared admitted grimly. He'd cancel the date if he could, but Candace was probably already on her way to André's and he might not be able to get hold of her. Even if he did manage to get hold of her, it would be unforgivable to cancel at such short notice. As well, such shabby treatment of his daughter would offend Candace's father, who was his mother's accountant. It was too damned complicated. "Did you bring a bottle with you?"

Maggie turned around and picked up the diaper bag. "I brought everything with me. Diapers, toys, bottles, the whole works. I even brought a carton of yogurt to eat while Sarah's having her formula."

Jared frowned. "I gather the groceries arrived. But you still haven't eaten?"

"How could I with Sarah so miserable...and so *loud?* It ties my stomach in knots."

"Didn't the Hot Hunk stick around long enough to help you out?"

"Are you kidding?" she said dryly. "As soon as Sarah started crying he was outta there."

Jared smirked. "I gather he's not anything like the nobleman he plays on your soap...pining for an heir?"

"No more than I'm like Monica," she said with a shrug.

Jared wasn't sure he agreed with that statement, so he said nothing in reply.

"Maybe Billie was right," Maggie continued as she walked into Jared's apartment, set down the bag and turned to face him.

"About what?" Jared asked cautiously.

"She said we should sign a truce for Sarah's sake. I know we got off to a wrong start with this apartment thing, but, like Billie said, Sarah seems to need both of us right now. How about it, Dr. Austin? Can't we join forces for a while to keep this baby from crying herself sick?"

Jared saw his chance and took it. "On one condition."

Maggie looked anxious but hopeful. "Which is?"

"We only join forces till Monday."

"What happens on Monday?"

"That's when the social worker is supposed to come out and determine your suitability as a foster parent, isn't it?"

"Yes. Unless the police find her guardian before then and something else is arranged. So?"

"So…you give Sarah to the social worker and have her put in another foster home. Keeping her with you is obviously not working out."

"But—"

"Yes, I know. You think she'll be unhappy wherever she goes, but you don't know that and neither do I."

"She'd miss you."

"Nonsense. She likes men, apparently. She'd probably become just as attached to a court-appointed foster father as she is to me."

Maggie looked doubtful. "She didn't like Greg."

Jared smiled sardonically. "Well, if Sarah is immune to his so-called charm, maybe he's not such a Hot Hunk after all."

Maggie laughed. "Everyone has an opinion, I suppose."

Jared found that comment interesting, but didn't dare ask her to elaborate on it. He waited, hoping she'd continue without prodding. No such luck.

"Well, to get the truce, I guess I'll have to accept your terms," Maggie said, moving close to grab hold of Sarah's hand, then looking down at her and smiling wanly. "I don't think either Sarah or I could get through the weekend if she continued to cry non-stop. I really do want her to be happy, you know."

There was a pause, during which Jared involuntarily took a deep whiff of Maggie's lilac-scented hair. Then

Maggie exclaimed, "Oh, look! She's smiling back at me!"

When Maggie lifted her face to share her delight with Jared, he was entranced by her expression. Real joy...or a very realistic facsimile of it...lit up her face like a million stars.

"That proves it! It's not that she doesn't like *me*, it's just that she likes *you* better!" she said happily.

"But the fact still remains that I have a date in an hour." He looked at his watch. "No, make that forty-seven minutes."

"Well, at least we've got a reprieve for forty-seven minutes," Maggie said philosophically, but she still looked worried about the impending separation.

"I have to shower," Jared pointed out. "What will you do with her while I'm...er...indisposed?"

"Why don't you give her the bottle now? That will only take a few minutes. Then maybe she'll go right to sleep and you'll be able to take your shower in peace."

"It's worth a try," Jared agreed.

They went into the living room and Jared sat down with Sarah and fed her the bottle while Maggie walked around the room, idly looking at the pictures on the wall as she ate her carton of yogurt. He couldn't help it; his gaze kept wandering to whatever part of the room she was standing in. She really was lovely. He could understand why millions of TV viewers were under her spell and riveted to the screen whenever her soap opera was on. They probably didn't care about the story, they just wanted to gape at the stunning Maggie Stern. Or should he say...Monica Blake?

Then he wondered what she was thinking, and felt his irritation build as he decided that she was probably comparing his cramped apartment with her much larger one and secretly congratulating herself on stealing it away from him. He stoked his anger, much more willing to be mad at her than under her spell.

Maggie stared determinedly at a seascape that hung over Jared Austin's fireplace. It wasn't that she was that fascinated by the pleasant picture, it was just that she was forcing herself to look at anything and everything but Jared Austin himself.

Sitting on the sofa, bare-chested, his blond hair tousled from removing his sweater, he was one luscious hunk of man. Add to that the fact that he was holding and feeding a baby who clearly adored him. The combination of sexy manliness and nurturing tenderness would throw any woman for a loop. Too bad he had absolutely no similar feelings of attraction for her.

She liked his apartment, she decided. It was smaller than hers, but actually more charming. However, she didn't dare speak such an opinion out loud. She knew it was in her best interests not to speak of the apartment situation at all.

"She's done," Jared suddenly announced. "But not at all sleepy."

Maggie turned and observed that Jared was absolutely right. Sarah seemed as alert as if she'd been chugging down a caffeinated cola drink instead of formula. And her loud burp seemed to support this theory.

Maggie laughed, then abruptly sobered. "What about your shower?" She wished he'd just cancel his date...the idea of which rankled her, anyway. What happened to all that paperwork he had to do?

He shrugged and smiled slyly. ''I guess you'll just have to hold her and bring her into the bathroom while I shower, standing *real close* so she knows I'm there. Either that, or let her cry. What'll it be, Ms. Stern?''

# Chapter Six

"Okay," Maggie readily agreed, taking Jared completely by surprise.

He chuckled nervously. "I was only kidding. I...er...usually take my showers in private. You know...without an audience?"

"The only audience you'll have is Sarah," Maggie informed him with a sniff. "She's too young to even know what she's looking at."

"I wasn't thinking about Sarah," he clarified stiffly. "I was thinking of you, Ms. Stern. You're certainly old enough to know what you're looking at."

"Humph! But *I* have no desire to see anything. I'll just hold Sarah and look the other way."

Jared couldn't help it; he laughed! "This is absurd! I'll take a quick shower. Surely Sarah can stand to be separated from me for such a short period of time."

Maggie frowned. "I don't know about that."

"Well, let's test the waters...no pun intended." He handed Sarah to her and backed away. Sarah watched him intently, but, so far, hadn't made a peep.

"She's anxious," Maggie warned.

"No, *you're* anxious," Jared countered. He backed away a few more steps. "See? She's going to be just fine.'' Then, slowly, stealthily, he turned and walked toward his bedroom, only to be stopped short by the sound of Sarah's screams. Sheepishly he trudged back into the living room.

"I told you so," Maggie said smugly, as Sarah immediately stopped crying.

"Well, come on, then," he muttered. "It's getting late."

Wide-eyed, Maggie followed Jared into his bedroom, hardly able to fathom the strange turn of events her life had taken since that fateful morning. "Now would be a good time to turn your back, or shut your eyes," he advised her. "I'm about to drop my shorts."

Maggie chuckled nervously and closed her eyes. "Is that how you tell your little patients to remove their pants to get shots? *Drop your shorts!*" she mimicked in a deep voice, sounding like a drill sergeant. "Seems a tad unprofessional."

"My nurse gives the shots," Jared informed her, unamused.

Maggie nodded, her own amusement fading as she listened to Jared "drop his shorts." The jangle of the belt buckle and the whoosh of fabric as his trousers hit the floor was almost as disconcerting...and tantalizing...as actually watching him undress.

"All right, I've got a towel around me and I'm headed for the bathroom. You'd better open your eyes as you follow me so you won't trip over something."

Maggie obeyed. And as Jared rounded the corner to the bathroom, she caught a glimpse of his bare back and long legs, his narrow hips wrapped in a blue towel. Nice. Very nice. She followed him, holding Sarah so she would always have a clear view of her idol. Sarah watched intently...and so did Maggie.

Inside the bathroom, Jared opened the shower stall door and turned around. His expression was one of embarrassed resignation. "I can't believe this is happening."

"It *is* odd that we met only yesterday, and we've already seen each other wearing just a towel," Maggie agreed.

"Odd doesn't even come close to describing this situation," Jared grumbled, whisking off his glasses and setting them on the sink. "Get ready. At the count of three the towel's coming off."

Maggie nodded and immediately squeezed her eyes shut. "Thanks for the warning, Dr. Austin," she said primly. "But, no need for the countdown. My eyes are already closed."

But they didn't stay closed. As the shower door snapped shut and the water came on, Maggie's eyelids seemed to lift of their own accord. After all, the shower door was made of that hazy glass you couldn't see through. What was the point of not looking when you couldn't see anything, anyway?

But Maggie was wrong. She *could* see something. Yes, the view was hazy, but the outline of Jared's slim, muscular body was certainly clear enough to the...er...naked eye to make Maggie's temperature shoot up a few degrees. Fortunately for her blood pressure, however, the room soon steamed up and she couldn't see past her nose.

Maggie had to admit she was disappointed...and so was Sarah. Maggie looked into Sarah's little face as it began to crumple and whispered to her, "Are you sure you aren't really Mae West reincarnated?"

Just as she started whimpering...Sarah, that is...Jared shut off the water, reached for the towel hanging on the outside of the shower door, and emerged.

Sarah cheered up, and so did Maggie.

"The worst is over, but I've still got to get dressed," Jared said in a businesslike tone as he reached for his glasses and put them on. "Shall we retire to the bedroom, ladies?"

Maggie followed, mesmerized by the way the water glistened on Jared's smooth brown skin. He was something to look at, all right, his body muscular without being bulky, his blond hair slicked back from his brow, the wet ends curling around the nape of his neck.

Maggie couldn't believe where she was and what she was doing. It was like being a fly on the wall in the house of someone you secretly lusted for, or having a very realistic fantasy...because stuff like this just didn't happen in real life. Again she wondered if she'd somehow slipped into the Soap dimension of the Twilight Zone.

"You might as well sit down," Jared invited, motioning toward a bed draped with a burgundy bedspread. Maggie sat down. "Now, close your eyes again. You can open them when I've got my pants on."

Speechless, still feeling a little overheated, Maggie nodded and closed her eyes. But she found herself picturing everything Jared was doing, which did nothing to cool her down. She wondered how Jared could be so blasé about this whole shower business.

JARED WONDERED how Maggie could be so blasé about this whole shower business. The last time he'd undressed in front of a woman without it being a prelude to physical intimacies was when he was four years old. That was when he and a female playmate had thought it would be so much more practical and fun to swim in her small plastic pool in the nude.

That was a long time ago and perfectly innocent, but in the present circumstances he felt a lot of sexual tension in the room. Adding to the tension was the vain part of him that wondered if Maggie liked what she saw. To stack things in his favor, he held his stomach in till he was fully dressed.

"Now what?" Maggie asked, as he stuffed his wallet and keys into his trouser pocket.

"I go on my date, I guess," Jared answered.

"But she'll cry all night!" Maggie objected.

"My *date?*" Jared asked dryly.

"No...*Sarah!* Why go to all this trouble to make her happy for a few minutes, then leave for several hours?"

"Because I've got no choice. Besides, she's bound to be exhausted. I'm sure she'll fall asleep very soon," he reasoned.

Maggie shook her head dolefully. "I don't think so."

"Well, what do you suggest, Ms. Stern?" Jared asked her, exasperated.

"I suggest that we come along with you on your date."

Jared felt his jaw drop like a drawbridge over a moat...only faster. "That's crazy. How would I explain you? How would I explain Sarah?"

"You don't have to explain either of us. Your date doesn't even have to know we're there. We'll just sort of...stick close."

His eyes narrowed. "How close?"

"Close enough for Sarah to see you...that's all."

"That's pretty damned close. Unless my date's a dunce, she'll suspect something."

Maggie blinked. "You don't know whether or not your date is a dunce?"

Jared grimaced. "We've never met."

Maggie's brows lifted. "Oh, I see."

"No, you don't see. But you would if you had a mother like mine," he grumbled. He glanced agitatedly at his watch. "I have to go or I'll be late."

Maggie stood up. "Please take Sarah and me with you," she begged. "We promise not to interfere with your evening."

"Oh, that's a good one."

"Since you're meeting your date at the restaurant, we could take the same cab," Maggie persisted. "Then once we got inside, we'd just sit at the table next to you and pretend you're a stranger. Sarah will be content to just look at you."

"Someone will recognize you," Jared countered, feeling himself beginning to relent.

"I'll wear my blond wig and a pair of sunglasses."

"At night?"

"We're in New York," she reminded him.

"It's cool out. Sarah—"

"I'll bundle Sarah up like an Eskimo baby. Besides, it will be much worse for her if she spends the entire evening crying."

"But what if we can't get tables together?"

Maggie smiled confidently. "You're going to André's, aren't you? I know the owner. He's a huge 'Rich and the Reckless' fan and a good friend. Don't worry, I'll get us some tables together."

Jared smiled back...grimly. "By all means, Ms. Stern, use your star power to get us tables together."

Maggie lifted her chin defiantly. "I will."

"What about afterward?"

"Where are you taking your date after dinner?"

"I don't know. We'll have to play it by ear." He gave her a malicious smile. "Are you up for a little skulduggery?"

Maggie's eyes gleamed determinedly. "I'm up for anything. Anything, that is, but listening to this baby cry her heart out for hours." She held Sarah so she could look into her face and asked, "How about you, Sarah Sunshine? Up for some skulduggery?"

Sarah gurgled and waved her arms in the air.

Maggie laughed. "I think that was a yes."

As it always was on a Saturday night, André's was busy, but Maggie had still managed to get a table right next to Jared's in the densely packed dining room that was fragrant with delicate seasonings and the succulent smell of roasted meat. And Jared had to give her credit; she was doing a marvelous job of pretending not to know him.

So far no one had recognized her, either. If people looked at her it was probably because they were wondering why a lone woman—a sexy-looking blonde wearing sunglasses and a calf-length black leather coat—was dining with a baby in an elegant French restaurant instead of feeding it mashed bananas and rice cereal at home.

As for his date, he had to give Claire the credit she deserved, too. Candace was nothing like the two other dates his mother had set him up with. So far, unlike Rhonda, she hadn't taken off a stitch of clothing, and unlike Kimberly, she hadn't repeatedly run off to the ladies' room. And he had his mother's word for it that Candace was definitely of the female sex. This was all good news.

The bad news was that Candace was as dull as yesterday's news. When his mother summed her up as "boring," she'd been right. Jared was beginning to wonder why he couldn't meet a woman whose personality and charm ranged somewhere in that normal zone between stripping, transvestite starlets and a pet rock.

A short, delicate blonde, Candace was attractive enough, but she looked as though she'd been caught in a time warp and had dressed with June Cleaver as her model of the perfect woman. She wore a white blouse with a Peter Pan collar and a full skirt with a wide belt that cinched her small waist. She wore a string of pearls, soft makeup, and pale pink lipstick. Her hair was coiled in a tight chignon with bangs feathering her forehead. She looked neat, sweet and petite. Which was all fine and good, even though it wasn't Jared's idea of style. He just wished he could get her to *talk!*

Candace answered his many questions with monosyllabic and flattering replies, forcing him to babble away like an idiot to fill the awkward pauses. He just hoped Maggie wasn't overhearing and labeling him an egotist. But when your date wouldn't talk, but seemed to prefer demure simpering and nods of the head, what was a guy supposed to do? Sit there like a bump on a log?

He did finally manage to drag out of her that she worked as a receptionist for her Uncle Sol's accounting firm. It was a fact he already knew, but he was hoping to get her to expand on the topic.

"So, Candace, how long have you been working for your uncle at the—"

A gleeful infant squeal interrupted Jared's question and several diners...Candace among them...turned and stared at Sarah, smiling.

"Isn't that baby darling?" she cooed. "Look at the way she's kicking her arms and legs!"

Maggie had propped Sarah in her carrier in a chair facing Jared, but she, herself, sat facing away. Their tables were very close.

"Yeah, she's cute," Jared replied shortly. "Now about your job—"

"And she keeps staring at you, Jared," Candace added, looking from Sarah to Jared, then back to Sarah.

"I'm the person sitting nearest to her," Jared explained. "Babies like to watch people's faces. Especially if that person is talking a lot...like me," he added pointedly.

"But look at the way she's smiling at you," Candace persisted. "Those dimples are as deep as the Grand Canyon. I think she's smitten."

Jared hid his growing nervousness with a shrug. She was finally talking, but not on a subject he would have chosen! "I'm a pediatrician. I like babies and they usually like me back. It's that simple."

Candace leaned toward Jared and placed her hand over his on the table. "I love babies, too," she gushed, squeezing his fingers. "They're just so—" She seemed to struggle for a suitable adjective.

"Young?" Jared joked uncomfortably.

Candace laughed affectedly. "Well, of course they're young. They're *babies!*"

"Cute, then. You must have been thinking 'cute.'"

"Yes, that's it. They're so darned cute. I want to have at least a half dozen of them!"

Maggie was hardly able to contain herself. Picking at her salad, she wondered where Jared's mother had dug up this relic. From the Sixties Sitcom dimension of the Twilight Zone, maybe? She couldn't help but overhear their conversation and it struck her that Candace had been determinedly playing the role of a demure, unopinionated female. She looked the part, too. And Maggie ought to know. She'd been playing parts for years. Heck, she was playing a part tonight!

And now the woman was rhapsodizing about babies…to a pediatrician. It all seemed pretty contrived to her. Every woman should just be herself, Maggie reasoned. If you got a man on false pretenses, how could you possibly hope to have a successful relationship or marriage, anyway?

All Maggie had ever wanted was to be herself with the opposite sex, but her battle had definitely been uphill. She wanted to be ordinary old Maggie, but her dates expected her to be the sultry *Monica.*

André interrupted her wandering thoughts when he walked up to the table and handed her a menu. Confused, Maggie looked up at the tall, dapper Frenchman and said, "But André, I've already ordered."

*"Oui, mademoiselle,"* he said in a low voice. "I know. But there is something new on the menu I think you will find most interesting." He raised an eyebrow and widened his eyes, then cocked his head toward the menu.

Curious and nervous, Maggie opened the menu and

looked at the front page of an early edition of the *Planet* that had been tucked inside. In a large photo that took up nearly the entire page, there she stood in her sexy white nightgown, holding Sarah and looking dazed. The caption read, Monica's Miracle—Soap Star Finds Baby on Doorstep.

"Great, just great," Maggie mumbled. "I was afraid of this."

André leaned close and whispered near her ear. "It was also on the seven o'clock news, *mademoiselle*."

"You're kidding?" she murmured. "How do *I* rate? It surely must be a slow news day. What about the deficit? Jeez, isn't there a war somewhere? Now the whole world knows about Sarah...and that includes my mother."

"I suggest you be very careful about hiding your identity tonight," Andre continued. "If someone discovers who you are, you will be *mobbed*."

Maggie shuddered. She felt sure André was being overly dramatic, but she agreed that she needed to be extra cautious. She certainly didn't want Sarah caught up in a paparazzi blitz.

"Thank you, André," Maggie said. "You're a good friend. How can I ever repay you?"

André smiled and bowed, but as he straightened up, his nose twitched and his lips puckered. Sliding a glance toward Sarah, he said, "It will be easy to repay me, *mademoiselle*. Take the *enfant* and change her diaper before I lose customers, *s'il vous plaît*." Then he quickly walked away.

Maggie frowned teasingly at Sarah. "Didn't anyone ever tell you it was impolite to take a potty break in the middle of dinner, Sarah Sunshine? Especially in *public*." But as she leaned close to affectionately pinch Sarah's smiling cheek, she noticed the odor that André's sensitive French nose had already picked up on.

Yes, Sarah definitely needed changing. But that was something that would have to be accomplished in the ladies' room...and fast, before the odor permeated the room and offended the other diners. The only hitch in this plan was that Sarah would probably scream bloody murder the minute they walked away from the table and she lost sight of Jared.

But Maggie had to take the chance. The odor was beginning to "waft."

Quickly picking up Sarah and holding her against her shoulder, then stooping to retrieve the diaper bag, Maggie walked toward the ladies' room. Sure enough, Sarah started to whimper, then to wail as if her heart were breaking. Maggie just walked faster, hoping to get the diaper change over with and return to the dining room as quickly as possible.

But as Sarah screamed in Maggie's ear, she also clutched at Maggie's shoulder-length blond wig, eventually clamping on to a firm fistful. Then she yanked.

Maggie could feel the front of the wig sliding away from her forehead. She stopped in her tracks, dropped the diaper bag, and grabbed for the wig...just a tad too late. Maggie turned around and looked down with horror at the platinum mop at her feet, then lunged for it, desperate to hide her identity. Unfortunately, as she bent for the wig, her sunglasses fell off and skittered across the floor and under Jared's table.

Maggie straightened up and stared around her in horror. By now, of course, she was the center of attention. But how could it be otherwise? Here was Monica Blake, soap siren, suddenly revealed for who she was after trying to hide behind a wig and sunglasses, holding a malodorous baby that was screaming at the top of her lungs. A baby, moreover, that had been left on her doorstep that morning by a delusional fan.

"Monica Blake! *It's Monica Blake!*" exclaimed a heavyset woman in sequins.

"And she's got the baby with her!" another woman yelled, standing up so abruptly she toppled her wine glass.

*"Mon dieu!"* André shouted from the sidelines as several women abruptly left their seats and approached Maggie like a herd of stampeding rhinos. It looked like a scene from *Jumanji!*

Maggie felt frozen to the spot. And she would have continued to stand there like Frosty the Snowman if Jared hadn't suddenly loomed before her, caught her hand, and pulled her down the hall toward the rest rooms and the entrance to the kitchen.

"Here! Through here!" André shouted, leading the way through the kitchen to the back door.

"I've got the diaper bag and the baby carrier!" Candace called from the rear.

They ran past rows of hanging pots and pans and astonished cooks in tall white hats to the back door. Maggie was glad she'd worn her flats so she could safely maneuver through the confusion and still hold tightly to Sarah. The one positive point of the whole episode was that Sarah had stopped crying.

"Hurry!" André urged them, waving them through the door. "There's always a taxi out front. Good luck *mademoiselle!*"

They made it into the taxi just before Maggie's fans burst through the front door of the restaurant. As the cab screeched away from the curb, she looked through the back window and saw a crowd of about twenty standing in the street.

"Whew, that was close. What a bunch of nutcases!" Jared said as he sat back in the seat. Maggie was sitting in the middle, with Jared on one side and Candace on the other, still holding Sarah and still trying to catch her breath. But, considering how Sarah still smelled, maybe breathing wasn't such a good idea.

"I can't believe this," Candace gasped, sitting forward and staring at Maggie. "Ms. Stern, I'm one of your biggest fans! I don't understand why Jared rescued you, but it's so exciting!"

Jared couldn't believe what had happened, either. And he was even more astonished by the animated way Candace talked and talked…and *talked*, during the ride back to the apartment building. She couldn't say enough about how much she admired Maggie's career and how much she wanted to emulate her. She also pulled the pins out of her chignon and shook loose her long blond hair, suddenly looking a lot less like June Cleaver and a lot more like a *Baywatch* babe.

Jared sat there, stunned and speechless. It seemed his mother had set him up with an actor after all, one that was only playing the part of a demure receptionist at an accounting firm. But *why?* Well, he sure as hell was going to find out.

When they arrived at the apartment building, they noticed a couple of paparazzi hovering near the front entrance. Jared and Ralph, the night doorman, blocked them while Maggie and Candace ran inside with the baby. Upstairs in Maggie's apartment, they all collapsed into chairs and on the couch in the living room.

"Is it always like this for you?" Jared asked Maggie, actually feeling sympathetic.

"No," Maggie said with a weary sigh. "Not always. This baby-on-the-doorstep story has evidently created quite a stir."

"Your producer will be happy," Jared murmured grimly. He wanted to add that she was probably happy, too, but he refrained...for the moment.

Maggie gave him a repressive look and pushed herself to her feet. "I'd better get this baby changed." She turned to Candace and smiled. "Thanks for grabbing the diaper bag and carrier."

"It was a pleasure, Ms. Stern," Candace assured her in a nasal voice because she was holding her nose. "But please call me Candy. Everyone does. It's been so great meeting you!"

"You, too," Maggie replied politely, picking up the diaper bag. "Although the circumstances were a little harried."

"I thought it was fun. I just hope I get chased by fans someday." Candy's brows furrowed. "But I still don't understand how you and Jared are connected. Claire never mentioned—"

"Ralph said he'd hold a cab for you. I'll tell you the whole story as I walk you down to the lobby," Jared interrupted, eager to keep his mother's name out of it. And he was reserving the right to decide what and how much he'd explain to Candy about his connection to Maggie.

"Could you wait till I've changed Sarah's diaper, then hold her while I warm a bottle?" Maggie asked. "I promise to hurry. It's just that she might need to be...er...calmed down after I change her."

Jared was about to advise her not to worry about

being polite and just change Sarah right there on the couch where the baby would be able to keep him in full view, but he was eager to talk to Candace alone. "Sure," Jared said, then waited till Maggie had disappeared down the hall before turning to Candace and demanding, "Before I tell you my story, I want to hear yours. What's with the act?"

Candace suddenly seemed to fall off the cloud she'd been walking on since meeting Maggie. "Your mother's going to kill me for screwing up," she said with a glum face. "But I thought I played my part really well till all heck broke loose. Then when we ran out of that restaurant with the one and only *Maggie Stern....*" She sighed worshipfully. "I just couldn't help it. I had to be me again."

Sarah had started crying as soon as Maggie carried her out of the room, and now her pathetic wails were a nerve-shattering background noise to Jared's already strained conversation with Candace. "You should have just been yourself from the beginning. I don't understand the point of this little charade in the first place. Why the insipid behavior, the demure getup?"

"It was your mother's idea. She said you needed waking up. She said you had very narrow, traditional views about how a woman should act and look. She said she was afraid that by limiting yourself so stringently you'd end up with some vacuous little woman that would bore your socks off."

"I see," Jared said with a grim nod. "And you were meant to typify the insipid little woman I might end up with and scare the hell out of me. Well, it was working. Trouble is, your act was just that. An act. There's got to be a happy medium somewhere between the character you played tonight and the transvestite Claire set me up with last time.''

Candace blinked. "No kidding? A transvestite?''

"Out of fairness, I should tell you she didn't know the woman was...well...a man.''

Candace's eyes opened wide. "You didn't...?''

"No. She, or rather *he*, repelled me from the beginning. But now maybe you'll understand why I get nervous whenever Claire decides to do a little matchmaking. I'm not as narrow-minded as my mother thinks, but I have to admit that I'm more traditional than she is. And this time, she even lied to me. She said you were a receptionist at her accountant's firm.''

"I really am Uncle Sol's receptionist,'' Candace assured him. "I do it part-time. The rest of the time I look for acting work. But since I haven't landed a job yet, Claire wasn't actually lying when she said I wasn't an actor.''

Jared shook his head ruefully. "You seem like a nice person, Candy. Are you sure you want to get mixed up in the wild and wacko world of show business? Take my advice. If you want a normal life...marriage, kids, sanity...become a teacher, or a dentist, or even a crossing guard. But don't be an actor. An actor is the last person on earth *I'd* ever hook up with.''

"But your mother is an—''

"Thanks for waiting,'' Maggie said as she returned from the bedroom. Jared stood up, turned around, and quickly took the wailing baby out of Maggie's arms. As usual, Sarah abruptly stopped crying. Uninterested in the baby now that she was no longer playing a part, Candy walked around the room and looked at Maggie's belongings.

Maggie went immediately into the kitchen to prepare a bottle, but when she returned just a couple of
minutes later, Sarah had already fallen asleep in
Jared's arms.

"She must be exhausted," Maggie said, peering
down at Sarah as she peacefully snoozed.

Jared gazed down at Sarah, too. "It's been an exhausting evening for *all* of us. Did Mrs. Fernwalter
bring the crib?"

"Yes, this afternoon." Maggie spoke briskly. "It's
set up in my bedroom, for now. The spare room is too
cluttered with boxes. But, don't worry, I'll put Sarah
to bed. You go ahead and take Candy downstairs."

Jared nodded and handed Sarah over to Maggie.
Even though the five-month-old had ruled his life for
the past few hours, putting him in the most awkward
and embarrassing situations, Jared felt a strange reluc-
tance to part with her.

He almost felt as though he were abandoning
her...which, of course, was ridiculous. Even though
she'd attached herself to him like a newly hatched
chick to its mother, he wasn't responsible for the little
rug rat. But despite this reasoning, he still felt a tender
ache in his heart at the sight of her peaceful, utterly
innocent little face as she slept.

"Sweet dreams, Sarah Sunshine," he whispered as
he gently kissed her forehead. *And please, please,
sleep through the night,* he added to himself.

"I'll drop by before going to my apartment," he
told Maggie after Candy gushed out a goodbye and
preceded him through the door.

"No, don't bother," Maggie said with a brittle
smile.

"But I promised I'd help out till Monday, remember? A deal's a deal.''*Why did she look so stiff?* he wondered.

"I'll be asleep by the time you get back up here," she replied.

"Well, okay, but here's my private number." He fished in his pocket and produced a card. "Call me if you need me during the night." He smiled. "I'm used to emergencies at all hours."

Maggie took the card absently, nodded perfunctorily, and quickly closed the door behind him. He walked toward the elevator with Candace babbling away beside him about Ms. Stern and how wonderful she was. Jared listened absently, puzzled and troubled by Maggie's sudden aloofness.

AFTER SHE'D PUT Sarah to bed, Maggie searched for and finally found a pair of green plaid flannel pajamas. She put them on, then made herself a cup of fatfree hot chocolate. Returning to the living room, she sank into her most comfortable chair and propped her feet on a plush ottoman, savoring the quiet.

After Jared and Candy left, she'd listened to her phone messages. There was one from Mrs. Fernwalter, one from Morty…who, so he said, had accidentally had his phone turned off all day…two from her married sisters, and, surprisingly enough, one from her limo driver, Chuck. All expressed concern about the publicity and offered help if Maggie should need it.

There were *seven* messages from her mother. But since it was after ten o'clock and Lorena Morgenstern kept early hours, Maggie didn't call her back. Besides, she had a feeling that sometime tomorrow her mother would show up in person, anyway.

With Lorena destined to drop by, Maggie knew

she'd better enjoy the quiet for as long as it lasted. But while the apartment was quiet and peaceful, her thoughts were not. She hadn't intentionally eavesdropped, but when she was returning to the living room after changing Sarah's diaper, she'd overheard the tail end of Jared and Candy's conversation.

Maggie's eyes narrowed as she took a sip of hot chocolate and swallowed. "So..." she murmured dryly, "an actor is the last person on earth the good doctor would ever hook up with. What's the deal? We've got leprosy or something?" She found his comment insulting. And hurtful.

Evidently she'd had two strikes against her from the beginning. First, she was an actor, and second, she'd "stolen" his apartment. There was nothing she could do about his prejudice against showbiz folks, but Maggie was tired of pussy-footing around the apartment bone of contention. The next time she and Jared were in the same room, she was going to make it perfectly clear that she hadn't stolen anything.

She lifted her chin, visualizing with satisfaction the shouting match they'd undoubtedly have. Then, hopefully, he'd skulk back to his inferior apartment with the distinct impression that he was the last person on earth *she'd* ever hook up with, too. Even though that wasn't quite true....

# Chapter Seven

Jared started off the evening by sleeping on the couch, fully dressed. When he woke up at 2:00 a.m. he felt like he was dying of heatstroke. He'd forgotten how the polyester material of the couch made him hot whenever he happened to fall asleep on it while reading or watching TV. But that was probably because it had been a long time since he'd had the leisure to read anything but medical journals and patient charts, much less watch TV.

He also had an ear-to-jaw crease in his face from the throw pillow he was resting his head on, an ache in the small of his back, and a numb right arm from lying on it at an awkward angle. At this point, putting on his PJs and going to bed seemed the smart thing to do. It appeared that Sarah was going to sleep through the night and there was no sense in him roughing it on a hot, cramped couch just in case the phone rang.

However, no sooner had Jared changed into his comfy pajama bottoms—not bothering with the top—and slipped between the cool sheets than Sarah's lusty screams could be heard through the thin wall between his apartment and Maggie's. He sat up in bed and

waited for the phone to ring…but it never did. He
waited for a half hour, pacing the floor and dragging
his hands through his hair, but he still received no call
for help from the queen of soaps.

"I knew it. She's mad at me for some reason," he
mumbled. He'd thought her behavior before he left her
apartment that night had seemed cool and strained, but
now he was sure there was something wrong. And
why that bothered him so much, he wasn't
sure…except, of course, that he was concerned about
Sarah.

Finally he couldn't listen to Sarah's crying any
longer and he threw on a robe, tied it haphazardly at
the waist, grabbed his beeper and keys, and went next
door.

First he rang the doorbell. When Maggie didn't answer, it occurred to him that maybe she couldn't hear
over Sarah's cries. So he knocked on the door…softly.
He certainly didn't want to awaken any neighbors or
draw any sort of attention to himself.

But when she still didn't answer, he knocked
again…*hard.*

In thirty seconds, Maggie swung open the door and
glared at him angrily. "What are you trying to do,
wake up everyone in the building?"

He slipped past her, murmuring, "No, but you will,
if you don't shut the door." She shut the door and
turned around, her eyes still flashing warning signals.

"Why didn't you call me?" he asked her, taking
Sarah out of her arms. He noted with surprise that
Maggie wasn't wearing a fancy nightgown, but then
maybe she realized that baby spit-up washed out of
flannel better than it did satin and lace. The pajamas
were so roomy, he figured she must have borrowed

them from Mrs. Fernwalter. Funny thing, even in plaid, oversized pajamas, she still managed to look damned sexy.

He watched as Maggie's full lips formed a pout as Sarah immediately calmed in his arms. He couldn't say he blamed her for feeling a bit resentful. He'd worked with enough parents with colicky infants to know that there was nothing more frustrating than a baby who wouldn't stop crying. And to add insult to injury, this baby seemed to have the ability to turn it off and on at will.

"I said," he repeated, "why didn't you call me?"

Her chin lifted in that defiant pose of hers he was becoming quite familiar with. "I didn't want to bother you."

His brows rose in supercilious surprise. "Oh, really? What's the matter, Ms. Stern? Why are you suddenly on your high horse?"

"I am *not* on my high horse," she snapped, sweeping past him. "I don't have a high horse. I don't even have a low horse. I, frankly, don't know why you think I have any kind of horse at all!"

Jared blinked confusedly and followed her into the living room. The television was on, but the mute button for sound must have been pushed. It was an old Cary Grant movie. The TV and a single lamp in the far corner were the only lights in the room.

"You've heard the expression 'on your high horse' before, haven't you?" Jared inquired.

"Yes, but it doesn't apply to me!" she snapped again, rounding in the middle of the room and majestically flicking her hand in the air. "I resent your use of the term. I am tired of you thinking I'm some kind of prima donna!"

She folded her arms and looked down her nose, appearing in that moment more like a prima donna than she ever had before, despite the baggy flannel PJs. Jared laughed. Sarah watched, wide-eyed and smiling.

"Don't laugh at me," Maggie warned him, moving close and shaking her finger in his face. "I know you think I stole this apartment from you, but you're dead wrong."

Jared sobered immediately. The apartment was a sore subject. "By my standards, your pressuring Mrs. Fernwalter into giving you the lease when she'd already promised the apartment to me was stealing, Ms. Stern."

"What makes you think my standards are different than yours, Mr. High and Mighty?"

"I never said—"

"For your information, I didn't pressure Mrs. Fernwalter into anything. I didn't even know she'd promised the apartment to you. I thought it was free and clear and available to the general public."

Jared scowled. "You didn't think it seemed a bit odd that such a choice apartment was so easy to snap up?"

"Of course I did! But I thought I'd just lucked out or...or something."

"'Or something' is right," Jared drawled. "You got this apartment because you're a star, Ms. Stern, and I'm not."

"And that really ticks you off, doesn't it, Doctor? But I'm trying to tell you I didn't do it on purpose. I would never have taken the apartment if I'd known you had first dibs. And if you don't believe me, that's your problem, 'cause I'm absolutely telling the truth."

Jared had no idea what to say to such an impassioned speech. She'd certainly taken him by surprise. But if she was telling the truth, that meant Mrs. Fernwalter, his landlady for the last four years, had blatantly lied to him. Thrown for a loop, Jared eased down on the sofa, cradling Sarah in his lap.

"I'll fix Sarah a bottle," Maggie said with a sigh. "While you 'digest' my little bombshell, she might as well be eating, too."

While Maggie was gone, Jared thought about what she'd said. He supposed it came down to Mrs. Fernwalter's word against Maggie's. Who should he believe? But by the time he'd considered Mrs. Fernwalter's recent behavior...her gushing over Maggie, her guilty reactions to Jared's presence, and her disregard for the rules of the building to accommodate Maggie's infant guest...Jared had to admit that Maggie looked like the innocent party in this little miscarriage of justice.

But one fact still remained; while Maggie hadn't purposely stolen the apartment from him, it was her celebrity status that had made Mrs. Fernwalter behave so unfairly toward him. He couldn't directly blame Maggie for the incident, but he still found it damned irritating.

When Maggie returned, Jared took the bottle and looked up with a frown. "I believe you," he mumbled.

Maggie leaned forward. "What was that? I didn't quite hear you."

"You heard me," he grumbled. "I said, I believe you. You didn't steal the apartment and I apologize for accusing you."

Her surprised and triumphant smile irked Jared, but he had to admit that it lit up her face, too. She had a beautiful mouth and straight, white teeth—*camera-friendly* teeth.

"I can't believe how easy that was!" she crowed. "Do you know that what we just did is *never* done on soap operas? On a soap, characters agonize over misunderstandings for weeks, months…heck, sometimes years…before it's cleared up. You just want to tell them, 'Folks, please, sit down and talk this out. It will take about thirty seconds of plainspeaking to realize you've been in a fret all this time for *nothing.*' But *noooo,* they can't do that 'cause that would relieve the tension and the writers would have to come up with another misunderstanding, or tragedy, to make their lives miserable again. Believe me, I much prefer real life!"

Jared wanted to tell her that if their lives were being directed by some omnipotent writer or writers, they needn't worry about creating more tension between Maggie Stern and himself. It was still there, simply because she was an actor. He didn't like the way the world pandered to people in Maggie's profession, and he never would.

Because he wanted Claire to be a part of his life, he put up with a lot of the baloney that went along with her show-business life-style, but he'd had no choice about who his mother was. He did have a choice about who his friends were and who he dated, however, and it would always be first priority with him to keep show-business connections to the barest minimum.

And then there was that "other" tension he felt in his dealings with Maggie. Sexual. Purely sexual. And he was having a hell of a hard time ignoring it.

So, naturally, he felt a great deal of misgiving when

she sank down on the sofa right next to him and tucked her legs under her, saying, "We got off to a bad start, but now that we've sort of cleared up the apartment thing, do you think we could be friends, Dr. Austin?"

Jared swallowed a lump in his throat. She looked so sweet and open and appealing in her baggy pajamas, and she was sitting so close. He was glad his hands were busy holding Sarah and the bottle or he might have been tempted to touch her skin and see if it was as soft as it looked...starting with her face, then her neck, then her shoulders, then her—

"Well?" she prompted him. "After all, we are neighbors."

Jared was growing more uncomfortable by the minute. It was one thing conceding he'd been wrong about Maggie stealing his apartment, but that's as friendly as he wanted to get with her. She might not fit his idea of the self-absorbed actor...in fact, like Claire, she might actually have a few good qualities he'd appreciate...but he didn't want to get close enough to find out. By then he'd be hooked, just like his dad had been hooked. And he was sure he'd live to regret it.

But how could he tell Maggie that he didn't want to be friends? The fact was, he couldn't. But he'd make sure the only friendly time they'd spend together would end Monday morning, when Maggie handed over Sarah to the social worker. Then their friendship would dwindle to polite greetings in the elevator and outside their apartment doors. Just like with Billie.

"Sure, we can be friends," he finally said. "It'll make it easier to take care of Sarah if we're not always squabbling."

Maggie looked pleased and relieved. "Good. And

since we're friends now, we should drop this formal stuff and call each other by our first names. Agreed...Jared?''

Jared hesitated, then finally answered, "Agreed... Maggie.''

"Good! Want some popcorn?''

Jared was taken by surprise. "It's nearly 3:00 a.m.''

"But Sarah is bright-eyed and bushy-tailed. I don't think we're going to get her to bed anytime soon, so we might as well watch this movie. Do you like Cary Grant?''

Jared tried to keep up with Maggie's rapid-fire conversation. *Was she this impulsive with all her friends?* he wondered. He checked out Sarah, who was just finishing the dregs of her bottle. She was as alert as he'd ever seen her, which meant he wasn't going to be able to go home for a while, so, like Maggie said, they might as well watch the movie.

He shrugged and smiled resignedly. "Why don't you turn up the sound?''

CURLED UP in an overstuffed chair near the couch—where Jared was half reclined, with Sarah propped on his chest—Maggie munched a handful of popcorn and stared at the television screen. The movie, titled *Room for One More,* was delightful. In a departure from his many roles as a debonair bachelor, Cary Grant was playing the dad of a family of five children. Three were his biological offspring, and two were foster children he and his sweet, saintly wife had taken in.

The trials and tribulations of raising a family were handled with the usual moralistic sentimentality of films of that era, with Cary Grant dispensing advice and solving problems with the same self-deprecating charm he used to woo women in other films.

A running gag through the show was Cary's frustration in finding "romantic" time alone with his wife. It seemed she was always needed by the children, even when Cary brought home champagne and flowers.

Maggie found that part of the show highly unrealistic. If she was married to a man who looked like Cary Grant...a man, moreover, who could qualify as father of the year and still be debonair and sexy...she'd sure as heck find time for "romance" with the guy! And the first thing she'd do would be to buy a lock for the bedroom door! Those kids went in and out of their parents' bedroom as freely as if it were a video arcade!

She slid a look toward Jared. Leaning against a pile of pillows, with one long leg stretched out on the couch and the other bare foot resting on the floor, with Sarah nestled against him and happily playing with her plastic keys, he looked fatherly and sexy at the same time. Just like Cary Grant in the movie.

His robe was gaping open, exposing his bare skin above Sarah's blond curls. Maggie watched as his chest rose and fell in long, quiet, comfortable breaths.

Suddenly, Maggie found herself daydreaming. She pictured Jared beckoning her to come and share the couch with him and Sarah. With so little room, she'd have to press close to him, sliding her arms around his waist and slipping her knee between his legs. She'd rest her cheek against his chest and listen to his heart beat strong...and fast. Then faster.

She'd look up and he'd be gazing at her like Cary Grant had gazed at Betsy Drake when she was reading their foster son a bedtime story. Longingly, hungrily, deeply in love. Then he'd say in a low, dreamy voice, "Sarah's asleep now. Let's put her to bed, then you and I can go to our own bedroom and—"

"Put butter on it."

Maggie blinked rapidly. "What did you say?"

"Are you awake?"

Maggie forced away the playful, sexy images Jared's words had unintentionally conjured up. She focused and saw Jared staring at her with an amused, slightly puzzled expression. "Yes, I'm awake," she said in a dull voice.

She was awake all right, and everything, unfortunately, was back to normal. She much preferred her daydream to reality. After all, "in her dreams" was probably the only place something as wonderful as what she'd been imagining could ever happen. Maybe Jared had agreed to be friends with her, but he probably was as firm as ever in his determination never to "hook up" with a woman in show business. She sure wished she knew why he was so prejudiced against actors. "Were you saying something about…butter?"

"I asked if you always eat your popcorn with just salt on it," Jared replied. "You know, the salt doesn't even stick to the popcorn. It's too dry. Call me crazy, but I think it would taste better if you put butter on it."

"Sorry. I don't even keep butter in the house," she said. "I have to watch my figure, so—"

"Everyone else will," he finished for her.

She shrugged. "Something like that. But I was going to say, so the wardrobe people won't have to throw out all Monica's clothes and shop for bigger sizes."

He gazed at her across the dimly lit room, the flickering light from the TV casting interesting shadows on his face and reflecting in his glasses. "You talk about Monica as if…well, as if she's not *you*."

"She isn't me. She's a character. I'm just plain old Maggie."

*Hardly plain or old,* Jared thought. Watching this Cary Grant flick had been fun, but frustrating. He really related to the poor guy's dilemma. Kids were great. Jared loved kids. But sometimes a man just wanted to be alone with his wife.

*Get a grip, Austin. You don't have a wife,* Jared reminded himself. But Maggie would make a marvelous stand-in. Even knowing what a big mistake he'd be making, he'd love to be alone with her for a little "romance."

"She's finally asleep."

Jared looked down, and sure enough, Sarah had dozed off. He immediately stood up, carefully and gently handling Sarah so he wouldn't disturb her. "Good. Now I can go home and get a little shut-eye."

He probably sounded eager to go, but not because he was so anxious to get some sleep. He needed to get away from Maggie before he forgot the hundreds of reasons why he couldn't get involved with her. Besides, he reasoned, she probably had just as many reasons, if not more, for not getting involved with him. And maybe Greg Moran was one of those reasons.

Jared was surprised at the sick feeling he got in the pit of his stomach at the thought of Maggie with Greg Moran. The guy was a conceited lout. He was an actor, for crying out loud!

But so was Maggie.

Why did he wish he could forget that?

Jared carried Sarah to Maggie's bedroom and laid her in the crib. As he covered her up, then lightly rested his hand on her blond curls, Maggie came in and stood beside him. He was aware of her presence even before he saw her. The faint, womanly scent of her, the warmth of her body, had preceded her by perhaps ten tantalizing seconds.

"She's beautiful, isn't she?" Maggie whispered, trailing her own slim, white hand over Sarah's sleeping form.

Jared couldn't resist it; he moved his own hand and covered Maggie's. It was the first time he'd purposely touched her. It was thrilling. It was risky, too, because he didn't know how she'd respond.

She turned startled eyes to his, and he realized that he probably looked just as surprised by what he'd done as she did. There was a question in the depths of her wide brown eyes...then a hesitant invitation. Or was that just wishful thinking on his part?

Jared took a chance. He drew her hand to his lips and pressed a kiss against her knuckles, gazing down at her, watching her reaction. He saw her swallow, then shiver delicately. That swallow and shiver were the result of either desire or revulsion, he wasn't sure which. But he figured he at least had a fifty-fifty chance of succeeding if he took this encounter a step further.

He put one hand on her shoulder and, with the other hand, he threaded his fingers through the soft layers of hair that fell against her cheek. In the dim light that filtered into the room from the hall, Maggie's hair shimmered with russet highlights.

"You're beautiful, too, Maggie," Jared breathed.

She laughed softly, nervously. "Even in this getup?"

He smiled down at her. "I realize it's not what you usually wear to bed, but—"

"Oh, but it is," she assured him. "I love flannel, except in the summer. Then I just wear a big T-shirt to bed."

Jared knitted his brows. "What about that flowy thing you had on yesterday?"

"Not my usual night gear," she said wryly. "I figure why dress up for bed when—"

She stopped suddenly and looked embarrassed. But Jared guessed she was going to say, *Why dress up for bed if you aren't going to share it with someone?* But did that mean she'd shared her bed Friday night with someone? And was that someone Greg Moran?

That sick feeling stabbed Jared's stomach again. But could he honestly expect a beautiful, desirable woman like Maggie to be celibate? She probably had men after her all the time.

Not that she slept with them all, of course. She didn't strike him as that type at all. But she must occasionally take a fancy to a man and get out her snazzier sleepwear to please him. Maybe as recently as Friday night....

But this was 4:30 a.m. Sunday morning, Jared told himself, and there were no men around except him. He was alone with Maggie and, if she'd let him, he was going to kiss her.

He bent his head. He watched as her eyes drifted shut, and that's when he knew that she wanted to be kissed as much as he wanted to kiss her. Pleasure rippled through him like a warm wave of water.

Their lips touched...and Jared was lost.

She tasted like popcorn, salty and delicious.

Her mouth was warm and mobile, and eagerly responsive.

His arms slipped around her waist and he pulled her fast against him. Her arms wrapped around his neck and her fingers drifted into his hair. Each kiss deepened, lengthened. He was breathless.

Every thought, every reservation fled before Jared's sudden passion for Maggie Stern, soap star. He couldn't imagine ever letting her go. The taste of her, the feel of her was more intoxicating than the finest wine. Her scent filled his head and made him dizzy. All he could think about was lying down with her and making love to her til—

Suddenly she pulled away and gazed up at him, her eyes hazy with passion and longing...and laughter?

"Have you got a vibrating beeper in your pocket—" her mouth slanted and her eyes brimmed with humor "—or are ya just happy ta see me?"

"My beeper!" He slipped his hand in his robe pocket and grabbed the beeper, turning it toward the hall light to read the message. "It's the hospital. The E.R. number. Can I use your phone?"

"Of course," Maggie said. "There's one by the bed."

Maggie watched as Jared sat down on the edge of her bed, flicked on the bedside lamp, and punched numbers on the phone. She marveled that he was suddenly so alert and businesslike. She still felt like she was in a daze. *Those kisses....*

"This is Dr. Austin."

Maggie turned away and leaned over the crib, fidgeting with Sarah's blanket. She didn't want to appear to be listening, but it was unavoidable. And if Jared wanted privacy, he'd have called from his apartment. Besides, now that they were friends....

Maggie frowned. Did friends kiss passionately, as they just had?

"How high is her fever? Is her neck rigid? Did the resident order blood tests? Prepare her for a spinal tap. I'll be there in twenty minutes."

When Jared got off the phone, Maggie had never seen him look more serious and distracted. It was obvious that their passionate kisses were the last thing on his mind.

"I have to go. A patient of mine, a four-year-old girl, was brought to the E.R. with symptoms that sound very much like spinal meningitis."

"Of course. I hope she's all right."

"I do, too," Jared said soberly. "Her parents have already lost one child." He looked at her keenly. "Will you be all right here with Sarah?"

"Of course." She made a wry face. "If she starts crying, I'll just start praying that you'll be back soon."

Her weak attempt at humor hadn't fooled him. "You'd like to come with me, wouldn't you? It's almost morning, Maggie, and you haven't slept a wink."

"But I won't rest anyway if Sarah starts crying," she reasoned.

"If you're recognized, you'll be mobbed again."

"I don't imagine my fans hang out en masse in emergency rooms in the wee hours of the morning. Or, if they do, they're probably thinking of anything but Monica Blake and her misadventures. Besides, I've got a red wig I've been dying to try out."

He smiled briefly, then looked thoughtful. "Unless the E.R. is busy, I could probably find a small, private room for you and Sarah to hang out in, then I could check on you periodically to make sure she's not screaming her lungs out.''

"Sounds like a plan to me," she said, encouraged.

"Well, thank goodness all this togetherness will no longer be necessary after tomorrow, when you give Sarah to the social worker," he said with a heavy sigh. "Now, hurry and get dressed. I'll be back to help you carry Sarah to the car. I'm parked under the building. If there are still paparazzi out front, they won't recognize you or the car, so we shouldn't be followed. See you in five."

"Yeah, see you in five," Maggie replied, feeling as if she'd just been slapped in the face with a pitcher full of cold water.

*Thank goodness all this togetherness will no longer be necessary after tomorrow.* Those had been his very words. Could there be a clearer indication of Jared's feelings? wondered Maggie.

Obviously he had just been playing around when he'd kissed her, had simply been stealing a smooch from a soap star for the sheer novelty of it. And when he'd questioned her about her "flowy" nightgown, he'd seemed disappointed, or mad or something, when she'd admitted to preferring comfort over glamour in the boudoir. When was everyone going to realize she wasn't Monica?

Maggie knew it was time she faced the hard facts. Despite the kiss, Jared didn't really want to be with her and was only hanging around for Sarah's sake. Brooding, she slipped out of her flannel PJs and into jeans, a black turtleneck, and a short red wig.

Why, she wondered, did she suddenly want to "play doctor" with a man who couldn't wait to end their forced togetherness?

# Chapter Eight

The parking garage was cold when Jared strapped Sarah's carrier into the back seat of his sedan and helped Maggie into the front. For this, he was thankful. He needed a bit of brisk night air to clear his head before arriving at the hospital.

Actually, what he really needed was a cold shower. Kissing Maggie had been much more of a thrill than he'd expected, and it had been almost impossible to think of anything else since then. Thank goodness, Sarah would be gone tomorrow and he and Maggie could go their separate ways.

Not that he wouldn't miss Sarah.... He would. But it would be best for her—and for him and Maggie— if she were comfortably settled in a loving foster home.

The drive to the hospital was almost surreal. Parts of the city were always open, but most of the downtown stores and offices were closed at this hour and the sidewalks devoid of pedestrians. Five in the morning seemed to be the ideal time for traveling into the city because they cruised along to their destination without any trouble with traffic. By six it would be fender-to-fender.

Jared was used to this off-hours, ghost-town aspect of Manhattan, but he wondered if Maggie found it a bit spooky and that was the reason for her silence on the way to the hospital. Or maybe she was feeling just as stunned and awkward as he did about the passion that had flared between them.

What had possessed him to kiss her? True, he'd been fighting an attraction since they'd first met, but he'd fought attractions before...and won. This time he'd gone down in a whistling trail of smoke.

Maybe he could blame that sentimental Cary Grant movie they'd watched—Hollywood's spin on domestic bliss, circa the 1950s. The perfect family in perfectly performed traditional roles.

Life just wasn't like that anymore. Maybe it never had been. Nowadays, most women worked outside the home. Many had to. Many wanted to, and Jared had absolutely no problem with that. But some careers were just not as conducive to the kind of stable family life a child needed. Claire had realized that and had bowed out early.

When they arrived at the hospital, Jared hurriedly parked his car in the lot reserved for physicians, then escorted Maggie and Sarah into the hospital through a side entrance. While she waited in the adjacent corridor, he went into the E.R. area and looked for a vacant room.

As orderlies, nurses, and medical technicians passed her in the hall, Maggie hunched into the upturned collar of her navy windbreaker and tried to appear as though she belonged there. Two nurses at two different times stopped and asked her if she needed to be directed somewhere, but when Maggie assured them she was just waiting for a friend, they smiled perfunctorily and hurried off. Neither had shown any sign of having recognized her, so they either weren't soap fans, or her red wig and sunglasses were working. Snuggled into her carrier, Sarah slept through it all.

Presently Jared poked his head around one of the double doors leading into the closed-off E.R. area and crooked a finger at her. Clutching Sarah's carrier, Maggie followed him through the doors and down a hall, then into a small room.

"I told the head nurse that you needed some privacy so you could nurse your baby," he told her. "This room is ordinarily reserved for infectious diseases that come into the E.R., but since there aren't any right now, it's free for us to use."

"Infectious diseases?" Maggie repeated doubtfully, taking off her sunglasses.

"Don't worry. The room is thoroughly scrubbed down after every use. You and Sarah are safer in here from germs than you are on the street, believe me," he assured her. He opened a closet and pulled a green surgical gown off one of the shelves. He slipped his arms into the sleeves over his heather-blue pullover sweater and felt for the little strings to tie in the back. Maggie set down Sarah's carrier and came to his rescue, quickly tying the garment in the back around Jared's waist.

Looking over his shoulder, he said, "Thanks."

"No problem," she replied, meeting his gaze shyly.

For just a moment, their gazes locked. Circumstances had forced an abrupt end to their kisses and Maggie couldn't help wondering what would have happened if they hadn't been interrupted. She wondered if Jared wondered the same thing. What else was he thinking? Did he regret the kisses?

"I'd better go. They're waiting for me to do the spinal tap." He glanced toward Sarah. "So far, so good, with Sarah Sunshine. I'll check back as soon as I can."

Maggie nodded, managing a weak smile, then Jared left the room. She watched him through a rectangular window in the door as he walked down the hall, the picture of authority and confidence in his surgical scrubs.

At the end of the hall, he stopped as a man and a woman approached him. Even from a distance, Maggie could detect the anxiety on their faces. Jared conversed with them briefly, taking the hand of the woman and squeezing it before he walked away. After Jared was gone, the woman looked up at the man and they smiled at each other tentatively, hopefully. Maggie felt sure they were the parents of the four-year-old girl about to undergo the spinal tap. They trusted Jared with their most precious possession...their child.

It was an affecting scene, and Maggie immediately had more respect for Jared. She realized how little she actually knew about him. But then they'd never really had a normal "getting acquainted" conversation. They'd got off to such a bad start, with him angry at her for mistakenly thinking she pirated his apartment. Then they'd clashed over what was the best thing to do for Sarah. Add to that the prejudice he already had against actors, and it was no big mystery why they hadn't become instant buddies.

Then the relationship took a sudden turn when she explained about the apartment and he accepted her overture to be friends. But two short hours later, they were kissing and embracing like lovers! Maggie had never been that bowled over by a kiss, and she'd kissed plenty of studly guys, both on screen and off. Where did they go from here?

Maggie paced around the small sterile room. Sarah, miraculously, slept on, leaving her with nothing to do but leaf through some old, battered copies of *Newsweek* she'd found in a magazine rack by one of the chairs. Restless, she stood up and walked to the door again and peered out through the narrow window.

She drew back when two female nurses stopped just opposite the door to discuss a patient. She started to walk away, but suddenly she heard Jared's name mentioned and couldn't resist eavesdropping. Flattening herself against the wall so she wouldn't be seen, she listened closely.

"I knew he'd come in to do the procedure himself. He really cares about that little girl."

"He cares about all his patients. He's a regular Dr. Kildare."

"With the looks to match."

There was a pause, during which Maggie could picture the women looking wistful. She could definitely relate.

"Any luck with him so far?"

"If you mean has he asked me out yet, the answer is no." The woman's voice was wry. "But I'm not giving up. We had coffee together in the cafeteria the other day."

"Well, that's something. Don't give up. Stacy used to date him and she says he's a dynamite kisser."

"Believe me, there's no way I'm gonna give up. Look, he's done with the spinal tap. I'm going to go see if there's anything I can do for him. You know...like rub his aching shoulders?"

"Oh, Nurse Molly, you're so efficient," the other

woman teased. Then their voices faded as they walked away.

Maggie peeled herself off the wall and pressed her cheek against the window, looking hard down the hall to try to catch a glimpse of "Nurse Molly" putting the moves on Jared. She couldn't blame the woman for being interested in him, but it irked her still the same. It also irked her to think that some woman named Stacy could also lay claim to Jared's killer kisses.

"How stupid, Maggie," she mumbled. "As if you're anything special." That sinking feeling she'd had before, the feeling that as soon as Sarah was out of her life Jared would be, too, came back full force.

Embarrassed by her jealousy and the silly way she was gaping out the window, Maggie resolutely sat down, picked up one of the old *Newsweek*s, and determinedly read an article about the 1992 presidential election. No surprises there....

Five minutes later, the door opened and Jared walked into the room. He was no longer wearing the surgical gown...but he was wearing a smile.

"She's going to be all right?" Maggie suggested hopefully.

"I think so. The labwork isn't back yet, but the spinal fluid was clear and that's a good sign. But I really don't want to leave till I know for sure what's going on with her."

"Of course," Maggie answered readily.

Jared nodded with a grateful smile that warmed Maggie's heart, and other parts of her body, too. But then Jared abruptly looked down at Sarah. He shook his head ruefully. "Still asleep. Amazing."

"I guess it really wasn't necessary to come with

you,'' Maggie said, feeling sheepish. She hoped Jared didn't think she was just using Sarah as an excuse to be with him constantly.

"Well, we didn't know if she'd sleep or cry. It's no big deal. Hopefully it won't be that much longer before we can—"

"Dr. Austin?"

Jared turned as a gray-haired female nurse stuck her head around the door. He deliberately shifted position and stood between her and Maggie, no doubt trying to block her from the nurse's view. "Yes, Joan?"

"We're going to need this room. There's a chicken pox patient outside. Is the young lady done nursing her baby?" The nurse came in and peered around Jared, fixing her curious gaze on Maggie, then Sarah. "Ah, I see she is. The baby's sleeping like an angel. It's a girl, isn't it?"

"Er...yes," Maggie muttered, avoiding direct eye contact with the nurse by finding it necessary at that moment to make several adjustments to her apparel...removing a piece of lint here, twitching a button there.

Joan walked further into the room and stood smiling down at Sarah. "What a precious little girl. And what pretty blond hair." She looked at Maggie again, inspecting her red wig with a perplexed furrow between her brows. "She must take after her father."

Maggie just smiled and plucked nervously at the titian strands of phony hair that curled over the top of her collar. When the nurse turned her attention back to Sarah, Maggie threw Jared a panicked look that she hoped conveyed her heartfelt desire that he get rid of Nurse Joan, pronto!

Jared just shrugged and looked helpless, then si-

lently mouthed some reassuring words that Maggie,
who was horrible at reading lips, couldn't make out
for the life of her. It looked like he said, "It's a cake.
Shells belong to midgets." But she was sure she must
be wrong.

"It's a shame to move her while she's sleeping so
peacefully, but this is the only room left to put the
chicken pox case." She turned to look at Maggie
again, her eyes narrowing. "You look familiar.... Who
did you come in with, anyway? Your baby's obviously
not sick. There's a Mr. Brady in room ten with a crou-
per. Are you Mrs. Brady?"

Maggie almost said yes, she was Mrs. Brady, just
to get Nurse Joan off her back, but since that revela-
tion would come as something of a shock to Mr.
Brady, she didn't. "No, I'm—"

"I know who you are!" Joan suddenly exclaimed,
her eyes widening to the size of gurney wheels.
"You're that soap actress, aren't you? You're *Monica
Blake!* I heard about you and the baby on the news!
*How exciting!* Can I have your autograph?"

Maggie groaned, and Jared turned quickly to shut
the door. But Joan had spoken so loudly, Maggie was
sure her voice had carried into the hall and, possibly,
down the corridor and into the main lobby of the E.R.

Sure enough, within a matter of seconds, several
nurses had crowded into the room and were gaping at
Maggie and babbling excitedly. The noise woke up
Sarah and she started screaming at the top of her lungs.

Maggie felt helpless. Across the sea of faces, she
sought a reassuring look from Jared, but his expression
was grim and frustrated. And at that moment, with
pandemonium all around her, Maggie couldn't blame

Jared for feeling the way he did about not "hooking up" with an actor.

IT TOOK JARED over an hour to extricate Maggie and Sarah from the infectious disease room at the E.R. It was appalling to him that so many of his colleagues at the hospital could behave so unprofessionally, neglecting their duties just to get an autograph from a celebrity. Thank goodness it was a relatively slow night at the E.R., and not all of the staff were soap opera fans, or the patients might have suffered.

He'd had to calm Sarah, shoo away the nurses, and sneak Maggie out to his car before word of her presence spread throughout the children's hospital and the paparazzi showed up. No easy task. Then he'd raced back inside to check his patient's lab work results, confirm a diagnosis, leave doctor's orders, and inform and reassure the parents, while Maggie drove the car around the block till he showed up outside the least conspicuous hospital exit...which happened to be the morgue.

Now, as they drove back to the apartment building, Jared heaved a huge sigh. It was eight-thirty in the morning and he was dead tired. Skulduggery was exhausting.

"I'm so sorry that happened," Maggie said. "I shouldn't have come with you."

Jared looked over at Maggie and realized that she was just as exhausted, if not more so, than he was. And dejected, too.

"It wasn't your fault," he admitted, but his tone was still a little grudging. "You didn't advertise the fact that you were there. I guess you're just too famous, Maggie."

"Only at the moment," she muttered. "This, too, will pass, you know. It's this baby thing. It's just really caught the fancy of the public, but once it's over I'll be able to move around like a normal human being again. Or, at least, *almost* like a normal human being."

Jared said nothing. What did she mean by "almost?" And did she think almost was good enough?

When they arrived at the apartment building, Dennis commandeered the elevator and took them non-stop to the twenty-first floor so they wouldn't be waylaid by other tenants. En route he warned them that guests awaited in Ms. Stern's apartment.

"Dennis, who did you let in?" Maggie asked him, horrified. "I never gave you permission to—"

"Sorry, Ms. Stern, but it was your mother...a Mrs. Lorena Morgenstern? She said you wouldn't mind. She had identification on her, so I knew she wasn't some reporter from one of those lousy birdcage liners." He shrugged and looked apologetic. "She was very persuasive."

Maggie nodded resignedly. "Yes, she always is. It's all right, Dennis."

"But you said 'guests' as in plural, didn't you?" Jared asked.

Dennis shifted uncomfortably. "Yes, sir, I did say guests. Two gentlemen came by after Ms. Stern's mother arrived, and she let them both in. I've seen the one before, but not the other. Here's your floor, folks."

Dennis seemed eager to get rid of them. No sooner had they stepped off the elevator than he pressed the button and was on his way down again.

"I was looking forward to getting some sleep,"

Maggie said, walking along tiredly beside Jared. He was holding Sarah, who, naturally, was wide awake.

"Well, sounds like you'll have plenty of people to watch Sarah while you nap," he said stiffly, wondering who the two men were that waited in Maggie's apartment.

"Not if Sarah doesn't like them," Maggie pointed out. And if Sarah cried as loudly as she usually cried, Jared knew he wouldn't sleep, either. He figured he had no choice but to go with Maggie to her apartment and stay put till Sarah went down for her morning nap. Of course, such a plan would also enable him to get a good look at Maggie's male guests.

He was curious, he told himself. Just curious.

But the first person he saw when Maggie opened her apartment door was a short, plump woman with hair teased to an impossible height and dyed an opaque shade of black. She wore a snug-fitting, green knit pullover decorated with cat faces, and a pair of black slacks. She also wore dangling silver earrings in the shape of cat faces, with tiny green gems for eyes.

"Margaret Morgenstern, where have you been?" she exclaimed fretfully. "I was just about to call the police!"

"Sorry, Mom, but—"

"Oh, this must be Sarah! But who are you?"

Jared found himself being addressed by Mrs. Morgenstern as she gave him a thorough once-over. She definitely wasn't shy, and her worried expression had all but vanished.

"This is Jared Austin," Maggie jumped in, looking a little embarrassed by her mother's lack of timidity. "He's my neighbor, and he's been helping with the baby."

"But, sweetie, why didn't you call me?" she demanded to know, looking much put out. "I've had scads of experience with baby girls, and you know it!"

Maggie sighed and set down the baby carrier. "He's a pediatrician, Mom, and Sarah likes—"

"You're a *doctor?*"

Jared recognized the look. Suddenly Mrs. Morgenstern was all smiles and checking him out with increased interest. Maggie winced, but Jared found Mrs. Morgenstern's open speculation and unabashed approval kind of amusing. He smiled. "Yes, Mrs. Morgenstern. I'm a doctor."

"Oh, your mother must be so proud," she said. "I know I'd be proud to have a doctor for a son." She smiled coyly. "Or even a son-in-law."

"Mom, who else is here?" Maggie hurriedly inquired.

"Last I looked, Mort was on the balcony, and Chuck's in the living room. Now, give me that baby, Dr. Austin. I've been dying to see her ever since I heard about her on the news. By the way, sweetie, I must say I was shocked to see you in that nightgown on the front cover of the *Planet*. What were you thinking wearing an expensive getup like that to bed when you're sleeping *alone?* For heaven's sake, Margaret, save it for your honeymoon!"

Jared tried not to chuckle as he handed Sarah over to Mrs. Morgenstern. He slid a look at Maggie to see how she was handling her mother's affectionate nagging. Her cheeks were bright pink, just like his would be in the same circumstances. Then his smile fell away as he caught a whiff of...cigar smoke.

"Oh, it's you," said Morty, dropping his hand behind his back, as if he could hide the smoking cigar he was holding as he appeared at the arched entry between the living room and the hall.

"Put it out, Morty," Maggie quickly ordered, saving Jared the job. "I told you—"

"The kid wasn't here," Morty reasoned with a shrug, sauntering past them to the kitchen. "And Lorena said she didn't mind. Says she likes the smell of cigar smoke."

"Well, the kid's back," Maggie called after him.

"Hey, I just came by to show you an early edition of the *Weekly Spectator*. You look good, Maggie, m'girl. And so does Greg. You make a great couple."

"Yeah, you do, Maggie," came Billie's voice from the kitchen. "Are you sure you two aren't...you know. After all, you did say he was a great kisser."

"I didn't know you were here, Billie," Maggie exclaimed, flitting Jared a nervous glance.

Billie appeared with a plate of marshmallow treats. "I slaved all day!" she quipped with a smile. "With a full house like this, Maggie, you oughta have more food on the premises. I had to raid my larder...whatever that means."

"Oh, don't worry. I brought food," said Mrs. Morgenstern, bouncing a happy Sarah in her arms. "A whole pan of lasagna. But that Chuck looks like he could eat half the pan himself."

"Who's Chuck?" Jared asked, still brooding about what Billie had said about Maggie endorsing Greg Moran's kisses. He hoped Chuck wasn't yet another soap actor!

"What's Chuck doing here, I wonder?" Maggie said, more to herself than to anyone else, slipping past Jared toward the living room.

"Who *is* Chuck?" Jared repeated. Maggie didn't

answer, so Jared had no choice but to follow her into the living room along with everyone else.

Sitting on the edge of the couch, his back stiff as a board and his hands clasped together in front of him, was a tall young man with blond hair. He was wearing a chauffeur's uniform. As Maggie drew near, he stood up and respectfully removed his hat.

"Ms. Stern. Hi. It's me...Chuck."

"I can see that, Chuck," Maggie replied with a chuckle. "I got your phone message last night. It was kind of you to offer to help with Sarah." She turned and motioned toward everyone else in the room and said wryly, "But as you can see, I've got more help than I can handle."

His eyes flitted from Maggie to Sarah, who was thoroughly enjoying being tickled and cooed at by Mrs. Morgenstern. "She looks happy," he offered, shifting nervously from foot to foot.

"As long as Dr. Austin's around," Maggie said.

Chuck's keen blue gaze shifted to Jared. He looked surprised. "Really?"

"I don't understand it, either," Jared admitted.

Chuck nodded, gazed at Sarah a minute longer, then suddenly said, "Well, as long as you've got everything under control, I'll just head out."

"Stay for lunch!" Mrs. Morgenstern practically shouted. "My lasagna is legendary."

"Thank you, but I can't," Chuck said politely. "I'm working today."

"Well...thanks, Chuck," Maggie said as she followed him out of the living room to the front door.

"Another guy with a crush on her," Billie lamented, munching on a marshmallow treat. "Why else would he be here? Some girls have all the luck."

"I just wish she'd marry one of them," Mrs. Morgenstern grumbled. But her expression brightened as she turned to speak to Jared. "But I've always told her to hold out for the right guy. Personally, I hope she marries a *professional* man."

"But you gotta admit, Mrs. Morgenstern—"

"For heaven's sake, Billie, call me Lorena." Another beaming look toward Jared. "You, too, Dr. Austin."

"There's something about a man in uniform," Billie finished. Her eyes lit up. "Speaking of which...."

Jared turned and observed Maggie walking back into the living room with the same young, burly policeman who had been there the day before. His face was flushed with pleasure as he gazed adoringly at Maggie.

"They flock like bees to nectar," Morty observed in a low voice, chewing on his stubbed-out cigar and watching everyone through hooded eyes that glinted with amusement.

Trailing behind the policeman, with an armful of teddy bears, was Mrs. Fernwalter. This was the first time Jared had seen her after finding out the truth behind the apartment situation, and he gave her a stern look. But she pretended not to notice and hurried over to show Sarah the teddy bears.

By now, Maggie's apartment was beginning to resemble the main hall at Grand Central Station, but Sarah seemed delighted by the activity. Her eyes were enormous and her lips were tilted in a perpetual smile as she took in everything and everyone around her.

As Maggie introduced everyone to the beefy cop, Officer Mulrooney, Jared thought it might be a good time to sneak away. Surely Sarah wouldn't miss him with so many people to entertain her. But first he'd listen to what the policeman had to say…if anything. He wouldn't put it past the guy to have come over with absolutely no news to report at all. Seeing Maggie again was probably the real reason for his visit.

And, sure enough, Jared was right.

"You've come up with absolutely nothing?" Maggie repeated, looking disappointed.

"So far, Ms. Stern," the officer admitted, then added importantly, "but we've got our best people on it. And we do feel reasonably sure Sarah wasn't kidnapped."

"Is there a chance you'll never find out who Sarah's parents are, and who this aunt is?" Jared asked him.

Officer Mulrooney tore his eyes away from Maggie and gave Jared a slightly irritated look, as if to say, *You're still here?* "It's possible," he replied to Jared's question, then turned back to Maggie with a smile. "But in that case, you'd be able to keep Sarah forever, Ms. Stern."

This comment drew everyone's attention and they all turned curious and questioning eyes toward Maggie. Especially Jared.

After glancing about the room and observing everyone looking at her, Maggie reluctantly met Jared's gaze. He waited tensely to hear her tell them what she'd promised to do…give Sarah to the social worker.

Just before Maggie's gaze shifted to the policeman, Jared thought he saw a sad expression in her eyes. But when she spoke, her tone was crisp. "Much as I'd like to, I'm really too busy with my career to keep Sarah, even on a temporary basis. I've decided to give her to the social worker tomorrow so she can put her in another foster home.''

While Jared breathed an audible sigh of relief, the rest of the occupants of the room erupted in noisy exclamations, with everyone expressing their opinion at the same time.

"Maggie, sweetie, have you thought this through?" her mother said. "I'm dying for more grandchildren, and at the rate you're going—"

"Look at this picture, Maggie," Morty said, thrusting the *Weekly Spectator* under Maggie's nose. "See how great the three of you look together? This is priceless publicity, sweetheart, and—"

"You're so good with her, Ms. Stern," the officer assured her. "And it's already been settled that—"

"Hey, you'd be getting a baby without losing your figure," Billie pointed out, biting into another marshmallow treat. "It's something to think about, Maggie. And remember—"

"You're *infertile!*" Mrs. Fernwalter wailed. "You and the Count may never get another chance to—"

Maggie closed her eyes and held up her hands for silence. Gradually the room stilled, then she opened her eyes and said, very succinctly, "I can't base my decision on what you want, or even what I want. I can only do what I think is best for Sarah. Understand?"

But by the looks on everyone's faces—everyone's but Jared's—no one understood or approved. And Sarah had begun to cry.

# Chapter Nine

At first Sarah had enjoyed having so many people around, but now Jared could see that she needed to get away from all the noise and confusion. Leaving Maggie to explain her decision to give up Sarah—or not to explain it, if that's what she preferred—Jared announced that it was time Sarah had a nap. He gently plucked her from Lorena's arms and bore her away to Maggie's bedroom, shutting the door and most of the noise behind them.

As Jared held Sarah against his shoulder, he walked around the commodious room and crooned a little non-sensical song to her. The motion and the singing, however discordant, soon calmed her and she was on her way to dreamland.

Jared, on the other hand, found that being in Maggie's bedroom didn't calm him at all. No, quite the contrary. There was the usual irritation of comparing his bedroom to hers and finding his lacking, and knowing that her bedroom ought to have been *his*. But worse than this old grievance was the fact that, despite its still disorganized state and all the boxes sitting around, the room was filled with the essence of Maggie.

Half her things were unpacked and piled here and there, and half still remained in the boxes. Books and perfume bottles and stuffed animals, scraps of lacy underwear and piles of sweatshirts and pants, pewter-framed family pictures, a thick, downy quilt and hand-stitched pillowcases, all seemed to illustrate Maggie's personal tastes and preferences. He was fascinated.

He wandered into the bathroom and looked at the large whirlpool tub, imagining her up to her chin in bubbles, a coy smile on her lips, motioning him to join her.... He saw her bathrobe hanging on a hook by the door and he caught it in his hand and pressed the cool material against his face, breathing in the delicate scent of her. But her scent was everywhere in the room, teasing him, taunting him.

"I need sleep as much as you do, Sarah," Jared mumbled into the ear of the drowsy child as he stroked her back. "And maybe after a little shut-eye—no, make that a lot of shut-eye—I'll be able to think more clearly and make smarter decisions."

Like never to kiss Maggie again. Of course it would be easier to make those smart decisions once Sarah was out of the picture, since caring for her together with Maggie had put them on such intimate footing. But as each hour passed, Jared was dreading the final separation more and more. It had been way too easy getting attached to Sarah...and to Maggie.

When Sarah was completely asleep, Jared laid her down in the crib, covered her up, then wearily sat down on the edge of Maggie's bed. He'd rest there for just a minute, then haul his rear back to his apartment, get a shower and take a nap before Sarah woke up again. In just a minute....

MAGGIE WAS GLAD that Jared had taken Sarah and left the room. It was easier to cope with all her well-meaning friends and relatives when he wasn't around. Within fifteen minutes she was able to get rid of Morty, Mrs. Fernwalter and Officer Mulrooney, and had appeased both her mother and Billie by eating a small square of warmed-up lasagna and a marshmallow treat.

"What else can I do, sweetie?" her mother asked her, her eager eye roving the apartment.

"Nothing, Mom. I just want to get some sleep."

"Can I do some unpacking for you? The study's still a mess and so is your bedroom."

"No, I'll have plenty of time for that after...after Sarah's gone." Maggie was surprised at how depressed she suddenly felt about parting with Sarah. She was probably just over tired. "Right now I want to rest while she's resting or I may never get the chance again today."

Lorena's forehead beneath the teased bangs furrowed into worry lines. "Don't you want to talk, sweetie? I'm not so sure you're happy about the decision you've made about that precious baby."

Maggie sighed heavily. "Thanks, but there's really nothing to talk about. I'm just trying to do the right thing."

"Is Doctor J going to keep helping you with Sarah till tomorrow?" Billie inquired, glancing with an arched brow toward the closed bedroom door. "He's pretty much got the run of the place, hasn't he?"

Maggie collapsed onto the couch. "After tomorrow I'm sure you won't see Jared in my apartment again." *Especially in my bedroom,* she added to herself.

"Is that good or bad?" Billie asked her, obviously

digging to find out Maggie's feelings about the good doctor.

"It's bad," Lorena interjected emphatically. "He's a doctor, Maggie. A baby doctor, no less. And as handsome as they come. Don't be stupid."

Maggie had opened her mouth to reply when the intercom buzzed. "Who could that be?" she groused, slowly rising to her feet. "I thought everyone I knew had already been here this morning."

She went to the intercom, pressed the button and said, "Yes, who is it?"

"It's Greg, Maggie. Tell Dennis to let me in, will ya, doll? I'm all alone. No paparazzi or reporters, I swear."

Maggie was about to politely but firmly tell Greg to take a hike when she caught sight of Billie's pleading expression. "*Please, please,* Maggie, let him come up," she begged. "I've been dying to meet that hunk for ages!"

"Are you sure, Billie?" Maggie asked. "He's nothing like the Count. He's pretty self-involved."

"Oh, but so cute!" Billie enthused, practically jumping up and down with excitement. "Don't worry, Maggie. I can take care of myself."

"Okay, but don't say I didn't warn you. I'll let him come up as long as you promise to get him out of the apartment right after you meet him," Maggie bargained.

"Believe me, I'll do my best," Billie promised fervently.

"Be careful, Billie," Lorena advised her. "He looks like a heartbreaker to me. Does he like lasagna?"

"He won't be staying long enough to eat lasagna, Mom, so please don't offer it, okay?"

"Maggie? Are you there?" Greg called.

Maggie pressed the intercom button. "Come on up, Greg."

Billie ran to look into the mirror over the mantel to check her hair and makeup, then draped herself on the couch in a suitably nonchalant, yet sultry, pose. Maggie summoned up just enough energy to laugh at her friend and answer the door.

Greg followed her into the living room, waving a copy of the *Weekly Spectator* and gloating out loud about the great publicity they'd be sure to get from the family-style photos of him and Maggie and Sarah. He pointed to a big heart he'd drawn around their photo with a red pen, and made a comical show of pretending his own heart was beating out of his chest with love for Maggie.

Then he saw Billie. Stopping dead in his tracks, he stared. She stared back. It was instant chemistry.

Ten minutes later, true to her word, Billie got Greg out of the apartment by suggesting that they try out the new espresso bar down the street. Maggie could tell that Greg was really smitten because he had chosen to spend time with someone who couldn't do anything to advance his career.

Stretched out on the couch and barely able to keep her eyes open, Maggie said, "I'm going to have to thank Billie for getting Greg out of my hair."

"Judging from appearances, I think she's going to be thanking *you*," Lorena said as she put on her jacket. "At least at first.... With guys like that, you never know."

"Where are you going, Mom?" Maggie asked drowsily.

"I'm going to get out of your hair, too. Looks to

me like you've got all the help you need from Dr. Austin,'' she said with obvious satisfaction, then picked up an afghan from a footstool and covered Maggie with it.

"Can't sleep," Maggie mumbled, already halfway gone. "Got to take a shower when Jared leaves."

"You'll have a long wait. I think he must have gone to sleep in your bedroom, sweetie. He and the baby. He's quite a guy, Maggie."

"Don't get any ideas, Mom. He doesn't like me...."

Lorena smiled smugly and gazed down at her sleeping daughter. "That's what you think, sweetie. He just needs a little nudging." Then she picked up the copy of the *Weekly Spectator* that Greg had brought over, the one with the big heart circling their happy family photo, and laid it on Maggie's lap.

WHEN JARED WOKE UP, he wasn't sure at first where he was. Then he took a deep breath and remembered. The room smelled like Maggie. It was Maggie's room. He'd fallen asleep on Maggie's bed.

Bleary-eyed, he sat up and looked at her bedside alarm clock. It was already one o'clock in the afternoon! A quick glance at Sarah's crib showed that she was still sleeping, too, which meant she'd be very alert all evening. And maybe half the night! He figured he'd better get back to his apartment while he had the chance and take a shower.

He carefully opened Maggie's door, relieved when he couldn't hear any voices, and tiptoed down the hall. Rounding the corner to the living room, he was even more relieved when his hopes were answered and he found the place empty. Then it hit him. Where was Maggie?

He hurried toward the kitchen, already mentally chastising her for leaving him with Sarah without telling him, when he caught sight of her out of the corner of his eye. She was lying on the couch, which faced away from the hall, and that's why he hadn't seen her when he first entered the room.

Turning back, he slowly approached the couch. Then he just stood and stared down at her, mesmerized. She was deeply asleep, her dark hair flowing over the throw pillow, her lashes stark and lush against her pale cheek, her hands neatly resting on her flat stomach. She really was beautiful. He was tempted to stoop down and—

But what was that? Pushed off a little to the side, but still in her lap, was a newspaper or something. Something she'd been reading, he guessed. He picked it up. It was the copy of the *Weekly Spectator* Morty Shuback had been waving around and bragging about that morning. But something had been added. Someone had drawn a heart around the picture with a red pen.

Jared wanted to be sick. He couldn't believe it was possible, but had Maggie drawn the heart around the picture? Did she have the hots for that phoney-baloney guy? But why else would she drift off to sleep with the paper in her lap?

Burning with a rage he could no longer deny was jealousy, Jared wanted to crumple up the paper and torch it with a match. Instead, he carefully put it back where he'd found it and resolutely left Maggie's apartment. He didn't like the way he was feeling and he was determined to get over such a stupid, ill-advised infatuation if it was the last thing he did.

JUST LIKE MAGGIE'S Sunday school teacher had always preached, miracles did happen. That day the miracle for Maggie was the fact that Sarah didn't cry when she woke up from her long nap. In fact, she didn't cry all day, all evening, or all night.

Maggie was grateful and decided that Sarah must have finally got used to her. But she was also disappointed. Disappointed because there was no reason for Jared to come over. He'd gone home while she'd been sleeping, not even sticking around to say goodbye. And he hadn't checked on them once during the entire day and night that Sarah had abstained from screaming her lungs out. It just proved to Maggie that Jared really was only interested in Sarah, and the kisses the two of them had shared had been just a momentary diversion.

On Monday morning, Maggie got up just as tired as the morning before. Sarah hadn't kept her up all night, but nagging thoughts had. She was going to miss Sarah. She'd had a lovely time with her the day before, feeding her, playing with her, dancing her around the room, bathing her. She'd found herself wishing Jared would call and come over so he could see that she really could take care of a baby, that she really did have more than a thimbleful of motherly instinct. But even without Jared, she'd had a great time with Sarah Sunshine. And now she had to give her up.

While feeding Sarah her morning bottle, Maggie looked at the time with misgiving. It was eight o'clock. In an hour the social worker would arrive and take Sarah away. She wondered if Jared would bother to come over on his way to work and say goodbye.

IT WAS EIGHT O'CLOCK and Jared was just finishing his second cup of coffee before leaving for the office. He was very tempted to just drop by Maggie's apartment for a minute on his way to work, to check on Sarah, but he talked himself out of it. It had been really strange not to be summoned to help with Sarah all day yesterday and all night. And it wasn't just that Maggie wasn't asking for help when she really needed it, because he hadn't once heard Sarah crying. Maybe, as Maggie had predicted, Sarah just needed to get used to her.

Jared rinsed his cup and set it on the counter, then grabbed his briefcase and headed for the door. Even though Sarah hadn't cried, that didn't mean Maggie should keep her. The longer she stood in as Sarah's foster mother, the harder it would be for Sarah to relocate to another family, another home. In Jared's opinion, giving Sarah to the social worker was still the best thing Maggie could do for her.

After Jared locked his apartment, he stared at Maggie's door and fought the urge to ring the doorbell. But if he saw Sarah that morning, she might start crying when he left and Maggie would have to listen to that till the social worker arrived. No, it was better for Sarah and for Maggie if he just didn't say goodbye. He sighed heavily and headed for the elevator. And better for him, too.

"HELLO, I'M Barbara Johnson...the social worker you were expecting?"

"Yes, Ms. Johnson, please come in."

Holding Sarah in her arms, Maggie stepped aside and motioned for Ms. Johnson to walk past her into the apartment. As she passed, Maggie scanned the social worker's neat appearance. She was a black

you do, Maggie. You have a wonderful talent that enables you to entertain people. Speaking for myself, escaping reality for a while, and simply watching a TV show for an hour or two, is exactly what I need sometimes.''

Maggie felt her spirits lifting. ''Do you really think so?''

''Yes, I do. And since you've earned two Emmys for your acting, I should think you're very good at entertaining people. If it makes you happy, I certainly wouldn't consider giving it up to have children. But you needn't give up children, either, to have a career.''

Maggie considered this for a moment, then said, ''To be honest, I've been so consumed by my career, I haven't given any of this much thought. I figured I'd probably have children someday, but it wasn't like a goal I was postponing. I was perfectly happy being single and carefree.'' Maggie looked at Sarah with fond chagrin. ''Then Sarah came along.''

''You seem attached to her. And she's obviously content to be with you.'' Barbara's concerned look returned. ''I really am confused, Maggie. I thought I understood that your employer had agreed to give you some time off to spend with Sarah. If your career isn't a conflict right now, why did you decide to give Sarah up?''

''She hasn't always been this happy with me,'' Maggie confessed. ''When I first got her, she cried constantly. The only person that could calm her and make her happy was my neighbor, Dr. Austin. He's thought all along that someone besides me should be taking care of her.''

''Why?''

''I think it's because I'm in show business. And he

does have a valid point. I've been ducking photographers and reporters ever since the story broke about Sarah's arrival on my doorstep. My life gets pretty crazy sometimes.''

"I see," said Barbara. "Well, Maggie, all I can tell you is that good foster homes for children are at a premium. I certainly don't think living with you would traumatize any child. You're intelligent and caring and financially secure. Your home is clean and spacious. You don't appear to be very 'showbizzy' to me, but even if you were, children are raised in many different kinds of environments and do just fine as long as they're given moral standards, education and love. All of which I'm perfectly convinced you could give Sarah for two weeks, or for the rest of her life.''

Maggie felt overwhelmed. "But you've just met me. And you've only been here ten minutes.''

Barbara smiled. "I did my homework. I know quite a lot about you, actually. And, after doing this for fifteen years, I have great instincts.''

Maggie wasn't sure what to think. How to feel. "So, you think I ought to keep her?''

Barbara firmly shook her head. "No, that's not what I said. I think you ought to do what you think would be best for Sarah…and for you. I'm sure lots of people have expressed their opinion one way or the other, but maybe some of their reasons are motivated by self-interest, or not founded on the real facts. You know what you can do, and why you're doing it, better than anyone.''

Maggie thought about Morty's and Greg's reasons for wanting her to keep the baby. Publicity. She thought about Mrs. Fernwalter, who clearly couldn't differentiate between the fictional Monica and the very real Maggie Stern. She thought about Officer Mulroo-ney who, because she was a glamorous figure to him, considered her eminently suitable to adopt Sarah. Her mother loved babies, but providing her with another grandchild was no reason to keep Sarah. Nor was it a good reason to keep Sarah simply because, as Billie had flippantly suggested, Maggie could have a baby without risking losing her figure.

Then there was Jared, who thought Sarah would be better off anywhere but with her. But he really didn't know her, and he'd had preconceived ideas about ac-tors before he even met her. And he'd gotten a bad impression of her from the start...thanks to Mrs. Fern-walter.

Maggie suddenly realized that Sarah's crying and Jared's doubts had undermined her confidence over the past two days. Add to that her overwhelming at-traction to such a difficult man and it was no wonder she hadn't been able to think clearly.

She was thinking clearly now and she knew exactly what to do. Sarah was happy and settled where she was. There was no point in uprooting her again, at least not till permanent decisions were made about her. Maggie had the time off and the means to care for this child...and she really wanted to.

Sure, there'd be challenges because she was famous, but she was a strong, capable woman and she could handle them. She'd promised Jared she would give Sarah to the social worker this morning, but she'd made that promise under duress. If he didn't like it, well, that was just too bad.

Maggie smiled at Barbara. "I'm going to keep her."

Barbara looked happy and relieved. "I'm glad. I think it will be the best thing for Sarah."

"You're an amazing woman, Barbara," Maggie told her.

Barbara shrugged and smiled. "So are you, Maggie. Now about that childproofing we were talking about—"

JARED HAD IMMERSED himself in his morning appointments, trying hard to put Maggie and Sarah out of his mind. By lunchtime, he figured the social worker had come and gone and Sarah was on her way to another foster home. He'd won the day. He'd convinced Maggie that it was in Sarah's best interests to give her up, and he still thought so...but he felt unaccountably sad.

With only half an hour before his next appointment, Jared headed for the lounge to grab some food out of the vending machines. It wasn't the most nutritious or tasty way to eat, but when you were pinched for time it was convenient.

Jared's office was in a clinic with several other doctors of varying specialties. He liked the clinic setup because he could have all his patients' lab work and X-rays done on the spot, without the hassle of sending them to the hospital and waiting forever for results.

As he entered the lounge, he noticed a group of nurses and medical technicians sitting around the television at the far end of the room, eating their lunches and, at the same time, getting their daily soap fix. He'd seen them doing this before and had never given it much thought, except to think that it was a waste of time to get involved in those preposterous melodramas. But today....

"Hi, Dr. Austin," chirped one of the nurses, patting

a vacant cushion beside her on the couch. "Wanna sit down? We're watching 'The Rich and Reckless.' Steamy love scene coming up!"

Jared could see that. He picked up the carton of orange juice he'd just bought out of the vending machine and, with his gaze fixed on the television screen, walked slowly forward. He stopped just behind the couch, resting his hands and the juice carton on the back, and just stared.

There was Maggie in living color. He'd never actually seen her playing the role of Monica Blake. She looked glamorous and sexy as hell in a black teddy, curled up on a huge bed that was draped in red satin, her thick lashes drooping over eyes that sizzled with passion for—

"Greg Moran," he muttered under his breath. His fingers clenched around the juice carton.

The same nurse looked up at him with a quizzical expression. "Oh, do you follow this soap? Yeah, that's the actor's name, but I can't think of him as anyone but the Count of Carsovia, Alexander Tolstoy! Isn't he a dream?"

*More like a nightmare,* Jared thought to himself. And only a passably good actor. But he and Maggie were very convincing at generating a great deal of heat on the screen. Like watching a gory scene in a horror movie, Jared was repelled and transfixed at the same time by the seduction scene being staged.

The Count had entered their candlelit bedroom in some apparent agitation. When he saw Maggie on the bed, he stopped in his tracks and stared. "Darling," he uttered in that strangely contrived accent of his. "I've been looking everywhere for you. In the garden, in the conservatory, in the grove…wherever beauty thrives.''

Maggie, or rather Monica, reversed her position on the bed, sliding around and down on her stomach with slow sensuality. Jared swallowed…hard. That black teddy she was wearing left little to the imagination. She rested her chin on her knuckles, kicked one shapely leg in the air over her nicely rounded bottom, and smiled coyly. ''I've been here all the time, Alexander…waiting for you.''

The Count's wolfish grin made Jared a little sick, but he thought he heard one of the nurses sighing. Then the Count shrugged out of his impeccably tailored sport jacket and began to unbutton his shirt.

''Come here, my royal stallion,'' Monica crooned as she crawled to her knees, revealing a great deal of luscious cleavage in the process. ''Let me undress you.''

The Count eagerly obeyed and Maggie took her time unbuttoning his shirt, kissing each inch of exposed chest as she went along. Jared's blood began to boil. His fingers curled tighter and tighter around the carton of orange juice. All he could think was, *It should be me she's kissing, not him!* Then he reminded himself it was just a show. She was just acting. But she sure as hell was convincing.…

Finally removing the Count's shirt, Maggie pressed herself against his naked chest and kissed him. He kissed her back. Boy, did he ever kiss back.… And Jared remembered Billie's comment about Maggie telling her what a good kisser Greg was.

Then, just when Jared thought he couldn't stand to watch another moment, they eased down onto the bed. The Count hovered over her, his gaze burning into hers. She smiled up at him, and breathed, "Tonight, darling. Tonight maybe we'll make a baby. Giving you a child is what I want more than anything in the world."

"Making love to you, Monica, is all that I want," the Count assured her. "For hours, and hours, and hours." As his head lowered to hers, the scene faded to a commercial...and Jared's carton of orange juice exploded all over the nurses who were seated on the couch.

# Chapter Ten

Jared worked with such single-minded energy during the rest of the afternoon, he finished with his patient load early and was on his way home well ahead of the rush hour traffic. It had proven to be a difficult and embarrassing day. After spraying the nurses with orange juice in the lounge, he had had to come up with some believable excuse for squeezing the carton so hard.

Since Jared had no intention of telling them the truth—that watching Maggie on the screen with Greg Moran had made him unusually "tense" and he'd unconsciously relieved that tension by squeezing the life out of an innocent juice carton—he told them he'd got a muscle cramp. The nurses and technicians looked dubious, but politely did not challenge his lame explanation.

Now, stepping off the elevator, Jared wasn't sure whether he was glad to be home or not. Walking toward his apartment, he couldn't help but look at Maggie's door and remember all the time he'd spent there over the past two days. But all that was over now. Sarah was gone. And so was his excuse to see Maggie....

Although, he reasoned, as he unlocked his own door and went inside, it would be perfectly natural...even considerate...to check in with her and ask her how it had gone that morning. He was sincerely concerned and curious about how Sarah had reacted when she was handed over to the social worker. He was even concerned about how Maggie was feeling about the whole thing. Relieved? A little sad, maybe...like him?

Reasonably sure he wasn't just making up an excuse to see Maggie, and telling himself he wasn't interested in a woman who could swoon over the likes of Greg Moran, anyway, Jared went into his bedroom to change out of his slacks and sport jacket into something more casual. That's when he heard it.

A baby crying. *Sarah.* Sarah was still next door!

Jared's first, and probably most revealing, reaction was happiness. Then puzzlement and curiosity. What had happened? Why was Sarah still there? Was it just that the social worker was unable to take Sarah right away...or had Maggie decided to keep her? That's when Jared felt his first prick of annoyance. What about the deal they'd made? She'd promised to return Sarah if he helped her out over the weekend. Had Morty or Greg talked her out of doing what was best for Sarah?

Without bothering to change, Jared left his apartment and went next door. He rang the doorbell and waited. A half a minute later, Maggie opened the door with Sarah in her arms. She lifted her chin and stared him down, looking defiant as hell.

"What's going on, Maggie?" he demanded to know, sweeping past her into the apartment.

"Oh, do come in," Maggie said with breezy sarcasm. "No need to wait for an invitation."

Jared took Sarah out of Maggie's arms, and Maggie turned to shut the door. Jared walked into the living room, bouncing Sarah and crooning to her, and Maggie followed.

Once he'd calmed Sarah down, he kissed her damp cheek, propped her against his shoulder, and rubbed her back. He wasn't going to mention how glad he was to see Sarah and hold her again. He wasn't going to allow Maggie to use his affection for Sarah as leverage.

"Why didn't you give her back?"

Instead of addressing this question, she crossed her arms and said accusingly, "You didn't even come by this morning to say goodbye to her."

"I was afraid she'd cry, then you'd have to deal with that till the social worker came."

Maggie raised a brow. "How considerate of you. Is that why you stayed away all day yesterday, too?"

"I wasn't needed. I was home all day and I never once heard her crying."

Maggie couldn't dispute that, so she gave a sulky shrug and sat down on the sofa, tucking her legs under her.

"What's going on with you?" he asked her, puzzled by her angry and defiant attitude. "Why didn't you keep your end of the bargain and give Sarah back to the social worker?"

"I realized that Sarah was better off with me than in a new home where she'd have to get used to a whole new set of people."

"How can she be better off with you if she's crying herself sick all day?"

"She hasn't been crying. This is the first time all day that she's made a single peep."

Apparently Jared's disbelief showed.

"I'm telling the truth," Maggie said emphatically. "You know for a fact that she didn't cry yesterday, so why's it so hard to believe she didn't cry today?"

"Hell, I don't know what to believe," Jared groused.

"It's like she's got her own agenda, you know?" Maggie said with a shake of her head. "Sometimes she wants you. Sometimes she's content to be with me. There's no second-guessing her."

"But the bottom line still is that she's better off in another foster home," Jared reminded her.

"Sez you," Maggie retorted, rising to her feet again and glaring up at Jared. "I don't agree, and neither does Ms. Johnson, the social worker."

"What does Ms. Johnson know?" he exclaimed, then realized how ridiculous he sounded.

"She knows a lot," Maggie informed him frostily. "She's been a social worker for fifteen years and has great instincts. She thinks this is a good temporary home for Sarah...or, for that matter, a great home for the rest of her life."

"What does she know about you...about your life?" Jared challenged.

"A heck of a lot more than you do," Maggie shot back. "You've had preconceived ideas about me and my ability to take care of a child from the beginning. But, the fact of the matter is, you don't really know me at all. All you know is that I'm in show business and you think that's reason enough to dismiss me as a competent foster mother. Or even a suitable date, for that matter."

At Jared's surprised and guilty look, she said, "Yes, I overheard the tail end of your conversation with

Candy. I know you don't date actors and such. I assume you've had some sort of trauma or something. I don't really know. But you don't seem to understand that whatever happened to you has nothing to do with *me*."

After a short, uncomfortable silence, Jared said, "This conversation has strayed from the main and most important topic. We were talking about Sarah, not you."

"But it's been about me from the beginning, Jared," Maggie insisted with a frustrated sweep of her arms.

"The apartment mixup gave me the wrong impression."

"There's more to it than that. Your big objection to me being Sarah's foster mother was because of my profession. Admit it."

"Okay, I admit it," Jared said stiffly. "Now can we drop the subject?"

"No, now I want you to justify your prejudice." Maggie waited, her fists on her hips, but Jared remained stubbornly silent. He wasn't about to talk about his own personal experience dealing with the oil and water combination of motherhood and show business. Besides, it wasn't that big of a deal. And Maggie was right, he suddenly realized. Right about... well...almost everything.

"Look, I'm sorry," he said finally. "I'm not usually so judgmental or narrow-minded. You're right. I haven't considered you as an individual. I stereotyped you right from the beginning. I did date a couple of actors when I first came back to New York from medical school, and, believe me, it was a terrible experience. Then, with you...first the apartment thing happened, which really ticked me off. Then I saw you wearing that fancy nightgown, and Officer Mulrooney and Mrs. Fernwalter falling all over you—"

Maggie's expression suddenly changed. It softened. It was as though she understood and actually sympathized. "I don't like to be treated that way either, Jared," she told him earnestly. "When I moved here I just wanted to blend in with everyone. I didn't expect or want special treatment. It makes me uncomfortable when people stare and gush and flatter. But it comes with the territory, and I won't give up acting just to get away from the unfortunate side effects of public exposure. I love it too much."

Jared thought about this as Sarah cooed happy gibberish in his ear. She didn't seem the slightest bit disturbed by their heated conversation.

"There must be some drawbacks to your profession, too," Maggie finally said, breaking the silence. "The hours, the stress, and constantly being on call are par for the course for you. But you couldn't quit being a doctor, could you? No more than I could quit being an actor. But does that necessarily preclude me from having other things in my life? Like a child, for instance?"

"Maggie, you aren't really thinking about adopting her, are you?" he asked.

"By your tone, I have to assume you still think I'm not mother material," she said with a disappointed sigh.

"That's not what I—"

"Never mind. It's a moot point, anyway. The police still haven't determined who's legally responsible for her. Right now I just think I ought to take it one day at a time."

"That's a good idea," Jared agreed. He paused, then impulsively added, "And I want you to know I'll be here for you—that is, for *Sarah*—whenever I'm needed."

Maggie smiled wistfully. "Okay. And...for Sarah's sake...I thank you."

For a moment they stared at each other. He wondered if his expression showed the same poignant mix of frustration and longing. If only they'd met under better circumstances.... But then they wouldn't have been forced to spend time together, which had allowed their attraction to grow. Under normal circumstances, he'd have been able to nip that initial attraction in the bud and go on with his life. It was too late for that now. But where did they go from here?

Maggie was grateful when the intercom buzzed. She wrenched her gaze away from Jared and went to answer it.

"Yes?"

"Ms. Stern, it's me, Chuck. I just came by to see if there's anything I can do to help out with the baby. Can I come up?"

Maggie was a bit puzzled by Chuck's continued interest in her baby problems. But it was sweet, and she didn't want to offend him, so she told him to come up. When she turned around, however, Jared's knowing look put her on the defensive.

"He just wants to help. He's young enough to be my...well...my younger brother. And if he is doing this because he's got a crush on me, I can't help that. I didn't encourage him."

"You're right. You can't help it if he's got a crush on you," Jared admitted grudgingly. He sat down on the couch, crossed an ankle over a knee, then laid

Sarah on his bent leg and gently bounced her up and down. She smiled happily. "Besides, he does seem like a nice kid."

"Yes, despite my scandalous profession, I do have some nice friends and even some nice business associates," Maggie said pointedly.

Jared conceded with a weary nod, then the doorbell rang and Maggie went to answer it. Chuck wasn't dressed in his chauffeur's uniform this time, but was wearing a sweater and cords. She was struck again by what a good-looking young man he was. In fact, he almost looked like a younger version of Jared...tall and blond and blue-eyed.

Strolling ahead of her to the living room, he wiped his palms on his pants and Maggie realized that he was nervous...just like last time. But Maggie chalked that up to the fact that their association over the past year, although very cordial, had always been work-related. Now, for some reason, he was coming around as a friend. She hoped he was just responding to her present crisis and didn't, as Billie had suggested and Jared suspected, have a crush on her.

"Hello, Dr. Austin," Chuck said respectfully as he entered the living room. "Still Sarah's favorite person?"

"She's come around with Maggie, too," Jared said, throwing her a look that said, *See, I can be fair.*

"We spent a wonderful day together yesterday and today," Maggie told Chuck, smiling at Sarah. "We played and danced and sang. We even took a bath together, didn't we, Sarah Sunshine?"

Chuck grinned from ear to ear. "That's great, Ms. Stern. I was really worried about you two at first. But sounds like Sarah just needed to get used to you, that's all."

"You're not married, are you, Chuck?" Jared asked.

Chuck blushed. "I'm only nineteen. I want to get through school first before I settle down with a wife and kids."

"That's smart," Maggie assured him. She cocked her head to the side. "Do you have lots of younger brothers and sisters?"

Chuck blushed deeper than ever. "No. Er...none. Why do you ask?"

"You just seem so interested in Sarah," Maggie said with a smile and a shrug. "That's unusual for a guy your age."

"I just thought I might be able to help you out, Ms. Stern. I know...well, I've *heard* how tough it is when you first get a baby. It can be exhausting and frustrating. I was just thinking of *you*."

Chuck's words, and the blush that accompanied them, seemed to support Billie and Jared's idea that he had a crush on her. Maggie found this fact more exhausting and frustrating than taking care of Sarah.

"Have you been away from her at all since she was dropped off at your door?" Chuck inquired.

"Away from her?" Maggie repeated.

"You know, *out*," he clarified. "Every new mother ought to get out once in a while or she'll go crazy."

Maggie got a sudden, horrible fear that he was about to ask her out on a date. "It's kind of hard for me to get out, Chuck," she said nervously. "What with everyone trying to get a picture of us. Not to mention the fact that I wouldn't have the slightest idea who to hire as a baby-sitter."

"I'll baby-sit for you," he offered, taking Maggie totally by surprise.

"Do you know how to take care of a baby?" Jared asked him.

"My steady girlfriend in high school took care of her younger brothers and sisters every day after school." Chuck smiled shyly. "I helped. The baby always liked me the best and I learned how to change her and feed her and everything."

"Well, why don't you take Sarah right now and change her?" Jared suggested. "She needs it."

Maggie was dumbfounded. Why was Jared encouraging this? Surely he didn't expect her to go out somewhere and leave Sarah with Chuck. Not that she had any objection to Chuck personally. She liked him a lot and had never heard anyone say anything bad about him. But Sarah didn't know Chuck. Surely she would put up a fuss if they left her with another total stranger.

But when Chuck took Sarah, Sarah didn't cry. Even when Jared took Maggie by the hand and led her out of the room and out of Sarah's sight, she didn't cry. And, from what Maggie could see, Chuck was as good at changing a diaper as he was at driving her safely through Manhattan during rush hour.

"I think we should take him up on his offer, Maggie," Jared said as they watched from the hall.

"We?" Maggie repeated. "Why both of us? If I went somewhere alone, at least I'd know you were next door in case Sarah needed you."

"But do you really want to go somewhere alone?"

She looked at him. They were standing very close and she could see the beginnings of a very sexy five-o'clock shadow on his face and smell the faint, spicy scent of his morning aftershave. And he was still holding her hand.

"Are...are you suggesting we go 'out' together?"

"Why not? We've both been taking care of Sarah for the past three days. I need a break, too."

"Maybe you need a break from me," she suggested.

"No, I don't think so. In fact, I think it would be nice if we went somewhere and kind of got to know each other. Getting-acquainted conversation has been sadly lacking in our relationship so far."

*Our relationship?* thought Maggie. What was he getting at?

"So you really think we ought to go out together? Are you sure Sarah will be all right?"

"Maybe she only likes Chuck because he looks a little like me," Jared said consideringly, "but, the point is, they're getting along. We can take my cellular phone, then if she does start crying, we can rush home. So, how about it, Maggie? After all, we *are* neighbors. And it appears, by Sarah's choice, that we're in this thing together. Wouldn't it be a good idea to know each other better?"

Maggie was surprised, but intrigued. Was it possible that after such a shaky start they could be friends...or more? She had to find out.

She smiled. "I'm willing to give it a try."

A HALF HOUR LATER, Jared had parked his car on a street that bordered Central Park, and he and Maggie were walking into a small grocery store to buy food for a picnic. He'd had a quick shower and a change of clothes, but there had been no time to shave. They were both casually dressed in jeans and sweaters and athletic shoes.

Maggie wore her usual sunglasses, but had not donned a wig. Instead she'd tucked her hair into a Mets cap, looking very much like the first time he'd seen her. He just hoped they could manage some time away from the apartment without Maggie being recognized. There was about an hour left of sunshine and they planned to eat in the park.

"I'm glad we kept this simple," Maggie said as she inspected the tomatoes. "Sandwiches and beer under a tree with yellow and red leaves falling all around sounds wonderful."

"Is fall your favorite season?" Jared asked, grabbing a hearty loaf of pumpernickel and sticking it in their basket.

"Most definitely. What's yours?"

"Spring. All the new buds and green leaves gives me a lift after a long hard winter."

"But I like winter, too," Maggie put in. "Fires, cozy quilts, Christmas."

"Let's not forget summer," Jared said with laugh. "It has its advantages, too. Sunshine, swimming, tennis, baseball, golf."

"With that tan, I suspected you were into sports," she said, grabbing a package of Brie cheese.

"See, we already know more about each other," Jared said.

"And so far, none of it is shocking," Maggie pointed out. "Despite the fact that I'm an actor." She drew out the word and made it sound very dramatic.

Jared smiled and wondered how good an actor she was, and his thoughts were drawn back, against his will, to her relationship with Greg Moran. Did she enjoy their physical intimacies on the set as much as she appeared to, or was it just acting? If it was just acting, why had she drawn that heart around their picture? Maybe in the course of the evening, he'd find out. But it was too soon to get that nosy. Their truce was still very fragile.

On the way to the park, Jared carried the sack of groceries in one arm and held Maggie's hand with the other. She didn't object, only looked up at him rather shyly. He had a hard time reconciling this dressed-down, almost demure woman in a Mets cap with the vampish Monica.

They found a table under a huge maple tree, brushed off the dry leaves that covered it, and laid out their impromptu feast. The sun slanted low in the sky and the pink rays streamed through the branches, giving Maggie's face a rosy glow. He resisted the urge to reach across the table and whisk off her cap so he could see her hair shining in the softly filtered sunshine.

"So, Maggie, tell me about your family. Where you grew up, et cetera."

"That's getting right down to the nitty-gritty," Maggie teased. "You either really do have some interest in getting to know me, or else you're playing social worker and finding all this out for Sarah's sake."

"I don't do everything for Sarah's sake," Jared assured her, smiling crookedly. "Some things I do just for me."

That seemed to satisfy her and she told him about her family. Her mother had been a widow for several years. She had four younger sisters, two of whom were married. She didn't say so, but something came up in the conversation that made him suspect she'd helped all her sisters with college expenses. When he asked her if she had, she blushed and shook her head, indicating that she didn't want to talk about it. That, of course, confirmed his suspicions. Immediately his opinion of her grew.

"You're from Long Island?"

"Do you even have to ask?" she said with an endearing little snort. "Can't you hear it in my mom's accent?"

"I'm from Long Island, too."

"Really?" She seemed delighted.

"My dad has an accent, but not my—"

Jared cut himself off. He'd almost alluded to Claire. He never talked about her. No one even knew she was his mother and he wasn't about to start advertising that fact to the world, starting with Maggie. He wasn't ashamed of her. He just didn't want any of that celebrity-circus stuff creeping into his life. Besides, although they'd never discussed it, he suspected that Claire would rather the world didn't know she had a thirty-three-year-old son, either.

"Not your who?" Maggie prompted.

"I meant to say, not *me*," he lied. "Want some Brie?"

"What about your mother? Does she have an accent?" she persisted, apparently not ready to let the subject die.

"No." He couldn't help a wry smile. "She hasn't spent much time on Long Island over the past few years." At her look of confusion, he clarified. "My parents divorced when I was one. I basically grew up without a mother."

She looked stricken. "I'm sorry."

"Don't be," he assured her. "My dad and I did fine."

She munched on her sandwich for a minute, then hesitantly asked, "But you still see her, don't you? Your mother, I mean. I thought she was the one who set you up with Candy?"

"Yeah, she was the one," he answered ruefully. "Want another beer?"

Maggie suspected that there was more to the story than Jared was letting on, but she didn't want to pry. She tactfully changed the subject to his medical career and heard about his schooling and internship in Boston, a city he liked almost as well as New York.

He turned the conversation to her work and, although she suspected he was still cynical about the whole entertainment business, he listened attentively and asked lots of questions. She told him about the good, and, with no sugar-coating, the bad aspects of the business.

As the sun set and the temperature dropped, they talked like old friends. Or new lovers....

When she shivered, he said, "I guess we'd better head back. It's a good sign, though, that Chuck hasn't called."

"I haven't even thought about Sarah," Maggie confessed with a guilty expression. "I've really enjoyed being out here with you."

Jared said, "Me, too, Maggie." Then, after a hesitation, he said, "Since we're being so open with each other, can I ask you something?"

"You can *ask*," she said with a cheeky grin.

But, after what appeared to be a bit of a mental struggle, he shook his head sheepishly and said, "No, never mind. Like I said, maybe we'd better head back.''

Maggie didn't press it. If he was hesitant to ask something, she might be just as hesitant to answer. They were off to a nice start on this new friendship of theirs, and it had been such a pleasant afternoon so far, she didn't want anything to rock the boat.

"You're right," she said with a bright smile. "It's probably time to pack up." She immediately stood up and began putting the remnants of their meal back into the grocery bag. Jared stood up, too, and was helping her, when suddenly he grabbed her shoulders and turned her to face him.

She stared up at him, her eyes wide and questioning. Then, without saying a word, he cupped her face and bent to press his lips to hers.

# Chapter Eleven

Jared had been unable to fight the urge to kiss Maggie one minute longer. And now that he was doing it, he wondered why he'd waited so long. His questions about Greg, his reservations about her career, the uncertainty of it all.... None of that was important. His arms wrapped around her and he pulled her close. All that mattered was how "right" it felt at that moment.

The brim of her cap was in the way, so he grabbed hold of it and pulled the cap off. Her long hair fell in a chestnut cascade down her back and he sank his fingers deeply into it, relishing its warm, silky feel.

He pulled her closer, and when she moaned with delight he seized the opportunity to deepen the kiss with experimental strokes of his tongue inside the warm, sleek contours of her mouth.

He was thrilled when she responded with kisses just as ardent. Her arms slipped around his waist and her hands moved up his back. She trembled.

He could feel her heart pounding and her quick, uneven breathing. His own heart seemed ready to beat out of his chest, his breathing as ragged and shaky as hers. His body ached with desire.

"Maggie," he breathed against her flushed cheek. "Maggie...."

"Isn't that Monica Blake? Hey, Monica, where's the baby? And where's the *Count?*"

Startled, Maggie and Jared practically jumped apart. Jared turned abruptly around to see who their unwelcome audience was. He'd been so caught up in their embrace, he'd forgotten they were in a very public park. And without her disguising sunglasses and Mets cap—even dressed down in a casual sweater and jeans, and with only a little daylight left to see by—there was apparently no mistaking Maggie Stern, soap star.

A white-haired couple, bundled in knit hats, colorful scarves, and bright red bulky jackets, and holding on to the leashes of two small terriers, was eyeing them suspiciously. "That's not the Count," the woman announced accusingly. "Look, Harold." She elbowed the elderly man standing next to her. "Monica's cheatin' on the Count."

"What? *Again?*" the man exclaimed, squinting in their direction. "If I were the Count, I'd ditch 'er. If she got a bun in the oven now, there'd be no telling who the father was."

The woman looked horrified. "You're right. The heir of Carsovia could turn out to be a bas—" She covered her mouth before the scandalous word slipped out in its entirety, making it sound as though she were predicting that the heir would slip out of its mother's womb in the form of a fish.

Maggie stifled a giggle, flitted an apologetic glance toward Jared, and stepped toward the outraged couple with her right hand extended and a big smile spread over her face.

"You're mixing me up with my character," Maggie

said cheerfully. "How do you do? I'm Maggie Stern, the actor who plays that devilish Monica Blake on television. Isn't she a piece of work?" Maggie resolutely stood before them, still smiling and still offering her hand to shake.

The couple stared suspiciously at Maggie for a minute, then exchanged a wary look between themselves before the woman finally shrugged and shook hands. The man, not quite as ready to be reasoned with and mollified, folded his arms over his chest. The movement tugged on the dog's leash he was holding, and the terrier began to yap excitedly. This got the other dog going, and now both of them were barking.

"So, you're Maggie Stern, eh?" the woman said, speaking loudly so she could be heard above the din.

"Yes," Maggie shouted back. "And you and your husband must be fans of the show."

"Oh yes!" the woman exclaimed. "We love 'The Rich and the Reckless.' We watch it every day while we're eating lunch. We haven't missed an episode in five years!"

"That's very nice to hear," Maggie told them. "And it sounds like you're quite caught up in the current story line." She paused, smiled again, then tactfully continued. "You do realize that I'm not actually married to the Count in real life? Monica Blake is a fictional character and Pleasant View is a fictional town."

The woman shot an embarrassed glance at her husband and then looked back sheepishly at Maggie. "Yes, of course. Sometimes we forget. But I thought I saw on one of those tabloid sheets that someone left you a baby? Is that true? Or is that just more 'fiction?'"

"It's true," Maggie admitted ruefully. "A fan got me mixed up with Monica and thought I was desperate for a baby."

"You mean you're *not* infertile?" the man inquired loudly, causing another passing couple to look over with curiosity and amusement. Jared held his breath, fearful that the other couple would join them. When they didn't, he breathed a sigh of relief.

Maggie's laugh had an embarrassed edge to it. "Am *I* infertile? Not that I know of. So far, I haven't attempted to find out."

The man turned and squinted at Jared again, who had stayed behind at the picnic table. He seemed to be taking his measure and was probably comparing him to the swaggering, bigger-than-life character of Alexander Tolstoy. Jared uncomfortably withstood this scrutiny and said nothing. He wasn't too eager to get involved in this strange encounter with a couple of Maggie's more zealous fans, and, besides, she was handling the situation admirably on her own.

Presently the man shifted his gaze back to Maggie and extended his hand, saying, "Sorry. Didn't mean to be rude. I just don't like to see couples cheatin' on each other." He smiled self-consciously. "'Cept on TV. Can we have your autograph, Miss Blake? I mean Miss Stern."

Maggie smiled warmly and shook the man's hand. "It would be my pleasure." The dogs, seeming to sense that the tension had diminished, stopped barking. Then the woman scrounged around in her fanny pack and eventually pulled out a pen and a scrap of paper for Maggie to sign.

Jared watched with wonder and respect as Maggie chatted and charmed, finally sending the couple on their way with happy faces. "Goodbye, Ms. Stern," they called. "And, you too, Mr. Stern," the woman added, waving enthusiastically.

Jared winced. *Mr. Stern?*

"I'm sorry about that," Maggie said with a look of pained consternation on her face as she joined Jared at the picnic table again. "I guess they just assumed—"

"It's okay," Jared said dismissively, making light of it. "I shouldn't be surprised. If they can get you confused with your soap character, how can I expect them to keep your real personal life straight?"

"Most of my fans aren't so confused," Maggie assured him. "Most of them are like the nurses at the hospital last night. They know the difference between me and Monica."

"But even *they* acted pretty juvenile," Jared couldn't help pointing out. "I'm just glad there weren't any critical patients that needed attention while most of the nurses congregated in your room. And I'm glad we only got waylaid by that old couple and not a crowd of demented fans. Or, worse still, photographers."

Maggie sighed. Things had been going so nicely. The kisses had been so *nice*. And, even though she thought she handled the situation with the elderly couple rather well, Jared was back to harping on the negative aspects of her fame. He seemed like such a fair-minded man in every other respect, she just wished she knew why he had so little tolerance for the silliness and inconveniences that were an unfortunate accompaniment to success in her chosen profession. There had to be something he wasn't telling her....

A strained silence fell between them as they packed

up the last of the picnic. It was quickly getting dark and, in this sparsely populated corner of the park they'd chosen for privacy, there wasn't a nearby lamp to light things up. In a way, Maggie was grateful for the darkness. Jared couldn't see how crushed she felt. How disappointed.

She put her cap back on and shoved her hair underneath it, he picked up the bag of food, then they walked, side by side, toward the street where the car was parked. She'd hoped he'd hold her hand like he had before, but he didn't. He seemed totally immersed in his own thoughts.

Suddenly the tense quiet was interrupted by the sound of the cellular phone ringing. "Oh, dear," Maggie said worriedly. "I'll bet that's Chuck. We probably should have called to check on Sarah."

Jared stopped in his tracks and snatched the slender phone from his back pocket and flipped it open. His eyes met hers and they exchanged a mutual look of concern before he answered, "Hello?"

As Jared listened to the caller, Maggie watched as his eyebrows drew together and his mouth thinned to a grim line. Maggie's throat went dry. Surely it was only Chuck, calling just to say that Sarah was being fussy. Surely nothing bad had happened.

"Thanks for calling, Chuck," Jared said at last. "I'll go right over." He flipped the phone closed and slipped it back inside his pocket.

"Go right over where?" Maggie inquired in some confusion. "Wasn't he calling about Sarah?"

"No," Jared said, already walking swiftly toward the car again as Maggie struggled to keep up. "Sarah's fine."

"Then what...who—?"

Jared turned and looked down at her, his glasses glinting in the light from the lamp they were passing under, his eyes narrowed, his expression worried and a little distracted. "It's my mother."

"Your mother?" Maggie was surprised. "Is something wrong?"

"Chuck said she called and needed me to come over immediately. Some sort of emergency."

Maggie frowned. "Why'd she call my place?"

"When she couldn't get hold of me at my apartment, she called yours...probably because she's talked to Candy since Saturday night."

Maggie was still stumped. "But I have an unlisted number."

"My mother is very resourceful," Jared said dryly. They'd reached the car by now and he unlocked the passenger side door and helped her in with a courteous hand on her elbow. But even that fleeting touch sent a thrill up Maggie's spine.

When Jared got in the car, he turned to her and said, "I hope you don't mind, but I'm taking you with me to my mother's apartment. She didn't tell Chuck what the emergency was, and maybe it's nothing too serious, but I'd rather not take the time to drop you off first."

"Of course I don't mind," she assured him. The fact was, she was quite curious to see Jared's mother. Maybe meeting her would shed some light on Jared's personality. But one question kept eating at Maggie, a question that she'd like answered before actually coming face-to-face with his mom.

"Jared?"

"Hmm?" He had pulled away from the curb and was headed south.

"I have a question that I'm not sure you're going to want to answer, and maybe it's none of my business, but—"

"Just spill it, Maggie," he advised her, keeping his eyes on the road.

"Well, I was wondering why your parents divorced," she blurted.

Jared was silent for so long, Maggie was convinced she'd been too nosy. But then, suddenly, he said, "It was her decision. She realized that she couldn't pursue her career and have a child, too."

"Why? What was her career?"

He turned and looked at her for a long moment, then said wryly, "You'll know the minute you meet her."

Mystified, Maggie leaned back in the seat. *She'd know the minute she met her?* Wild images presented themselves to Maggie's imagination. Was Jared's mother a circus performer...the bearded lady, perhaps? That certainly would be immediately obvious. Or maybe she was a bodybuilder with huge, unfeminine muscles bulging under her sweater? That would be hard to miss, too. Or maybe her career required a uniform that she might be wearing. Was she a nurse? An airplane pilot? A waitress? Or maybe....

MAGGIE'S IMAGINATION had run wild on the short drive to Jared's mother's apartment. But not even a vivid imagination had prepared her for the elite address of the building they pulled in front of. The doorman knew Jared and immediately arranged for a valet to drive his car into the underground parking while he and Maggie caught the elevator. Jared wasn't even required to announce himself. He obviously had the run of the place.

They got off on the tenth floor and hurried down a plushly carpeted hallway to apartment 1050. He pulled out his keychain, found the right key, then inserted it into the lock and opened the door. Maggie followed him inside and stood gaping at the luxurious and ornately decorated apartment. There were Persian rugs, Chinese vases, an elegant chandelier, fat throw pillows covered in silk, and vases and vases of fresh flowers filling the air with their heady scent.

"Claire?"

Although softly lighted by lamps set discreetly about, the living room appeared to be unoccupied.

"Claire?" Jared repeated, and Maggie wondered if Claire was his mother's maid or something. Why didn't he just call out "Mom" like she did when she walked unceremoniously into her mother's house on Long Island? But maybe things were done a little differently in this posh New York palace.

"Wait here," Jared ordered, a note of real concern in his voice. "I'm going to check her bedroom." But no sooner had he headed toward the doorway leading to the hall than his mother suddenly floated into the room.

Maggie found herself gaping again. This woman couldn't possibly be Jared's mother...could she? This woman was the famous stage actress, Claire DeSpain! But he *had* called out Claire....

"Mother," Jared said, advancing. "What's wrong? Why did you call me? Are you sick?"

Dressed in a multicolored silk caftan, with jewels dripping off her ears and fingers and glittering on golden chains around her neck and wrists, Claire DeSpain looked *extremely* well, especially for a woman who had to be in her early fifties, at least. She was a glorious bottle-blond, her face still wrinkle-free, her makeup impeccable...and dramatic...and her teeth, when she smiled, as white as polished pearls.

"Dahling," Claire uttered in that unmistakable throaty voice of hers. "So glad you came. Aren't you going to kiss me?" She offered her cheek and Jared stooped to give her a perfunctory kiss. He didn't have to stoop too low, however, since Claire was majestically tall...at least five foot ten, by Maggie's estimation. They'd met once at a benefit dinner and Maggie remembered her towering over her.

"I see you've brought Maggie Stern with you," Claire said with a warm smile for Maggie. "Delightful. I was hoping you would."

"Claire, what's the emergency?" Jared said, clearly exasperated.

"I'll explain in a moment, Jared. But where are my manners? Maggie, won't you sit down? You don't mind if I call you Maggie, do you? I recall that we've met before and formalities are such a bore, aren't they?" She motioned toward the couch.

Maggie sat down, thrilled that Claire DeSpain had remembered their prior meeting, although it had been early in Maggie's career and very brief. "Thank you, Ms. DeSpain."

"Call me Claire," she admonished her, sitting down next to her on the couch. "My son does," she added with a sly look toward Jared.

Jared did not reply. He simply stood where he was, crossed his arms and looked like a thundercloud. Maggie thought she understood why he was so unhappy. It appeared very much as though he'd been duped. Claire DeSpain, relaxing on the couch, did not look as though she were in a state of emergency.

"I've been following your career, Maggie," Claire continued, undaunted by Jared's stormy demeanor. "I was so thrilled for you when you won your first Emmy, then your second! I always knew you'd do well."

"Thank you," Maggie replied, really flattered. "I've always been a fan of yours, Claire."

"Are you two going to talk shop all night?" Jared grumbled.

"Oh, for heaven's sake, Jared, don't be such a fuss-budget." She gave an airy wave of her hand. "Be a dear, make yourself useful and pour us a glass of sherry, won't you? And perhaps a double bourbon for you. You seem rather tense. There's ice in the kitchen."

"Where's Isobel?" Jared inquired, looking about.

"I gave her the night off," Claire replied, then added, "oh, and when you get the drinks, Jared, dahling, try and find those German cookies I like so well. They're in the pantry...*somewhere*."

As Jared stalked off, Maggie couldn't help but chuckle. "I had no idea you were Jared's mother," she confessed. "But then I didn't even meet Jared till last Friday."

"Jared doesn't tell anyone I'm his mother," Claire revealed, still smiling, but with a wistful note in her voice. "As far as the world knows, I've never had any children. He's afraid that if it were suddenly to become known that he's my son, photographers would be constantly ambushing him for pictures to sell to the tabloids. I can't blame him for that. I can just see the headlines—Claire DeSpain's Secret Love Child Surfaces."

"But he's not your 'love child,'" Maggie objected. "You were married when you had Jared."

"Yes, but the tabloids don't let the facts get in the way of a good story. You should know that, dahling."

"Yes." She sighed dismally. "And now, because of me, he runs the risk of being in the tabloids, anyway. It's ironic, isn't it?"

"Ironic, but *meant to be!*" Claire said dramatically.

Maggie blinked with surprise. "What do you mean, 'meant to be?'"

"It's time Jared got over being so squeamish about a little media attention. You and I both know it can be embarrassing and tedious at times, but we manage just fine."

"But we put up with it because we love what we do."

"And Jared must learn to put up with it because he loves me," Claire said emphatically. "I want the world to know I have such a brilliant, handsome son." Then she looked coy and added, "And he must learn to put up with it because—judging by what Candy's told me and from what my psychic predicts—he's on his way to being in love with you, Maggie, dahling."

Maggie was stunned. "That's...that's impossible. He...he hates the fact that I'm a celebrity."

"He says so, I know. But that won't stop him from loving you. I think he's secretly very proud of me and very excited by you. He talks of being traditional and wanting a traditional wife, but there are loads of those types of females around and he hasn't married one yet, has he?"

"But what about...you know...what happened."

"You mean the divorce? The fact is, I would have stayed in the marriage had Victor been more tolerant.

I wanted a career on the stage and my husband and child, but Victor forbade me to work.''

"Forbade you?'' Maggie said indignantly.

"Remember, dahling, all this happened over thirty years ago. Victor's attitude was the prevailing one at the time. In the end, I had to choose between raising Jared on my own and pursuing a career, or leaving him with his father to be raised. I figured he'd have a more normal childhood with his father. As well, Victor thought he'd do better if I stayed completely out of the picture, and I agreed. But I regret that decision now. I should have been a part of my son's life. What could it have hurt? I'm a little eccentric...but *so?* I mean, after all, what *is* a normal childhood, anyway? When there's love and education and a set of moral rules to live by, what more does a child need?''

Maggie smiled. "You sound just like Sarah's social worker, Ms. Johnson.''

"She must be a very sensible woman,'' Claire concluded with satisfaction.

"Of course, Jared doesn't agree with her. But now I understand why he's been so dead set against me taking care of Sarah. He figures you made the *right* decision all those years ago.''

Claire nodded understandingly and scooted closer, snatching a glance toward the door. "I've put together pieces of the story from talking to Candy and reading the tabloids, but now, quickly, before Jared gets back from hunting for those nonexistent cookies, tell me exactly how you and he managed to get thrown together with this adorable baby.''

Maggie hurriedly gave her the basic, incredible facts. As she listened, Claire's smile broadened. "Better and better,'' she murmured delightedly. "I'm convinced now that you and Jared are meant to be. Even Sarah thinks so! You're just what he needs, Maggie, dahling. Now, leave the rest to me. I have a scheme. It's called *reverse psychology*."

Maggie was a little startled by Claire's assumption that she would be willing to participate in a "scheme," presumably to make sure Jared was equally convinced that she was "just what he needed." She also found it hard to believe that Jared could be falling in love with her so quickly, as Claire seemed to think. And she didn't put much store in predictions from psychics, either!

Maggie was about to make a feeble protest and request details of this so-called reverse psychology scheme, when Jared came back into the room with their drinks on a tray, looking more irritated than ever.

"I couldn't find the cookies," he announced in a beleaguered tone, setting the tray on the coffee table in front of them.

"Well, perhaps Isobel didn't buy any after all," Claire said with a shrug and a brilliant smile. "So sorry, dahling, to make you search for nothing."

Jared picked up his drink—it looked as though he'd taken his mother's advice and had mixed something potent—and sat down in a wing chair opposite the couch. Claire handed Maggie a dainty glass of sherry and then picked up the other for herself. They all sipped for a minute, then Jared set down his half-empty glass and leaned forward in the chair, resting his elbows on his knees.

"All right, Claire," he said. "I want to hear what your emergency is. It had better be good, because—"

"You were worried? I'm sorry, dahling. But, then

again, if you hadn't been worried, I'd be crushed. After all, I *am* your mother.''

"After you've explained the emergency, you can explain Candy, too," he added grimly. "No getting off easy tonight, Claire, just because you've got company."

"I wouldn't dream of it," Claire assured him, also setting down her drink. "It's actually because of Candy that I called you. Naturally she told me everything that happened Saturday night. She seems to think you disapprove of Maggie taking care of that baby that was left on her doorstep. I couldn't wait to tell you that I firmly—"

"I know," Jared said, wearily waving a hand. "You firmly disagree with me and think I've been giving Maggie too hard a time. Save it, Claire. There's no point in arguing—"

"Oh, no, dahling," she said, her elegantly shaped brows lifted in surprise. "That's not what I was going to say at all. I was desperate to get you over here to tell you I support you *one hundred percent!*"

Jared looked dumbfounded. "You do?"

"But of course!" She patted Maggie's knee. "Maggie's a darling girl, of course, but, with her career and all, hardly likely to be a suitable mother to any child!"

Jared flitted an alarmed glance toward Maggie, and Maggie, playing along, dropped her gaze to the floor and looked chastised. "Well, I wouldn't go so far as to say—"

"I hear the child cries constantly when she's alone with Maggie, and that can only mean she hasn't got what it takes to be a mother. No instincts at all...at least not in *this* life."

"Sarah doesn't cry *all* the time—"

"And what about all Maggie's eccentric friends? You know what show-business people are like! You've frequently thought my friends were odd. And, of course, Sarah must be sheltered from all that. An average, quiet, unalarming childhood is exactly what she needs. She might grow up a little *dull*, but isn't that better than taking the chance of her being *odd?*"

Jared shifted uncomfortably in his chair. "Well, I don't necessarily think she should be sheltered from every—"

"And think of all that publicity folderol she'd have to learn to cope with growing up as the child of a celebrity. Why expose her to that? After all, she'll learn the skills of poise and patience one must have in those circumstances some other way...I suppose."

Maggie snatched a glance at Jared, who looked momentarily arrested, as if his mother had made a point he hadn't considered before. But it was true, you did have to learn poise and patience to deal effectively with fans and the paparazzi.

"Besides," Claire concluded with a decided nod, "everyone knows that a single woman can't possibly have a demanding career and raise a child. What was true thirty years ago, is still true today!"

Claire took a breath and a sip of sherry, then sat back against the sofa cushions to watch Jared's reaction. By now, he was getting the picture. His intelligent blue eyes were alight with sudden understanding and insight. His mother, the consummate actor, had just finished a stunning performance.

"Good show, Mother," Jared drawled. "You're right. What was true thirty years ago, is still true today. I'm not stupid, you know."

She smiled her brilliant, beguiling smile. "That's what I'm counting on, dahling."

*So am I, Claire,* Maggie thought with a surge of hope. *So am I.*

# Chapter Twelve

When Maggie and Jared returned to her apartment, she purposely hesitated outside the door, fumbling with her keys. Fearing it might be her last chance to bring up a certain subject before she permanently lost her nerve, she turned around and gazed up into Jared's face. The incredible blue of his eyes, as he looked back at her, nearly knocked her over. Surreptitiously, she leaned against the doorframe for support. Heaven forbid that he should ever realize how much he affected her.

"You haven't uttered a word since we left your mother's," she said.

"I was thinking."

"About how angry you are with me?"

He smiled crookedly and shrugged. "Because you colluded with my mother to show me what a jerk I've been?"

"Well…yes."

He laughed and shook his head. "You were supposed to say, 'Oh, Jared, you haven't been a jerk.'"

She smiled ruefully. "But you *have* been a jerk. Not every day in every way, of course. You've been a godsend for Sarah, but you've definitely been hard on *me.* Although I realize now where you've been coming from.''

Jared sobered. ''You mean because of Claire? No, don't cut me any slack because of that, Maggie. I take full responsibility for my behavior over the past few days.'' He flashed a chagrined smile. ''Hopefully I've seen the error of my ways. But neither of us can be completely sure of that till I've been tested.''

She raised a dubious eyebrow. ''Tested? What kind of test are you talking about?''

''I don't know, but I'm sure we'll both recognize it when it happens.'' He gently grasped her shoulders, the pressure of his warm fingers so comforting and so thrilling at the same time. ''Meanwhile, you'll just have to accept my good intentions on faith. Can you do that, Maggie? Can we be friends and work together to try to do what's best for Sarah?''

As he smiled down at her, Maggie went all quivery inside, her legs growing as weak as water. She was more than willing to be friends with Jared. In fact, she was *more* than willing to be *more* than friends. She swallowed past a tightness in her throat and was about to stutter something that would probably come out all wrong, when the door opened and Chuck stuck his head out. ''I thought I heard voices. Did you forget your key?''

''We were just talking,'' Maggie said, turning regretfully away from Jared to smile at Chuck. ''Sorry to keep you waiting. You must be anxious to get home.''

''I do have some studying to do, but I've still got plenty of time.''

Maggie followed him into the apartment and down

the hall to the living room, with Jared just behind. "Is Sarah asleep?"

"Yes. She dozed off about a half hour ago. She's probably down for the count. She usually— I mean, most babies sleep through the night by the time they're five months old." He turned to Jared for confirmation. "Don't they?"

"Every baby's different," Jared replied, his hands stuffed in his pockets as he looked keenly at Chuck. "But, yes, by five months old, most babies don't need a feeding during the night. Sometimes, of course, they wake up for other reasons."

"She didn't sleep through the night Saturday," Maggie reminded them. "But that was probably because it was the first night away from her aunt…or whoever. I think she feels more secure now."

"I'm sure she does," Chuck said with a decided nod. "You'll be a great mom, Ms. Stern."

Maggie gave a disclaiming shake of her head and smiled modestly. "So you didn't have any problems with her?"

"Nope."

"You seem to have a natural rapport with kids, Chuck," Jared remarked. "Either that or you learned *a lot* while helping your girlfriend baby-sit in high school."

Chuck shrugged. "I don't know. I guess Sarah and I just get along, that's all."

"I wish she'd taken as quickly to me," Maggie complained good-naturedly. "I guess she just goes for tall, blond men."

"Looks that way," Chuck agreed, shrugging into his jacket. "When you need a baby-sitter again, give me a call, Ms. Stern."

"Chuck, you've got your job and your classes, and I'm sure you try to have a social life, too. I wouldn't dream of—"

"I really don't mind, Ms. Stern. In fact, I enjoy baby-sitting Sarah. Call me anytime. Seriously."

Maggie couldn't argue against such sincere persistence, but she also couldn't figure out why Chuck was so eager to be Sarah's baby-sitter. She didn't want to believe it was because he had a crush on her. She didn't want to take advantage of him for any reason, but especially not that one. Because of these concerns, she was relieved when he finally left. But Jared's knowing expression when she returned to the living room made her squirm.

"He really likes Sarah," Maggie suggested weakly.

"You and I both know there's more to it than that."

Maggie tried to shrug it off. "No, I *don't* know—"

"Yes, you do," Jared insisted. "He's not doing this just because he likes kids and he wants to do you a good deed." Jared's brow knitted and he rubbed his jaw. "And I don't think it's because he has a crush on you, either."

Maggie was surprised. "Really? I'd love to believe that! So, what's your theory?"

"I don't know, it's just a feeling I've got. I could be dead wrong."

"Tell me!"

Jared shook his head and smiled. "No. Not till I've thought this through a little more. Anyway, it's nothing to worry about. And, since Sarah's out for the count...as Chuck so aptly put it...I guess I'll go back to my puny apartment next door. You know, the one without the study, the extra closets, the whirlpool tub, and the view?"

"You know I couldn't help that!" Maggie exclaimed, punching his arm.

Instead of arguing, Jared surprised her by grabbing her wrists and drawing her close, then wrapping his arms around her waist. He smelled wonderfully of brisk autumn air, bourbon, and aftershave. "Maybe you could make it up to me?" he whispered, sporting a sly smile.

"Why, what are you suggesting, Dr. Austin?" she managed to quip, but she was so nervous and excited her knees were shaking.

"A good-night kiss," he answered her. "That's all."

"That's all? Well, I guess I could—"

But he was already claiming his consolation prize. And what had begun as a light, flirtatious advance almost immediately became much more serious.

Jared had only intended to kiss her. To kiss her once, quite thoroughly, then say good night. But the feel of her in his arms, the scent of her, the taste of her, was making him dizzy with desire. Her arms laced behind his neck, and she pulled him closer.

Responding to her evident eagerness, he deepened the kiss, probing her mouth with his tongue. He had never felt such an overpowering urge to make love to someone, to claim her with kiss after kiss after kiss.... His arms tightened around her slender body, crushing her small, firm breasts against his chest.

"Maggie," he murmured, trailing kisses along her neck, from her ear to the pulse point just above the neckline of her sweater. "Maggie...."

Then his hands were at her waist and inside her sweater, inching up her warm, smooth skin to the sheer, lacy fabric of her bra. He cupped her breasts, gently teasing the taut buds of her nipples between thumb and forefinger. She gasped and arched into his palms.

*This is crazy,* Jared told himself. *And much too soon.* They'd squabbled all weekend and now he was holding her, kissing her, as if he never wanted to stop. Well, he *didn't* want to stop. But it had only been a few hours since he'd actually admitted to himself that she was different, special. That he didn't need to consider her off-limits just because she was an actor. Or that she wouldn't make a wonderful friend, a great wife, even a fabulous mother.

His brain was spinning with ideas. Sexy ideas. Scary ideas that had to do with long-term commitments. Like raising Sarah. Like making more babies. Like buying a house in the suburbs big enough to put both of their apartments into it and filling it up with grandchildren for Claire DeSpain and Lorena Morgenstern. Clearly he'd taken leave of his senses. But if this was insanity, bring on the padded cell....

Maggie was convinced she was losing her mind. With all her relationships with men, on both physical and emotional levels, she was always the proverbial turtle. Slow-going and cautious, keeping close to home, and guarding her heart inside a hard shell.

With Jared, she couldn't go fast enough. After just four days, it was terrifying to realize she was falling in love with him. When she was a kid, she used to ride her bike down a steep grade called Amelia Hill. Halfway down she'd let go of the handlebars and slice through the air like a sleek sailboat on a brisk sea. The sense of joy and freedom were overwhelming, exhilarating...and so was the fear. She felt the same way in Jared's arms.

She was nuts. That was all there was to it. It was crazy to expect Jared to be having similar feelings for her, which would be the only thing that would make this state of blissful misery bearable.

He'd asked her to take his good intentions on faith, but he was talking about friendship and about their joint concern and affection for Sarah. She knew she could trust him to take good care of Sarah, but could she trust him to take care of her heart if she gave it to him?

She didn't dare give it to him. But if she gave him her body, her heart would be dragged into the fray, too. She knew herself too well. She didn't have casual love affairs.

Despite these reservations, she couldn't stop touching him, or from wanting him to touch her. Her hands were inside his sweater now, under his T-shirt, creeping up till her fingers splayed over the hard planes of his chest. Soft, springy hair teased her palms. She'd seen his chest before. Now she wanted to see it and touch it at the same time, to explore and caress every inch of his beautiful, tanned body.

"Maggie," Jared groaned, walking her backward toward the couch. "Sarah will sleep for hours. Let me make love to you."

Second thoughts. Suddenly those darned second thoughts hit her like flying debris from a twister. She wanted to make love with Jared more than she wanted her next breath, but it was too soon, too fast, too risky. She was the turtle again. She was playing it smart. *Slow and steady wins the race,* she told herself as she gently pushed Jared away.

Naturally Jared looked confused and...endearingly

dazed. Her heart cartwheeled at the idea that she'd put that loopy expression on his face.

"Please don't think I'm a tease," she begged him, wiping the stain of her lipstick off his chin with her thumb. "But I'm not ready for this, Jared."

To his credit, Jared did not argue. He pulled himself together with admirable grace, but when he finally spoke, his voice was still husky with passion. "Okay," he said. He cleared his throat, embarrassed by the telltale hoarseness. "I understand. You're right. We're moving too fast."

"We haven't even actually been out on a date," she said with a helpless chuckle, her own voice a notch lower than normal. "I'm not sure we can count tonight."

"You mean you want to be properly courted, ma'am?" he teased. Then, perfectly serious, "You really don't live in the fast lane, do you? Despite the vamp you play on 'The Rich and the Reckless,' you're pretty much just an old-fashioned girl, aren't you?"

"How many times have I told you I'm not Monica?" she retorted, poking his chest with her finger. "Maybe now you'll believe me."

He caught and squeezed her shoulders. "I've always believed you, Maggie. Well…maybe not at first. But when I was holding you and kissing you, whose name did I whisper?"

She smiled tremulously. "It wasn't Monica."

"Point made," he said, releasing his grip on her shoulders, sliding his hands slowly down her arms, then, reluctantly, letting go. He sighed and smiled. "Now about courtin'…. When can we get started?"

"How's tomorrow night for you? Can you come to dinner? I'd love to cook for you. Besides, it would be difficult to go out somewhere. Sarah can be our chaperone.''

"She's been our chaperone all along, hasn't she?"

"Only tonight she's sleeping on the job."

He grinned. "I don't mind."

"I know you don't," she admitted with a coy look over her shoulder as she led him to the door. "And, as you may have noticed, neither did I. That's why we need a chaperone. Till tomorrow, Jared? Say…six-thirty?" She opened the door and stood to the side, her lips curved in a tantalizing smile. "Don't forget to bring your appetite."

He waggled his brows. "No chance of that."

"Your appetite for food," she clarified, laughing.

MERCIFULLY, SARAH did sleep through the night, allowing Maggie to catch up on her rest. She woke up the next morning in an elated mood, looking forward to dinner with Jared that evening. Now that she understood him better, and now that he'd seemingly made peace with the fact that she was an actor…just like his mother…she felt there were endless possibilities to what might happen between them. But she still believed they needed to take things slow.

Maggie also figured that if Sarah fussed and cried all day, at least she'd know there was fun in store for later when Jared showed up. He'd make Sarah happy, too. Then they'd all three be happy.

But Sarah woke up in a mood as blissful as Maggie's, which was certainly a promising start to all the hours they'd spend alone together till dinnertime. While Maggie changed her diaper and fed her a breakfast bottle, Sarah cooed and kicked her tiny fists and feet with the zeal of an aerobics instructor. In fact, she was so much fun, Maggie spent the entire morning playing with her.

By noon, Sarah peacefully went down for a nap and Maggie undressed for a shower. She was just about to step into the stall when someone rang her doorbell. She thought about ignoring whoever it was, but then they started pounding on the door. She threw on a floor-length terry robe, cinched it at the waist and went to see who was there. Since they hadn't called up on the intercom, she figured it was either Mrs. Fernwalter or Billie or maybe the police with news about Sarah.

However, when she peeked through the peephole, it was Greg Moran's distorted face grinning back at her. "What's he doing here?" she grumbled. "And how'd he get past the doorman without buzzing up?"

She swung open the door, a scowl on her face. "Greg, how'd you—"

"Don't get mad, Maggie," said Billie, peering around Greg's broad shoulder with her arms wrapped around his waist, clinging like a vine. "He's with me."

"Oh, hi, Billie," Maggie said, relaxing a bit. "What are you two up to? If you've come by to visit, this really isn't a good time. Sarah's asleep and I was just about to step into the shower."

"We've been jogging in the park," Greg announced, sliding Billie a sexy smile. "Worked up quite a sweat."

Maggie observed them and raised a brow. "I can see that." They were both wearing tight-fitting running shorts and sweatshirts with the sleeves cut off at the shoulders. Moisture glistened on their arms and trim, muscular legs. Their hair was wind-tousled and their faces glowed with warmth from their exercise.

They made quite an attractive pair...and apparently couldn't keep their hands off each other. Considering Greg's reputation, Maggie just hoped Billie wouldn't someday blame her for introducing them to each other.

"We're dying of thirst," Billie added. "Have you got some water?"

"Well, sure," Maggie said, confused. "But don't you? You're...er...so close to home." She glanced at Billie's apartment door, not ten feet away. *And maybe you'd like some privacy,* she added to herself.

"I locked myself out," Billie cheerfully chirped. "Can you believe that? And Mrs. Fernwalter's not home, so we can't get her to open the door with her spare key."

"What about Dennis? Can't he let you in?"

Billie giggled and, standing on tiptoe, nuzzled Greg's neck. "I never thought of Dennis. Can we buzz him on your intercom? Meanwhile we could get something to drink out of your fridge before we expire. I've got rehearsal in a couple of hours and I need to start rehydrating now."

Maggie reluctantly opened the door. "All right. Come in, but be really quiet, okay? I don't want Sarah to wake up till I get my shower." She motioned toward the kitchen and managed a smile. "Help yourself to whatever I've got. You can even squirt yourself down with the spray hose on the sink, if you want," she said dryly, but then immediately regretted the joking comment when she saw a gleam appear in both pair of eyes...and Greg already stripping off his shirt.

"Lock the door on your way out, and please don't do anything *I'll* regret," was her parting warning as they headed for the kitchen and she headed for her long-awaited shower.

"Maggie? Wait a second, will you?"

Maggie turned reluctantly at the sound of Greg's voice. He'd followed her into the living room, leaving Billie behind in the kitchen. "What is it, Greg?"

He smiled disarmingly. He really was a handsome guy and Maggie could see why Billie was attracted to him. But she didn't know him as well as Maggie did. "I was wondering if you'd consider getting another publicity shot with you, me and the kid."

"Greg, I already told you—"

"The other one went over like gangbusters, Maggie," he interrupted urgently. "Our ratings skyrocketed, and I even got called in to audition for a part in an Arnold Schwarzenegger flick."

"You know how I feel about involving Sarah in publicity stunts, Greg. The answer is—"

"Arnold Schwarzenegger, Maggie!" he pleaded. "You know, from the Terminator movies?"

"And will always be—"

"Come on! Be a sport!"

"No."

Greg scowled. "It's that baby doctor, isn't it? He's the one who's making you so stubborn about this."

"No, Greg, Jared has nothing to do with this decision. I've never approved of exploiting Sarah for publicity. And don't think you can *trick* me into doing what you can't *talk* me into doing, either. Dennis knows better now than to let you sneak by with more paparazzi. Now, please go back to Billie and leave me alone so I can take a shower, okay?"

"I still think it's that damned baby doctor," she heard Greg mutter as she walked away.

RIDING UP ON THE ELEVATOR, Jared congratulated himself on finding a perfectly good excuse to come home during lunch break. He needed to pick up some patient records that he'd left scattered on his disorganized coffee table. He supposed that he could have taken the papers in the following day, but now he had an excuse to check on Maggie and Sarah, too.

Jared got off the elevator and headed directly for Maggie's apartment, completely and immediately forgetting about the patient records. He was trying hard not to get too excited about their budding relationship, but if the amount of dreaming about her he'd done last night was any indication, he was failing miserably.

He rang the doorbell and waited. He didn't hear any crying coming from the other side of the door, so he assumed that Maggie and Sarah were having another peaceful day. *Maggie was right all along,* he thought to himself, unable to subdue a smile. Sarah just needed to get used to her, that's all. And he knew from personal experience that getting used to Maggie Stern wasn't at all difficult.

The door opened...and Jared's smile disappeared.

Greg Moran seemed surprised at first, then a taunting little smirk curved his lips. "Dr. Austin. Shouldn't you be at the office at this hour?"

Jared's narrowed gaze flitted over Greg's naked torso, his damp, mussed hair, his tight runner shorts. "I could ask you the same thing. Aren't you wanted on the set, Mr. Moran?"

"My big scenes are with Maggie, and Maggie's on leave to take care of the kid...remember?"

Jared gave a curt nod and told himself not to jump to conclusions. Things were not always as they seemed. "Where are Maggie and Sarah, anyway?"

"Sarah's asleep and Maggie just stepped into the

shower.'' Greg raised his brows and waved an arm in a mocking invitation toward the living room. ''Want to come in and wait? I'll go and tell her you're here.''

He'd tried to suppress it, but jealousy reared its ugly head. Jealousy, shock, and disillusionment. After all, what's a guy supposed to think when he drops by the apartment of a woman he's falling head over heels for, and a damp, half-naked man answers the door and informs him…with a smirk on his smarmy face…that the aforementioned woman is in the shower?

This half-naked man, moreover, is someone the woman kisses and cavorts with on a regular basis as part of her job. And then the half-naked man offers to ''go and tell her'' she has company. If this didn't smell of off-hours cavorting, then Jared needed his olfactory senses checked out.

''It wasn't important,'' Jared muttered, suppressing the urge to reorganize the perfect features of Greg Moran's matinee idol mug. For all he knew, someone could be lurking around with a camera. ''I'll talk to her later.''

''I'm sure if she'd been *expecting* you—''

But Jared wasn't going to stand around any longer and let that phoney-baloney Count rub it in. He turned and walked resolutely to the elevator. Last night he'd wondered if Maggie's desire to slow down their relationship had anything to do with Greg Moran. Today, perhaps, he'd gotten his answer.

Jared had been jealous of Maggie's ''Hot Hunk'' costar from the beginning, even before he'd admitted to himself that he was developing feelings for her. Then he'd found that tabloid picture with the heart drawn around it, and he'd been wondering about the two of them ever since. He'd almost asked her at the park about her relationship with Greg, but then chickened out. And Maggie's response to his kisses last night had been pretty reassuring. Now, it seemed, it had been a mistake to be so easily reassured. He'd taken too much for granted.

Jared stepped onto the elevator and politely smiled at two other tenants, then turned his back to them and faced the front. His score was pretty bad when it came to successfully dating women who made a career in the entertainment industry.

First a stripping starlet—strike one. Then a transvestite—strike two. Then a beautiful soap star who seemed to combine the best of everything. She was an exciting woman with old-fashioned standards. Just his cup of tea. And, apparently, too good to be true. Strike three.

Three strikes...and he was outta there.

"JUST THOUGHT I'd drop by and check on you on my way back to the studio," Morty said as he stepped past Maggie and walked into the living room.

"Back to the studio, Mort? Working late?"

"Yeah. What smells so good? Did you fix me dinner, Maggie, m'girl?"

"I fixed dinner, Morty, but not for you," Maggie said with a teasing twinkle in her eyes.

Morty's eyes skimmed appreciatively over Maggie's short black dress and high heels. He raised his brows. "Looking good, sweetheart. Expecting company?"

"No, Morty," Maggie said with sweet sarcasm. "I always settle in for the night to take care of a baby wearing high heels and my best date dress. And I always fix Cornish game hens for myself and a five-month-old who's only got three teeth to call her own.'' She smiled. ''Jared Austin's coming to dinner.''

''So it's like that, is it?'' Morty inquired, his scraggly brows suddenly lowering. He scanned the room. Maggie had set her dining-room table with pretty china on a white tablecloth. Candles decorated the middle, just waiting to be lighted.

''You're not going to get all domesticated on me and get married, are you?'' he groused. Sarah gurgled and bounced in her infant carrier in the middle of the floor and Morty turned his scowling, suspicious gaze on her, too.

Maggie gave an elaborate shrug. ''Getting married and having babies doesn't dictate the end of a woman's acting career, Morty.''

''Famous last words,'' Morty snorted. ''I'm beginning to think giving you time off to baby-sit this kid was a big mistake.''

''Well, maybe it didn't turn out the way you planned it,'' Maggie replied unsympathetically. ''You didn't get as much publicity as you'd hoped for, but you still got plenty. But, as far as I'm concerned, becoming Sarah's foster mother was no mistake.''

''I didn't think you'd get so attached to her,'' Morty muttered. ''And why isn't she cryin' anymore? You two getting along now?''

Maggie smiled at Sarah, bending over to gently squeeze her fat little feet, all snug and warm inside her ''feety'' pajamas. ''Like two peas in a pod.''

''When you coming back to work, Maggie?'' Morty abruptly demanded. ''Haven't the police come up with anything on this kid yet?''

'' 'I don't know' to the first question, and 'no' to the second. But I'm in no rush.''

"Well, I'm beginning to be," Morty said, patting his pockets for a cigar. "Still can't smoke in here, I suppose?"

"What do you think?" Maggie answered. "But don't stress yourself out, Morty. If you need a cigar, go ahead and leave so you can have one." Maggie threw her arms wide. "I'm fine. Just fine." She glanced at her watch. "Besides, Jared will be here in fifteen minutes and I have to make hollandaise sauce for the broccoli."

"Cornish game hens and hollandaise sauce," Morty grumped as he trudged toward the door. "You're playing hardball, Maggie, and I'm gettin' indigestion just thinking about what's goin' to happen between you and that damned baby doctor."

"Thanks for coming by, Morty," Maggie said sweetly as she herded him out the door. "Good night!"

"Good night," Morty grunted, lighting up his cigar.

Maggie closed the door behind him. Alone at last. Well, sort of.

Maggie walked into the living room and scooped up Sarah from her infant carrier. She smiled into Sarah's big blue eyes as she trundled her off to the bedroom. "Before I make the hollandaise sauce, I'd better spruce you up for your favorite guy, Sarah Sunshine. Time for a diaper change!"

Sarah cooed and blew a few bubbles. Maggie laughed. "We need to buy you a proper dress, too, for showing you off to company and such. A girl can't lounge around in pajamas all the time."

Sarah squealed and pumped her arms and legs. "You like my dress, you say? Well, I think you're still a little young for black. Wouldn't do justice to your complexion. Pink's your color, I think. We'll ask Jared's opinion when he gets here, okay?''

But an hour later, Maggie and Sarah still waited. The hollandaise sauce had congealed on the back burner, the broccoli was soggy, and the cornish game hens were drying out fast.

*Where was Jared?*

*Chapter Thirteen*

Maggie told herself that Jared probably had a perfectly good reason for being late. Doctors frequently had emergencies. But why hadn't he called?

"He probably hasn't called because he can't get to a phone," Maggie told Sarah, but Sarah didn't appear to be buying into that theory. She was getting fussy. It was eight o'clock, time for her bedtime bottle. Glancing glumly at the phone, then at the mantel clock one more time, Maggie picked up the infant carrier and took it with her into the kitchen.

"I hope you enjoy *your* dinner, Sarah," Maggie said, as she set Sarah's carrier on the floor and reached inside the fridge for a bottle. "Mine's ruined...in more ways than one." Maggie sighed and put Sarah's bottle in the microwave to warm. She wrinkled her nose at the smell of overcooked broccoli.

After Sarah finished her bottle, Maggie expected her to go right to sleep. She'd been awake and active since her short nap at noon. But despite Maggie's burping her, singing to her, even slow-dancing her about the room, Sarah just got fussier and fussier.

"You need your daily dose of tall, blond and male,

don't you?'' Maggie muttered. ''I could use a little of that medicine myself, Sarah.''

Maggie glanced at the clock again. It was eight forty-five, and there was no longer any point in deluding herself. She'd been stood up. And, even if Jared had a valid excuse for not showing up, he could have called, or, at the very least, had someone call for him. Even if he'd had a *phony* excuse, it would have been much more polite of him to call.

''If this was the test, Jared,'' Maggie murmured to herself, ''you failed.'' Toeing off her high heels, she sank into a chair with a wailing Sarah draped on her shoulder.

The second she got off her tired feet, the phone rang. Maggie couldn't help herself; she fervently hoped it was Jared calling, full of contrition and with a good solid explanation. Cradling Sarah in one arm, she leaped up and hurried to answer the phone. Surprised by the sudden movement and the ringing of the phone, Sarah quit crying and looked around the room with big, wet, spiky-lashed eyes...as if she were expecting to see someone.

''Hello?''

''Maggie, m'girl.''

Maggie's heart sank to her toes. ''Morty. Hi.''

''Am I interrupting something?''

*She wished.* ''No.''

''How'd your date go?''

''It didn't. Something...er...came up.''

''Gee, I'm sorry.''

*Sure you are.* ''No big deal. So why'd you call?''

At this point, Sarah apparently decided that she'd got her hopes up for nothing and began to cry again, her internal volume dial switched to ''high.''

"Is that the baby crying?" Morty asked.

"No, it's the landlady," Maggie replied dryly. "Of course it's Sarah, Morty."

"I thought she wasn't doing that anymore? I thought you and she were like two peas in a—"

"All babies cry sometime. She's just tired. She'll settle down...but probably not as long as I'm on the phone."

"I'll get to the point."

"Good idea."

"I'm sending Chuck over with some scripts for you to look at."

"But I told you, I don't know when I'll be back, Morty. What scripts are you talking about?"

"The writers want your input on two scenarios we're considering, Maggie. One script gives a rough idea of how we'd go if we continued with the infertility story line and you and the Count adopted a child. The other script shows how we'd go if the Count got...well...run over by a bus, or the equivalent."

Maggie blinked. "You're thinking of not renewing Greg's contract?"

"It's a possibility. He's so full of himself these days, Maggie, and he's demanding a huge salary increase."

"He *is* quite popular with the ladies," Maggie reminded him.

"He's replaceable," Morty said shortly. "You decide which story line you like best, then we'll decide what to do with Greg Moran."

Maggie frowned. "I don't want to be the reason anyone loses his job."

"You won't be. As the executive producer, *I'll* make the final decision about Greg...and I'll base it on the whole picture, not just on your story-line preference. Feel better now?''

''Yeah, I guess so.'' She glanced down at Sarah's tear-stained face, her tiny mouth wide open and screaming at the top of her lungs. Maybe there was someone besides Jared who could give Sarah her daily dose of tall, blond and male. ''Morty, when will Chuck get here?''

''Any second, sweetheart. He left twenty minutes ago.''

''Good. I'll call you tomorrow after I read the scripts.''

''Thanks, Maggie. Er...sweet dreams.''

Maggie hung up the phone just as the doorbell rang. ''Great timing, Chuck,'' Maggie murmured. ''Just like in a soap opera, no wasted air time.''

Maggie hurried to the door and swung it open without bothering to look through the peephole. Big mistake. Her hand came up to shield herself from the blinding flash of a camera shoved in her face. She nearly tripped over backwards from surprise. Startled, too, Sarah cried even louder.

At first Maggie couldn't see past the spots in front of her eyes, but then the creep with the camera came into view. When she saw who the paparazzo was, Maggie was furious. ''Greg! I didn't invite you up. How'd you get past Dennis? And what do you think you're *doing?*''

He smiled smugly. ''I've been in Billie's apartment since we got back from our jog. She's at rehearsal now. And to answer your second question, it's not what I'm *doing,* it's what I've already done. I just took your picture, Maggie. A very unflattering picture, I might add, with the kid screaming and you looking about as motherly as a killer shark.''

Maggie tried to calm Sarah, looking right and left down the halls, not at all eager to attract a crowd. "Come inside," she hissed. "We'll cause a commotion.''

"I don't mind commotions," Greg informed her. "It's great publicity.''

"What are you trying to accomplish by acting this way, Greg?'' she pleaded, growing desperate.

"I'm offering you a bargain, Maggie. I won't sell this picture to the tabloids if you'll agree to pose with me for another one. A 'nice' one, where you and I and the kid are all smiling.''

Down the hall, Maggie heard the "ding" of the elevator. "You're trying to blackmail me, Greg Moran,'' she accused disbelievingly. If she wasn't holding Sarah, she'd tackle him and yank that camera out of his hand...although even unencumbered she'd probably have a hard time bringing down a former trophy-winning runningback.

Greg was well aware of his advantage over her. He smiled with supreme self-confidence. "That's exactly what I'm doing, Maggie. So, what'll it be?''

She was about to slam the door in Greg's smug mug, when she saw over his shoulder the unmistakable glint of blond hair bobbing in their direction from the elevator. Blond hair on top of a very tall frame. Unfortunately, at the same time, doors began to open up and down the hall. Yes, it seemed the tenants were about to be treated to a show.

Maggie leaned to the side, peering past Greg, and that's when she realized that there were two tall frames topped with blond hair traveling down the hall in their

direction! Not able to see that far, but somehow sens-
ing that rescue was at hand, Sarah stopped crying.

Yes, Sarah Sunshine was going to get a double dose
of tall, blond and male. Like a sheriff and his trusty
young deputy, Jared and Chuck stalked down the hall,
grim-faced and purposeful. It was high noon and Greg
Moran was the varmint in a black hat about to get
measured for a box and a spot of real estate on Boot
Hill.

By now Greg had turned to see what Maggie was
looking at and it gave her immense pleasure to watch
his complexion change from a healthy pink to a sickly
white. Then, before he even had time to rattle off some
explanation or get all puffed up and belligerent, Chuck
snatched the camera out of Greg's hand and Jared
drew back his fist and punched Greg square on the
nose. His arms circling like a couple of windmills,
Greg toppled backwards and fell with a hard
"oomph" on his rear.

Jared, rubbing his knuckles, stared down at him
with a fiery expression in his eyes that gave Maggie
goose bumps. She knew it was a pretty primitive reaction, but she couldn't help but be thrilled by the fact
that Jared had defended her in such a physical way.

While other tenants gathered around, oohing and
aahing, Chuck plucked Sarah out of Maggie's arms
and went into the apartment, removing her from the
fray.

"He was going to blackmail me into doing another
publicity shot with Sarah," Maggie said to Jared,
moving to stand next to him.

"So we gathered," Jared said, still staring at Greg
with a challenging glint in his eyes.

Greg just sat there, gingerly examining his nose.

Finally he looked up and said peevishly, "You might have broken it! If you've ruined my profile, I'll sue, Austin!"

"A bump on the nose might give your face a little character, Moran," Jared retorted coolly. "Too bad nothing can be done about your basic personality."

Turning neatly on his heel, Jared grabbed Maggie's arm and gently propelled her before him into the apartment, closing the door behind them.

Glancing up at his tight-lipped profile as he continued to guide her into the living room, Maggie decided it wasn't the best time to ask Jared where the heck he'd been…say…around dinnertime. She had a feeling she'd find out soon, anyway.

When they entered the living room, Maggie saw Chuck sitting on the couch with Sarah in his arms, the child heavy-lidded and happy. She appeared ready to doze off any second. By unspoken agreement, everyone kept quiet till the blessed event occurred and Chuck carried Sarah into the bedroom to put her to bed.

Maggie hurried ahead to pull back and straighten Sarah's blankets and flick on a newly purchased nightlight. Then they returned to the living room to find Jared standing with his back to the fireplace, his hands clasped behind his back, looking stern. And he remained as grimly silent as ever. Maggie got the perplexing—and annoying—impression that instead of being allowed to indignantly inquire where he'd been at six-thirty and why he hadn't called, he was itching to interrogate *her* about something. Either way, Maggie didn't want an audience.

She turned to Chuck, who was hovering uncertainly just inside the room…also saying nothing. If no one else was going to get the ball rolling, Maggie decided it was up to her.

"Chuck, thank you for grabbing Greg's camera," she said, smiling warmly. "I'll take the film out, then return the camera to him later."

"You don't think he'll call the police, do you?" Chuck inquired.

"No. He wouldn't take the chance of bad publicity, and I don't think it would do his macho image much good if it was revealed that you outsmarted him and Jared socked him in the nose and made him fall flat on his fanny."

"Good," Chuck said, pulling two shelves of paper from his shoulder bag. "I'll just leave these scripts and be on my way."

"No, you'd better stay. The police will have to be called, anyway, Chuck," Jared said, speaking for the first time since he'd entered the apartment. "They'll want to ask you some questions."

Maggie turned and gave Jared a puzzled frown. "Why do the police have to be involved at all? Greg won't press charges. I told you, he doesn't like bad—"

"Maggie, Chuck has another reason for needing to talk to the police...don't you?"

The two men stood facing each other across the room, their gazes locked in a sort of combative communication she didn't understand. Finally Chuck's gaze dropped and he sank into the nearest chair. "How long have you known?"

"I began to suspect yesterday, but I had to do a little investigating before I was sure." Jared's gaze shifted to Maggie. "That's why I wasn't here for dinner, Maggie. I'm sorry I didn't call, but this was important and I knew you'd understand."

"You're wrong, Jared," Maggie confessed with a bewildered shake of her head. "I don't understand what you're talking about at all. Why does Chuck need to speak to the police? What did you begin to suspect yesterday?"

Jared looked back at Chuck. "Do you want to tell her? Since I still don't know the whole story, I'm sure you'll explain it better than I could."

Chuck hesitated, looking guilty and apologetic, then finally blurted, "I'm Sarah's 'aunt,' Ms. Stern."

"Sarah's *aunt?*" she repeated incredulously. "What do you mean? Were *you* were the person who—?"

"Yes, I'm the person who left Sarah on your doorstep Saturday morning. I'm friends with Ralph, the night doorman. He let me in because he knows I drive you to work and back, and I told him I had some fruit to deliver to you,"

"In an infant carrier?" Maggie couldn't help exclaiming.

"Ralph doesn't know fruit baskets from infant carriers."

"How on earth did the police miss such an important piece of information?" Maggie wondered.

"The police were looking for a woman," Chuck said, shrugging. "A crazed fan. I didn't fit the description."

"And the police were a little distracted during their initial investigation, if you remember, Maggie," Jared pointed out.

Maggie sat down, shaking her head. "I suppose none of that matters anyway, not now that you've confessed that you're Sarah's—" Maggie cocked her head to the side. "How exactly are you related to Sarah?"

"I'm her uncle. She's my younger sister's baby."

Maggie was almost afraid to ask the next logical question, but Chuck wasn't readily volunteering information. "What happened to your sister? She's not...you know, like the note said...she's not—"

"Yeah, she died when Sarah was born. Back home in Oklahoma. Kathy wasn't married, our folks have passed on, and there just wasn't anyone else who could take care of her."

"You never said anything, Chuck," Maggie said wonderingly. "I never had a clue you were taking care of a baby and working and going to school, all at the same time."

"I've been leaving her at daycare centers. A different one every week, so no one would be able to recognize her when I finally gave her to you."

"You've been planning this for a long time."

"Yeah," Chuck admitted. "The infertility story line at your soap supplied me with the perfect front."

"Was the convenience of using my story line as a front the only reason you gave Sarah to me?" Maggie wasn't sure why, but if he said yes, she'd be crushed.

"No, absolutely not, Ms. Stern." Chuck was adamant. "I've been driving you for a year now, and I decided after the first week that you were one of the nicest people I'd ever met. I knew you'd be good with Sarah and that she'd have a wonderful home with you."

Maggie was gratified by Chuck's confidence in her, but shook her head modestly. "Jared was good with Sarah right from the beginning, but she had to get used to me." Then, suddenly putting together another piece of the puzzle, she exclaimed, "Was that why Sarah took such an instant liking to Jared? Because he reminded her of *you?*''

"That's probably a part of it," Chuck conceded, "but she wouldn't have continued to warm to Dr. Austin if the only attraction was a bit of physical resemblance between the two of us."

Maggie nodded, still bemused by the whole situation. "This is all so incredible. I don't know what to say, Chuck."

He leaned eagerly forward in the chair, his elbows on his knees, his palms pressed together, prayerfully. "Just say you'll keep her. She's happy with you. I can't take care of her like she deserves and I don't want her to go to a foster home. Adopt her, Ms. Stern. Make Sarah yours legally."

Chuck looked so earnest, so serious, Maggie's heart really went out to him. He was awfully young to be shouldering so much responsibility, and she didn't blame him for what he'd done. He'd been motivated by his love and concern for Sarah.

Maggie's first instinct was to say "yes." Unequivocally. She loved Sarah. She knew it would be an adjustment to her life, but she was ready for an adjustment that came in such an adorable package. But instead of answering, Maggie turned her gaze toward Jared. At the beginning, he'd doubted her ability to care for Sarah. She thought his opinion had changed, but now she wasn't so sure. He'd been acting so strangely this evening. Obviously he was angry with Greg, but it almost seemed that he was angry with her, too.

"Do you want my opinion, Maggie?" Jared finally asked her.

"Yes, I do," she admitted.

Jared fished in his pocket and handed Chuck his keys. "Would you mind going to my apartment for a few minutes so Maggie and I can talk privately? If anyone's still out in the hall, just ignore them."

Chuck nodded and left.

Maggie held her breath as Jared moved to the couch and sat down beside her. He took hold of her hands and clasped them between his two. The gesture should have been comforting, but Maggie was sure he was setting the stage to break bad news to her gently. She gazed into his intensely blue eyes and waited nervously.

"I think you should adopt Sarah."

Maggie's heart soared with happiness. "You do?"

Jared shook his head and gave a self-mocking chuckle. "I was so wrong about you...right from the beginning. And then, even when I should have known better, I jumped to wrong conclusions."

"What do you mean?"

"I came by on my lunch break. Greg answered the door wearing nothing but a pair of brief running shorts. You were in the shower."

Her eyes widened. "And you thought that I—that *he and I*—"

"He certainly led me to believe that there was something going on between you two. And, as jealous as I've been of the guy since he locked lips with you the minute he walked in the door on Saturday, I fell for his little farce."

"Oh, Jared, Billie was here, too! She must have been in the kitchen. I'm so sorry Greg made you believe—"

"No, *I'm* sorry," Jared said emphatically. "Greg didn't make me believe anything. I should have known better. I asked you to have faith in me, then I didn't show any faith in you. I should have known that you couldn't fall for a smarmy creep like Greg Moran.''

''You're right about that,'' she agreed.

''Then later in the day when I was thinking more clearly, I realized that Greg had been yanking my chain.''

''So your missing our dinner date—?''

''Had nothing to do with my encounter with Greg. I really was busy with a friend of mine who moonlights as a P.I. Because of my suspicions, I had him do a background check on Chuck. When I found out about his younger sister dying in childbirth five months ago, I knew I had my man.''

Maggie squeezed Jared's fingers, her eyes brimming with sympathetic tears. ''How sad for her...and for Sarah. And especially for Chuck.''

''Chuck's going to be fine, and Sarah will be, too—'' He smiled and his face lit up. Maggie felt as though she could believe anything he told her. ''—with a great mom like you.''

Maggie lifted her hand and lovingly traced the line of Jared's jaw with her fingertips. ''And with a great—'' She shrugged and smiled, uncertain what to call him. ''—*next-door neighbor* like you!''

His eyes gleamed with tender amusement, then shifted to settle intently on her lips. ''I hope to be much more than that, Maggie. To Sarah, and to you.''

He leaned forward, and Maggie's eyes drifted shut, anticipating.... That's when the doorbell rang.

Nose to nose, breaths intermingled, Maggie and Jared exchanged rueful looks. ''When am I ever going to get to court you, Margaret Morgenstern?'' he asked her.

"Patience has its rewards," she assured him, then she went to answer the door. Peering through the peephole, she announced, "It's Billie."

She opened the door and Billie stomped in and stood in the middle of the living room, her fists on her hips. She leveled a scowling gaze at Jared and inquired, "Dr. J, did you belt Greg in the nose?"

# Chapter Fourteen

Jared and Maggie exchanged glances. He could tell she agreed with him that it was time Billie knew what a creep Greg really was. Jared stood up, slipped his hands in his trouser pockets in a casual pose, and carefully began, "Yes, Billie, I did...er...belt Greg in the nose. But he—"

"*Deserved it!*" Billie finished for him, giving Jared a hearty congratulatory thump on the arm. Then she crossed her own arms and paced up and down the carpet, her eyes flashing indignation.

"When I came home from rehearsal I found him examining his swollen nose in my bathroom mirror," she revealed. "At first I thought he'd had an accident or something, but when I finagled the whole story out of him, I couldn't believe he'd stooped so low! Trying to force Maggie to pose for another publicity shot! The guy's got the biggest ego I've ever seen, and that's saying something in New York! I told him I never wanted to see him again."

Jared could see that Maggie was relieved that Billie wasn't devastated by Greg's fall from grace. It was much better for her to be angry, because then she could vent her feelings and get over him much faster.

Maggie walked over and gently caught hold of Billie's arm, leading her to the sofa to sit down, then sat next to her. "He plays such a wonderful guy on the show, and everyone expects him to be the same way in person. It's a hard act to follow, no pun intended! I've worked with Greg for two years now, and learned to put up with his inflated ego and to dodge his amorous advances because, in other ways, we worked well together. He's not exactly a Laurence Olivier, but he's a reliable actor and he has a lot of screen charisma."

Billie sighed. "Ain't that the truth."

"But lately he's gotten out of control. I was worried about introducing you two, but I figured you could decide for yourself if he was worth your time."

"He *is* a helluva kisser, Maggie. And so cute. Can't a guy be cute, a good kisser, and a nice guy?" Billie lamented.

Maggie looked up at Jared, her eyes warm and blatantly appreciative. Despite the fact that he was a grown man and not exactly inexperienced with women, Jared felt himself blushing. "Yes, a guy can be cute, a good kisser, and very, *very* nice. But they don't grow on trees. And they come along at the most unexpected times."

Billie couldn't miss the exchange of tender looks. Arching an eyebrow, she inquired, "You got a brother, Dr. J?"

Jared laughed and shook his head. "No, I don't. Sorry, Billie. But Maggie's exaggerating my merits."

"Maggie doesn't exaggerate," Billie contradicted him. "Even after knowing her for only four days, I've figured out that much about her. She warned me about Greg." She turned back to Maggie. "How will you be able to put up with seeing him on the set, day after day, Maggie? Kissing him and...and...everything?''

Jared was wondering the same thing. More to the point, he was wondering how *he* was going to put up with Maggie seeing Greg on the set, kissing him, cavorting with him on a satin bedspread in a black teddy, et cetera. He could tolerate her being in some other actor's arms, but not Greg Moran's. Not after everything that had happened.

Jared gave himself a stern mental shake. No, none of that was true. He was prepared to put up with this Greg Moran situation, no matter how difficult, because he wasn't going to jeopardize his relationship with Maggie over dumb jealousy. He knew she was only acting in all those bedroom scenes. He just wouldn't torture himself by watching again. So, he guessed he'd better keep clear of the staff lounge at the clinic during lunch hour!

"I'm not too worried about having to deal with Greg Moran much longer," Maggie confessed, idly toying with the tassel of a throw pillow.

Billie perked up. "Oh really? Why? You're not booting him off the show, are you, Maggie?"

"I don't boot anyone off the show," Maggie said. "Morty is the only one with power to 'boot.' But I *do* have something to say about story lines, and Morty's considering two possibilities for the Count and wants my feedback." Maggie looked coy and, in Jared's eyes, utterly adorable. "One of those story lines has the Count getting tragically run over by a bus."

Jared's mood suddenly lifted...sky-high!

Billie laughed gleefully. "No, Maggie, not really!" she exclaimed. "Oh, it's just too good to be true!"

"I couldn't do it, of course, if I thought he'd be

standing in the soup line the next day. But Greg will get another job right away, probably on another soap, or maybe even a film role. He's very hot right now.''

Maggie looked at Jared for his reaction, and without saying a word, he knew he'd conveyed his heartfelt and slightly chagrined relief. When they were alone...if they ever managed to succeed in that quest...he'd tell her he'd been prepared to cheerfully share her with the fictional Count. Well, perhaps ''cheerfully'' was too strong a word. In the meantime, there were other matters to be settled.

''It's getting late, Maggie,'' he announced. ''I'm going to get Chuck back over here, then call the police.''

''The police?'' Billie repeated, her eyes wide and curious.

''You explain,'' Jared suggested, winking at Maggie. She smiled and nodded, then he turned back to Billie. ''Wait till you hear Chuck's story, Billie. It won't need any exaggeration to amaze and entertain.''

Jared left the apartment and went to his, as amazed and entertained by his own story as he was by Chuck's. Who would have thought he'd be caught up in the middle of a real-life soap opera like this one...and loving every minute of it?

THAT NIGHT and the next two days were filled with police interviews and reports and dealings with the child welfare department, guardianship papers, negotiations with Morty on an extended vacation leave, discussions about story lines, and necessary press releases. In the end, Chuck wasn't charged with breaking any laws, Maggie had filed adoption papers, and Greg was looking for another job.

Maggie's real-life soap opera was still the talk of the town, only now everyone knew the real story, the whole story, because Maggie had agreed to a hurriedly set-up interview with Dianne Sawyer which aired live on Thursday night. So many false versions of the story were being circulated that Maggie wanted to set things straight.

She had also hoped to lessen the paparazzi's interest in her by scooping herself, but so far that hadn't happened. The tabloid shutterbugs were still skulking around outside her apartment, limiting her activities. But she knew it wouldn't last forever. Some other celebrity would get married or pregnant or arrested and Maggie's "little miracle" would fade into the obscurity of yesterday's news.

At 5:57 p.m. Friday, Maggie was again waiting for Jared. They'd barely crossed paths since Tuesday night and both had been counting the minutes till they could have that dinner they'd planned and spend a long-awaited evening together. This time Maggie wore a sage-green silk dress, and, being somewhat superstitious, she'd dispensed with the hollandaise sauce and broccoli and went with French green beans with almonds instead, and filet mignon in place of Cornish hens. Angelo's delivered everything.

Through it all, Sarah had been, and still was, behaving like an angel. It was as if she'd gotten what she wanted and no longer had any reason to cry. It was already settled that Chuck would be her godfather and a frequent visitor. As for Sarah's other favorite tall blond male, Maggie knew that Jared wanted to be part of Sarah's life…and *her* life, too…but she didn't know exactly what that meant. She didn't think Jared knew what it meant, either. Maybe tonight he'd figure it all out.

Maggie had already figured out what she wanted. She was in love with Jared and she wanted to spend the rest of her life with him. Sure, she'd only known him a week, but that didn't matter. She felt she knew him, his character, his heart, already. If her dreams came true, the delicious details could be filled in over the long, lovely years ahead.

At exactly two minutes to six, the doorbell rang. Maggie smoothed her hands down the slim lines of her short dress and glanced in the mirror over the mantel to make sure her hair still looked good. She wore it down, the different layers curving against her cheek and resting on her shoulders.

Then she glanced at Sarah, seated in the infant carrier on the couch, her bright blue eyes watching Maggie's every move, her little arms and legs pumping energetically. She had on a dress, too, a pink one with lots of ruffles that "Grandma" Morgenstern had obligingly shopped for. She looked as excited as Maggie felt.

"He's here," Maggie whispered conspiratorially, flashing Sarah a beaming smile. "Our favorite guy."

Sarah gurgled her approval and Maggie walked eagerly to the door. A little more careful since Greg's unexpected attack with the camera, Maggie made sure she looked through the peephole first. It was Jared. If what she saw with her own two eyes wasn't proof enough, her heart was performing a frantic version of the Macarena that had become the usual response to Jared being somewhere nearby.

Taking a deep, sustaining breath, she opened the door.

As it turned out, she was glad she'd taken that extra breath. Jared was wearing a tuxedo. Tall and blond decked out in "sleek and black" was a sight designed to knock the air out of any red-blooded female. Add to that the fact that Maggie was in love with the man inside the drop-dead gorgeous packaging, and it was no wonder she couldn't squeak out a single word of greeting.

A tawny eyebrow arched over one of Jared's sky-blue eyes. "Surprised that I'm on time, I suppose?"

"No...not that," she said, her voice an embarrassing croak.

He smiled, and Maggie was dazzled. "Then what?" He glanced down his six-foot-plus frame. "Is it the monkey suit? Too clichéd? Too much?"

Maggie made an effort to gather her scattered wits. "Oh, it's 'too much,' all right. But in the very best sense of the words. You look...wonderful."

"So do you," he whispered, his eyes traveling from the top of her head, down her trim-fitting dress, over her silky nylon-clad legs, to the tips of her strappy high-heeled shoes.

"I feel as though I've just been examined, doctor," Maggie teased.

"And you passed with flying colors, Maggie," Jared assured her, his advance slow but purposeful, his smile sly and sexy. "You look very...*healthy*. Now, don't you think we ought to shut the door before we've got a hall full of gawkers?"

Maggie stepped back only slightly as Jared moved forward. The lapels of his suit skimmed the front of her dress, making her nipples tingle. The scent of him was in the air. Clean, manly skin and the expensive fabric of his suit mixed enticingly. He shut the door.

Now they stood only inches apart. Biting her lip, she tilted her head and looked up and into his eyes.

"Where's Sarah?" he asked. "Is she…sleeping?"

His voice sounded hopeful. Maggie's heart skipped a beat. "She's in the living room, waiting for you. And if you don't make an appearance pretty soon, she'll start squawking. She's a girl who knows exactly what she wants." Maggie lifted her hands and rested them lightly on his chest. "Kind of like me."

Maggie watched as Jared swallowed hard. "I can't wait to see her. You know I love Sarah to death, but I was hoping that you and I could be alone tonight. So I—"

"You're worried she won't go to sleep after dinner? So was I." Maggie began to toy with the buttons on his shirt. "I've taken care of that. I've arranged for a baby-sitter."

"You have?" His arms circled her waist and pulled her close. "Who? Chuck?"

"No." Her hands began to move. She watched her fingers glide over his chest, enjoying the silky texture of the tuxedo over the hard, muscled chest underneath. "I didn't want to bug Chuck on a Friday night. The kid needs a social life. So I asked my mother to come over. I didn't think you'd mind if she took Sarah next door to your apartment while we ate dinner and…stuff."

Jared tilted her face with a finger under her chin. "You asked your mother to come over?" Amusement curved his lips in a teasing grin. "I'm flattered, Maggie. You really do want to be alone with me if you're inviting your mother over."

"She's been a great help with Sarah already," Maggie admitted.

"Yes, she's a wonderful woman," Jared agreed. "And I know you love her. But she's as much of a busybody as my mother." He paused, stroking his thumb across her lower lip. "Coincidentally, you also ought to be flattered. I asked my mother to baby-sit tonight, too."

Maggie burst out laughing, then suddenly sobered. "Oh, my gosh! That means, any minute now, they'll both be here! It's too late to cancel on either of them! Do you think they're ready to meet each other?"

"Don't you mean, are *we* ready for them to meet each other?"

"That's exactly what I mean," she agreed with a rueful smile. "Two busybody moms with matchmaking on their minds might be a bit overwhelming. Are we up to it?"

"The matchmaking's already been done," Jared said with a shrug. "There won't be anything left for them to do."

"You underestimate our mothers, Jared," Maggie told him. "I'm sure they think there's lots left to do."

*Like corral us into a quick engagement and a church wedding with all the trimmings.* Maggie wouldn't mind having the courtship hurried along to culminate in such a dream come true, but she was pretty sure Jared wasn't ready yet.

The doorbell rang and Maggie and Jared exchanged wary looks. "It must be *my* mother," Maggie said. "Dennis and Ralph both know to let her come up now without checking with me."

Jared looked through the peephole. "You're right. It's your mother." He turned around and lifted his brows in an ominous expression. "And my mother, too. They must have met and made the connection downstairs."

"Oh, Jared, what if they don't like each other?" Maggie whispered, biting her nails. "What if they argue over who should baby-sit Sarah?"

"You're probably fretting over nothing," Jared said soothingly, but Maggie could see the telltale pinch of worry between his brows. "But there's only one way to find out." He opened the door.

*"Dahlings!"* exclaimed Claire, the first through the door, a huge fur collar nearly hiding her face, her arms filled with brightly wrapped packages. She "kiss-kissed" the air on either side of Jared's cheeks and Maggie's, too. "I'm so glad you called me to baby-sit. Here's a few trinkets for Sarah. Where is the precious child?"

"Sweetie!" Maggie's mother waddled in next, bundled in a neon-purple, down-filled jacket that made her look like a stack of shiny tires, her arms weighted down with Tupperware containers of every shape and size, filled with food. She beamed at Jared. "And Dr. Austin! Why didn't you tell me Claire DeSpain was your mother? I think I like you even better now...though I didn't think that was *possible!*"

Claire emptied her packages into Jared's arms and turned a brilliant smile on Maggie. "A charming woman, your mother. We became *intimately* acquainted on the elevator. I think we must have known each other in several previous lives. I'm sure she and I were the Brontë sisters, Charlotte and Emily. I was Emily, of course, the one who created Heathcliff." She got a faraway, longing look in her eyes as if imagining something deliciously decadent. "So dark and brooding.... Just my cup of tea."

"Put these casseroles in the fridge, sweetie," Lorena instructed, piling Maggie's arms with the Tupperware containers. "You won't have to cook for a week."

"More like a month," Maggie muttered.

"Where's the child?" Claire again demanded.

"I'll show you the way, Claire," Lorena chirped happily. "You're going to adore her."

"Oh, I know," Claire replied. "My psychic already told me."

"Your psychic? Tell, me...does she read tea leaves? My grandmother, Myrtle, used to read tea leaves and she said—"

Jared and Maggie again exchanged looks, this time of utter amazement. They staggered into the kitchen, Maggie unloading the Tupperware containers into the freezer, and Jared dumping his packages on the counter. "I don't think we need to worry about them getting along," he said unnecessarily. He gave Maggie a grim look. "But I do think we might have to worry about getting rid of them, so we can be alone."

Maggie nodded and they hurried into the living room to assess the situation. Apparently Jared couldn't have been more wrong. Claire had already bundled Sarah in blankets and was putting on her knit hat with the fuzzy tassel on the top that made her look like a pixie, and Lorena had the diaperbag and carrier firmly in hand.

"You're already off to my apartment?" Jared inquired, obviously trying not to sound too delighted.

"Of course not, foolish boy," his mother scolded him. "Lorena and I are taking Sarah to *my* apartment. My driver's waiting for us downstairs in the underground parking. We didn't want you two to feel inhibited at the thought of your mothers right next door…if you know what I mean."

Maggie knew exactly what she meant. She blushed hotly and didn't dare look at her own mother. But she needn't have felt embarrassed about Lorena's reaction. On her way to the door she whispered in Maggie's ear, "Now, Maggie. Now would be the time to put on that gorgeous white nightgown. Or maybe something red…?"

"What if Sarah cries?" Jared found the presence of mind to inquire as the eager baby-sitters marched out the door.

Claire turned and displayed Sarah's ear-to-ear smile for all to see. "She won't cry. The three of us are going to have a ball." She raised a brow. "Maybe even a slumber party…if we don't hear from you by midnight. *Hasta la vista, dahlings!*"

"*Ciao,*" added Lorena, getting right into the Continental spirit. Then she winked at Maggie and closed the door.

The quiet after the whirlwind arrival and departure of Claire DeSpain and Lorena Morgenstern was deafening. Maggie stood in the living room, and Jared stood several feet away, near the door. With dazed expressions, they looked at each other across the distance that separated them.

"Do you think it will be all right?" Maggie asked in a small voice.

"You mean, our mothers spiriting Sarah away?"

"Yes."

"If she cries too much, I'm sure they'll call. But, judging by her expression when she left here, I don't think she will."

Maggie nodded uncertainly. "It seems so strange."

"Yes. For the first time since we met, we're alone."

"Yes...*alone*."

They stared at each other for a long time, his piercing blue eyes boring into her smoldering brown ones, the sexual tension in the room suddenly as tangible as the goose bumps on Maggie's arms.

"Are...are you hungry?" she eventually inquired in a strangled voice.

He took a purposeful step forward, then another. "I told you I'd bring my appetite."

Desire knotted in Maggie's stomach. "I made filet mignon and...and green beans with almonds."

"Sounds delicious." He took another step. "But I wasn't thinking about food."

Maggie's heart was in her throat. "What were you thinking about?"

Three more steps and he was only an arm's length away. "About the fact that you and I are alone, and there's nothing I'd rather do than make love to you."

Maggie's chin lifted. Her gaze met his with an endearing blend of shyness and determined desire. "Then what's stopping you?"

Nothing was stopping him, Jared realized. Nothing at all. No hangups. No reservations. No worries about tomorrow or yesterday. He wanted to embrace Maggie and everything about her, including her passion for acting. And if that meant giving up a little privacy, he was more than willing. The realization was liberating, stimulating. He swooped her into his arms and carried her into the bedroom.

Sarah's night-light was on, illuminating the room to a sultry softness. He laid Maggie gently on the bed and gazed down at her. A wry smile curved his lips. "I rented the tux," he said.

"Then you'd better take it off right away, before it gets irreparably wrinkled," she advised him with mock earnestness.

He thoroughly enjoyed her playfulness and immediately took her advice, slowly removing his clothes while she watched, her eyes seeming to caress every inch of flesh as it was exposed. By the time he was stripped down to his Skivvies, he was fully aroused.

"Did you rent the dress?" he inquired with a wickedly raised eyebrow.

She started to say no, then caught on and played along. Smiling demurely, she said, "You're right, I'd better take it off before it gets wrinkled, too."

She got up on her knees and turned her back to him, peering coyly over her shoulder. "But I need help, Jared. Unzip me?"

Jared was more than willing to help. He bent over, unzipping the dress with excruciating slowness, just a few teeth at a time, kissing her bared shoulders and back as he went along. It was nearly driving him mad with anticipation, and he hoped it was having the same effect on her.

Maggie thought she must have died and gone to heaven. Once Jared was through unzipping her, he inched the sleeves of her dress down her arms with slow deliberation, all the while nuzzling and kissing the nape of her neck.

She felt the bed dip under his weight as he knelt beside her. He turned her around and lowered her to the mattress, pulling the front of her dress down to her waist, baring her lacy scrap of a bra that was the same shade of pale sage green as her dress. Her taut, rosy nipples peeked through the netting.

"Pretty sexy, Maggie," Jared rasped, his eyes

sparking with desire. "I expected practical white cotton from a flannel-pajamas-and-baggy-T-shirt gal like you."

Maggie smiled and lifted her arms to lock behind Jared's neck. "I never said anything about what I wore underneath the flannel pajamas and the baggy T-shirt...now, did I?"

He swallowed hard. "I think you're a lot more like Monica than you let on."

She wet her lips and smiled provocatively. "Or is Monica like...me?"

That comment nearly sent Jared over the edge. He lowered himself beside her and pulled her firmly into his arms, then pressed his lips to hers in an urgent kiss. His hands roamed her soft body, over her hips and breasts, up her leg from ankle to calf to thigh. That's when he discovered the garter belt; the lacy strap, the warm, soft flesh above the silky stocking.

"Maggie," he whispered against her neck, laughing shakily. "How you continue to surprise and delight me."

"That's exactly what I want to do to you, Jared," she told him in a dreamy voice. "That...and other things."

He groaned and quickly divested her of her dress by drawing it over her slim hips and tossing it to the ground without the least concern about wrinkles. Her bra and matching panties came off next, then, last of all, the lacy garter belt and stockings...but those came very, very slowly.

She was naked now and Jared gazed at her, spellbound. She was so perfect, so sexy. And she felt so good beneath his hands, quivering and responsive to his every touch. He caressed and kissed her breasts, then stroked her stomach and gently probed the damp heat between her thighs.

"Now, Jared," Maggie breathed, weak with need. She tugged on the waistband of his boxer shorts, drawing them down. "Make love to me."

He helped her remove his boxer shorts and she wrapped her fingers around his arousal. He was so hot and tumid. So male. She opened to him and he entered her, burying himself deep inside her. She sighed with pure sensual satisfaction as the tension continued to build.

Pleasure enveloped him like a warm glove, but Jared braced himself and savored the moment. He felt something unfolding inside him like a huge, fragrant flower...some emotion even more intense than his urgent physical need. He gazed down at Maggie's hair spread out like a fan on the pillow, her face etched with tenderness, her eyes radiating desire...and love?

He hoped it was love, because he suddenly knew that that was exactly what he was feeling for her. He loved her. He wanted her to be part of his life from now on. And what a perfect time to realize just how important she was to him. He'd show her how much....

He began to move. They gazed into each other's eyes as Maggie's hips rose to meet each of Jared's thrusts. Slow and easy at first, then harder and faster till their bodies took over in a mindless rhythm.

Jared saw Maggie's face tense, felt the tension throughout her body as she reached a climax. Then came the shuddering release and the flow of color to her cheeks, the parted lips and soft moan.

It was beautiful to watch, and as erotic as anything

he'd ever imagined. His own release came quickly afterward, racking his body with waves of pleasure.

In the aftermath, as they rested in each other's arms, her cheek pressed against his chest, their damp arms and legs intertwined, he whispered, "I love you, Maggie."

He felt a tear roll onto his chest and the curving of her lips as she smiled. "I love you, too, Jared."

At midnight, the phone rang. Having just enjoyed a snack of various odds and ends from the kitchen, including cold steak and marshmallow squares, and some titillating foreplay for round three of their love-making marathon, Jared and Maggie were naturally not too thrilled to be interrupted.

"Hello?" Maggie answered in an embarrassingly faint and husky voice. She cleared her throat and tried again. *"Hello."*

"Sweetie!" came her mother's voice, loud and clear.

"Mom." Maggie sat up in the bed, pulling the sheet over her breasts as if her mother could actually see what was going on. She glanced with some alarm at Jared, but he just smiled back at her, his face pressed against the pillow, his hair a mass of golden, unruly waves. Maggie smiled back. "Is Sarah all right?"

"Of course. She's been asleep since ten. Claire and I have been talking to her psychic, Madam Natasha."

"Oh?"

Jared reached over and trailed his fingers down Maggie's arm, pulling her hand to his lips and lingeringly kissing the tender palm. She shivered, finding it difficult to pay attention to the phone conversation.

"We thought you might want to know what she told us, Maggie."

"About what, Mom? What was the question?" Maggie watched avidly as Jared kissed each of her fingertips, then drew her pinky into his mouth up to the knuckle and gently sucked. A delicious shiver ran down her spine.

"We asked her what month and day you and Jared should get married. You know, a time when all your planets would be aligned?"

Maggie smiled. "What did she say?"

"New Year's Eve, Maggie. She said New Year's Eve would be perfect."

"Sorry, Mom. That won't be possible."

"Maggie! Why wait, sweetie?"

"Oh, we don't plan to wait," Maggie assured her, sinking down into the sheets and blankets, shifting closer and closer to Jared's clever, questing hands. "We plan to get married at Christmas. In the meantime, Jared's moving into this apartment so he and Sarah and I can get a head start on being a family."

"Christmas, Claire," Maggie heard her mother exclaiming to her new friend and future in-law. "They're getting married at *Christmas!*"

"Marvelous, dahling," Claire drawled in the background.

Laughing, Maggie held the telephone receiver so Jared could also hear their reactions.

"I hope Jared realizes that I'll be inviting all my friends," Claire continued complacently. "Then everyone will know he's my son."

"About time," Jared murmured, smiling.

"Now, hang up the phone, Lorena. I'm sure they've got better things to do than talk to you."

"Good night, sweetie," Lorena said, speaking directly into the receiver again, her happiness obvious in the ecstatic tone of her voice. "Tell my future son-in-law, the doctor, good-night, too. And sweet dreams!"

Maggie hung up the phone and slipped back into Jared's waiting arms. "My mother says sweet dreams."

"She doesn't need to worry," he murmured as he drew Maggie close and playfully nipped her ear. "My dreams are going to be sweet from now on. After all, I've got everything I want. You and Sarah and—"

"Me and Sarah...and what?" Maggie prompted.

"You and Sarah and the best apartment in New York, with a study and a whirlpool tub. Speaking of that tub, I've had some fantasies...."

Maggie laughed. "Oh, you have, have you? So your real goal all along was to romance this apartment out from under me!"

"No, not at all," Jared softly denied, kissing her nose, her chin, her waiting mouth. "My goal was, and still is, to make love to you for hours and hours without a single commercial break."

"I always hated the lead-in for those breaks, anyway," Maggie murmured, returning his kisses with an enthusiasm that matched his. "Do we need to rehearse, or can we do this in one take?"

"There'll be lots of rehearsals and lots of 'takes,' Maggie," he assured her.

"In that case, we'd better get started." She kissed him, and... "Lights," she kissed him again.

"Camera." She kissed him one more time…putting into it all the love she felt for him.

"And *action*."

Jared more than willingly obliged.

Can tossing a coin in the Trevi Fountain really make wishes come true? Three average American women are about to find out when they throw…

# 3 COINS IN A FOUNTAIN

For Gina, Libby and Jessie, the trip to Rome wasn't what they'd expected. They went seeking romance and ended up finding disaster! What harm could throwing a coin bring?

### IF WISHES WERE HUSBANDS…
Debbi Rawlins—September

### IF WISHES WERE WEDDINGS…
Karen Toller Whittenburg—October

### IF WISHES WERE DADDIES…
Jo Leigh—November

## 3 COINS IN A FOUNTAIN
*If wishes could come true…*

### HARLEQUIN®
*Makes any time special* ™

Available at your favorite retail outlet.

Look us up on-line at: http://www.romance.net

HAR3C

# Take 2 bestselling love stories FREE

## Plus get a FREE surprise gift!

## Special Limited-Time Offer

**Mail to Harlequin Reader Service®**

### 3010 Walden Avenue
### P.O. Box 1867
### Buffalo, N.Y. 14240-1867

**YES!** Please send me 2 free Harlequin American Romance® novels and my free surprise gift. Then send me 4 brand-new novels every month, which I will receive months before they appear in bookstores. Bill me at the low price of $3.34 each plus 25¢ delivery and applicable sales tax, if any.* That's the complete price, and a saving of over 10% off the cover prices—quite a bargain! I understand that accepting the books and gift places me under no obligation ever to buy any books. I can always return a shipment and cancel at any time. Even if I never buy another book from Harlequin, the 2 free books and the surprise gift are mine to keep forever.

154 HEN CH7E

Name _____ (PLEASE PRINT)

Address _____ Apt. No. _____

City _____ State _____ Zip _____

This offer is limited to one order per household and not valid to present Harlequin American Romance® subscribers. *Terms and prices are subject to change without notice. Sales tax applicable in N.Y.

UAMER-98                                    ©1990 Harlequin Enterprises Limited

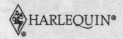

# Not The Same Old Story!

 Exciting, glamorous romance stories that take readers around the world.

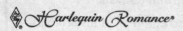 Sparkling, fresh and tender love stories that bring you pure romance.

 Bold and adventurous—Temptation is strong women, bad boys, great sex!

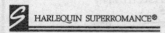 Provocative and realistic stories that celebrate life and love.

 Contemporary fairy tales—where anything is possible and where dreams come true.

 Heart-stopping, suspenseful adventures that combine the best of romance and mystery.

LOVE & LAUGHTER™ Humorous and romantic stories that capture the lighter side of love.

Look us up on-line at: http://www.romance.net          HGENERIC

# THE RANDALL MEN ARE BACK!

Those hard-ridin', good-lovin' cowboys who lassoed your heart—Jake, Chad, Brett and Pete Randall—are about to welcome a long-lost kin to their Wyoming corral—Griffin Randall.

Big brother Jake has married off all of his brothers—and himself. How long can Griffin escape Jake's matchmaking reins?

Find out in
**COWBOY COME HOME**
by Judy Christenberry

*They give new meaning
to the term "gettin' hitched"!*

Available at your favorite retail outlet.

Look us up on-line at: http://www.romance.net          HAR4B4

# HARLEQUIN ULTIMATE GUIDES™

**A series of how-to books for today's woman.**

Act now to order some of these extremely
helpful guides just for you!

*Whatever the situation, Harlequin Ultimate Guides™
has all the answers!*

| | | | |
|---|---|---|---|
| #80507 | HOW TO TALK TO A | $4.99 U.S. ☐ | |
| | NAKED MAN | $5.50 CAN. ☐ | |
| #80508 | I CAN FIX THAT | $5.99 U.S. ☐ | |
| | | $6.99 CAN. ☐ | |
| #80510 | WHAT YOUR TRAVEL AGENT | $5.99 U.S. ☐ | |
| | KNOWS THAT YOU DON'T | $6.99 CAN. ☐ | |
| #80511 | RISING TO THE OCCASION | | |
| | More Than Manners: Real Life | $5.99 U.S. ☐ | |
| | Etiquette for Today's Woman | $6.99 CAN. ☐ | |
| #80513 | WHAT GREAT CHEFS | $5.99 U.S. ☐ | |
| | KNOW THAT YOU DON'T | $6.99 CAN. ☐ | |
| #80514 | WHAT SAVVY INVESTORS | $5.99 U.S. ☐ | |
| | KNOW THAT YOU DON'T | $6.99 CAN. ☐ | |
| #80509 | GET WHAT YOU WANT OUT OF | $5.99 U.S. ☐ | |
| | LIFE—AND KEEP IT! | $6.99 CAN. ☐ | |

*(quantities may be limited on some titles)*

| | |
|---|---|
| **TOTAL AMOUNT** | $ |
| **POSTAGE & HANDLING** | $ |
| ($1.00 for one book, 50¢ for each additional) | |
| **APPLICABLE TAXES\*** | $ _____ |
| **TOTAL PAYABLE** | $ _____ |
| (check or money order—please do not send cash) | |

To order, complete this form and send it, along with a check or money
order for the total above, payable to Harlequin Ultimate Guides, to:
**In the U.S.:** 3010 Walden Avenue, P.O. Box 9047, Buffalo, NY
14269-9047; **In Canada:** P.O. Box 613, Fort Erie, Ontario, L2A 5X3.

Name: _____

Address: _____ City: _____

State/Prov.: _____ Zip/Postal Code: _____

\*New York residents remit applicable sales taxes.
Canadian residents remit applicable GST and provincial taxes.

HARLEQUIN®

Look us up on-line at: http://www.romance.net                    HNFBL4

## Catch more great
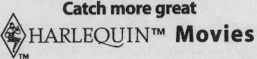
**HARLEQUIN™ Movies**

featured on **the movie channel** tmc

## Premiering August 8th
### *The Waiting Game*
Based on the novel by *New York Times*
bestselling author Jayne Ann Krentz

Don't miss next month's movie!
Premiering September 12th
*A Change of Place*
Starring Rick Springfield and
Stephanie Beacham. Based on the novel
by bestselling author Tracy Sinclair

If you are not currently a subscriber to
The Movie Channel, simply call your
local cable or satellite provider for more
details. Call today, and don't miss out
on the romance!

 **the movie channel** tmc    **HARLEQUIN®**

*100% pure movies.*
*100% pure fun.*

*Makes any time special* ™

Harlequin, Joey Device, Makes any time special and Superromance are trademarks of
Harlequin Enterprises Limited. The Movie Channel is a service mark of Showtime Networks, Inc.,
a Viacom Company.

An Alliance Television Production

PHMBPA898